Praise for Mel Sherratt:

We hope you enjoy this book. Please return or
renew it by the due date.

You can renew it at www.norfolk.gov.uk/libraries or
by using our free library app.

Otherwise you can phone 0344 800 8020 -
please have your library card and PIN ready.

You can sign up for email reminders too.

GOOD GIRL

Mel Sherratt is the author of fifteen crime novels, all of which have become bestsellers. For the past four years, she has been named as one of her home town of Stoke-on-Trent's top 100 influential people. She regularly appears at festivals and speaks at writing conferences throughout the UK, and pens a column for her local newspaper, *The Sentinel*, as well as feature articles for other newspapers and magazines. She lives in Stoke-on-Trent, Staffordshire, with her husband and terrier, Dexter.

MEL SHERRATT

GOOD GIRL

avon.

Published by AVON
A division of HarperCollins*Publishers* Ltd
1 London Bridge Street
London SE1 9GF

www.harpercollins.co.uk

HarperCollins*Publishers*
1st Floor, Watermarque Building, Ringsend Road
Dublin 4, Ireland

A Paperback Original 2021

3

First published in Great Britain by HarperCollins*Publishers* 2021

ISBN: 9780008371876

Typeset in Minion by Palimpsest Book Production Ltd, Falkirk, Stirlingshire
Printed and bound in UK by CPI Group (UK) Ltd, Croydon CR0 4YY

To Maddy Milburn, thank you for everything.

WEDNESDAY

ONE

Sara Ellis glanced at the large pile of ironing beside her and sighed. How did so much accumulate in just a few days? She stood in the middle of the room with the TV on, listening to it more than watching it, while she pressed a pair of jeans.

Coronation Street was playing. She could still remember a time when she'd sat down to watch the soap religiously at half past seven every evening, but now, aged thirty-eight, she often found herself catching up with it after she'd finished everything for the day. Or, in this case, half-watching while ironing at gone nine of an evening.

There was so much to fit in around her full-time job at the solicitors she worked at: the cooking, the housework, and tending to the demands of her two children. Her youngest, Nat, was ten, and her eldest, Erin, sixteen – but still very much a child at times.

Since her ex-husband Rob had walked out on them three years ago, doing everything by herself had been hard. Money was tight, child care made it near on impossible for her to go out and socialise, and she was still reeling from the fact that he had left her for someone younger who had three children of her own. Rob hardly ever came to see his two any more – not that she would argue with him too much about it. It was better for the three of them if they didn't see him at all. It only caused disruption.

Rob sent maintenance money, though it wasn't enough – not by a long shot – but it meant Sara and the kids had a roof over their heads, and their home was clean and tidy. They managed as a unit of three, and they were much better off than some families. For starters, they owned their own home, even if she did struggle with the mortgage payments every now and then. Rob had left the house to her, stating it was the least he could do. Well, yes, that would have been true if the home had been paid for. Sara struggled to make the repayments on just her one wage, and she hadn't been able to take the kids on holiday since Rob had left. But that was all changing soon. She'd booked them a fortnight in Tenerife for next summer; she'd been saving up little by little for a good while and was looking forward to it, despite it being several months away.

A loud banging almost had her jumping out of her skin. Quickly, she switched off the iron and rushed to the window. She popped her head around the curtain, giving her a clear view of the door. It was Erin's best friend, Molly. Sara looked along the drive but couldn't see her daughter, which was strange as they mostly came as a pair.

Molly spotted Sara and ran towards the window. 'Let me in!' she cried. 'Please, let me in.'

Erin. Sara raced to the door. On opening it, Molly rushed into her arms, sobbing.

'What's the matter?' she asked. 'Where's Erin?'

'She's . . . she's hurt,' Molly sobbed.

'What do you mean?' Gently, she pushed the young girl away from her. 'Molly, what's happened?'

Molly held up her hands. It was then Sara noticed they were covered in blood.

'Where is she?' Sara demanded.

'On the walkway. We were coming home and—'

Sara placed her hands on Molly's shoulders and bent down slightly to look her in the eyes. 'I need you to stay here while I go to her.'

Sara reached for her phone on the table and made a call to Lucy, Molly's mum, while she searched out her keys. Sara and Lucy had been friends since school. The Redferns lived eight doors down on the opposite side of the road.

'Lucy,' she cried as soon as her friend answered the call. 'I have Molly with me and she says that Erin is hurt. I need to go to her. No, she hasn't said. She's only on the pathway. Will you watch Nat for me? Thanks.'

'Is she coming right now?' Molly asked.

'Yes.' Sara disconnected the call, noticing the young girl was shivering. 'She'll be here in a minute. Stay here and—'

'I'm coming with you.'

'No. Please. Stay with Nat and your mum.'

It struck her then that Molly hadn't told her what had happened. But there was no time for that now. She had to get to her daughter.

She left the door on the latch and ran towards the road. She met Lucy at the pavement.

'Go,' Lucy said, rushing past her. 'And call me as soon as you know.'

Sara ran towards the path that led to the main road. She could hear Molly behind her, found no comfort in it. All she wanted was to see Erin.

The path was well lit as she raced along it. On the ground ahead, near to the grass, she spotted a shadow. As she drew level, she saw it was Erin and dropped to her knees.

'Erin, love, what's happened?'

But Erin didn't respond. Her eyes were glazed over, her skin pale. If it weren't for the blood, Sara would have said she'd taken some kind of drug. There was so much of it, dark red seeping through her jacket and onto the tarmac. She wiped a hand across Erin's forehead, crying out when her daughter still didn't respond. Instinctively, she pulled her into her arms and fumbled to get her phone out of her jacket pocket.

'Ambulance, please. My daughter – she's unconscious and covered in blood.' She gave the details required, all the time cradling her child; trying not to notice how cold she was, not to see the blood on the tarmac in the light of the lamp. By her side, she could hear Molly's snuffles but she couldn't take her eyes off Erin.

'It's okay,' she whispered as she stroked Erin's hair. 'Help will be here soon. I'll keep you warm and safe until then. You just stay with me. Do you hear?'

TWO

Detective Sergeant Grace Allendale was sitting on the settee when her mobile rang. At first she thought it might be Teagan, calling for a lift. Simon had collected his daughter from college and the three of them had eaten dinner together before he'd dropped her off at her friend's house for a couple of hours. As it was half-term, Teagan was staying with them, and going in to work with Simon as she wanted an insight into the running of a newspaper. She was taking a course in media at Stoke-on-Trent College, hoping to be a journalist like her dad, once she'd finished university.

But it wasn't Teagan on the phone. It was Grace's DI, Allie Shenton.

'There's been a mugging,' Allie said. 'A young woman, sixteen, has been stabbed in a walkway off Sampson Street, Baddeley Green. I'm heading up a team. Can you join us to liaise with the family?'

'Yes, of course. I'm on my way.' Grace disconnected the call and got straight to her feet, Simon looking over at her sudden movement. She knew his journalistic senses would already be activated. Last month he'd been promoted to crime editor of *Stoke News* after his boss had retired. Grace had never got on

7

with Phil Thurston – he'd always tried to get one over on her, especially when he'd heard of her relationship to the notorious Steele family.

'What's happened?' Simon asked.

'A mugging resulting in a stabbing. Female, teenager.' Grace told him all she could as she pulled on her boots and coat. She grabbed her keys, adrenaline pumping through her. 'Say goodnight to Teagan for me. I'm sure this is going to be a late one.'

'Will do, and Grace?'

She was already at the front door but stopped to wait for him to join her. He kissed her. 'Be careful.'

'I'm always vigilant, but thanks.' She gave him a faint smile.

Last month, an officer from their station had been killed in the line of duty. PC David Cunningham had been attending a burglary when he was attacked by one of three men who had gone out with intent. A fatal blow to his head had put him in a coma and all machines were switched off a week later, when there was still no sign of life after tests had been carried out. His killer, a sixteen-year-old, had been remanded into youth custody but that didn't alter the fact of the matter. An officer hadn't gone home at the end of his shift.

It had affected them all deeply. When it was one of your own, someone who you saw on a regular basis, it hit you hard. Dave had been a practical joker, always up to something to make the days go by with a smile. He was compassionate and a good officer too, liked by a lot of people out on the streets of Stoke-on-Trent.

Grace gave Simon a hug.

'I'm going to ring Teagan, tell her to go straight home to her mum,' he said.

'So you can come to the scene of the crime?' Grace knew he would be concerned for his daughter's safety but equally he'd want to report the case as it happened.

'Well, I—'

She pressed a finger to his lips. 'Just keep out of everyone's way.'

'Yes, ma'am.' He grinned.

'I'll ring you when I can,' she told him as she climbed into her car.

The incident had happened across the main road from the Bennett Estate, in the north of the city. In her own car, Grace had no means of getting there quickly without the sirens and flashing lights, but the roads at that time were fairly quiet anyway. The October night was clear and dry; a light breeze rustling through the trees.

Grace could see lights on in houses as she drove along Dividy Road. People safe in their beds, mostly out of harm's way, and here she was going to the stabbing of a sixteen-year-old. It wasn't going to be easy policing.

At the top of Sampson Street, the cul-de-sac where the path was located, she saw blue lights flashing. Parking as close as she could, she headed towards the crime scene tape, which was already in place across the road. The incident had been reported over the radio waves as she drove and she'd learned that the victim had been taken to the Royal Stoke University Hospital.

She drew level with her colleagues, DS Perry Wright and Allie.

'Hey,' Grace said. 'Any update on the victim?'

'Erin Ellis,' Allie said gravely. 'She's in a critical way. They were struggling to stabilise her enough for the ambulance to move off.'

Grace shook her head. 'Do we know what happened?'

'She was with a friend, Molly Redfern. They were walking home and someone came running up at them, grabbing for Erin's phone. Molly tried to stop him stealing it but he hit out at her, knocking her backward. Then he pulled out a knife and stabbed Erin in the chest. Molly reckoned it could have been either of them who was attacked.'

'She doesn't know the suspect?'

'Apparently not. She's not saying much more than that at the moment. She's with her parents. Can you come with me while I speak to her and get a first statement? I think your skills will be an advantage on this one. Molly is sixteen too. Apparently the girls' mums are good friends – both families live in this street.'

'Ouch.'

'Exactly. She could be either witness or suspect, but we'll be sympathetic until we know more.'

Grace shuddered involuntarily. A female teenager stabbing another wasn't unheard of, but she hoped it wouldn't be what had happened here.

DC Frankie Higgins was a few minutes behind Grace in arriving. 'How's the victim?' he asked when he reached them.

'We're waiting to hear,' Grace said. 'Can you start house-to-house? Take a few uniforms with you until the search team can coordinate things.'

As Frankie moved off, Grace glanced around Sampson Street. She hadn't yet attended an incident in any of the properties. From first impressions, they all looked to be privately-owned detached houses, about twenty in a row either side of the road. Mostly, cars were parked in double driveways, hedges were neat and tidy, outside lights shining in welcome. Neighbours were beginning to congregate at the end of their gardens in groups of threes or fours.

The cut-through where their victim had been attacked was off the cul-de-sac at the far end, four houses at its head. Grace could see more crime scene tape across the walkway, officers in uniform and CSIs busy going about their work.

She'd bet her life that no one living here would have ever imagined there'd be a stabbing that evening.

But then again, things like this happened all the time, no matter where she policed. Rich or poor, there would always be something that shocked her as she did her job.

Grace moved to join Allie, who was talking to the search team manager. 'Anything I can do out here?'

Allie shook her head. 'This is going to be hard to contain so we have to do all we can to get as much information in the dark tonight. I think it's all under control here with Perry. You and I can head up to the hospital to talk to Erin's mum after speaking to Molly.'

'Yes of course.' Grace moved aside for two uniformed officers as they passed. 'Nothing come through about our victim?'

Allie shook her head and Grace sighed. Allie was right. In the morning, they'd be able to dig around a lot more.

They also had to think of the residents of Sampson Street. They deserved their sleep and privacy, because nothing was going to be quiet around here for the foreseeable future.

One act of violence had seen to that.

THREE

While Perry stayed outside to coordinate, Grace and Allie made their way in silence towards the Redferns' home. Grace had thought that Sampson Street was a row of identical properties but looking closer, she could see each house had something slightly different. One had a porch; the next a window above the garage. The property to her right had a double garage; the one next to that a driveway just big enough to park one vehicle as it had an extra room downstairs.

The houses reminded Grace of where she used to live in Manchester – a community of new-builds, only a decade old at a guesstimate. Here in Stoke, her semi-detached house was a modern box and it had taken her a while to give it a character of its own. Everyone liked to feel individual, she mused.

They squeezed past a parked car in the drive in front of the Redfern home to find the front door ajar. As Allie was about to knock, she spotted a young boy sitting inside at the bottom of the stairs. He was wearing pyjamas with a Superman emblem on the top, and thick red socks on his feet.

'Hello. Who might you be?'

'Nat.' The boy looked to the floor for a moment. 'She's dead, isn't she? My sister, she's dead.'

'We haven't heard from the hospital yet.' Allie exchanged a look with Grace. 'But we do know she's in the best hands with the doctors there.'

He nodded. 'I couldn't go in the ambulance so Mum let me stay with Lucy and Phil. Our dad doesn't live with us any more.'

'And how old are you, Nat?'

'I'm ten.'

'So you're the man about the house then?' Grace smiled, trying to put him at ease and hoping he understood her statement.

A man and a woman appeared from the living room. They appeared to be in their late thirties. The woman had long dark hair, her eyes red from crying. She wore jeans and a white shirt, slippers on her feet. The man was dark-haired too, but with a receding hairline. He was wearing black jogging bottoms and a red sweatshirt.

Grace's heart went out to them. They'd had their cosy night in crashed, with a drama unfolding that could end in a fatality. The woman seemed shell-shocked, to say the least, perhaps thinking it could have been her daughter too. The man's skin was pale, his demeanour one of devastation.

'Mr and Mrs Redfern?' Allie held up her warrant card and Grace followed suit.

'Yes, I'm Lucy. This is Phil.'

'DI Shenton and DS Allendale. May we come in please?'

'Of course.' Phil beckoned the boy to him. 'Come on, Nat. Let's get you a drink and watch the TV in the kitchen.'

They were shown into a large room with a seating area at the front and a dining table at the back. Numerous family photos adorned the walls and mantelpiece over the fire. An imitation log burner shed a welcome warmth, the lights in the room on low. Lucy picked up the remote control from a coffee table and switched the TV to mute.

A teenage girl, who Grace assumed to be Molly, was sitting on a cream coloured settee, hugging her knees to her chest. She looked a slight thing, with long brown hair. Her hands were caked in dried blood, her face blotchy and red from crying; eyes raw and swollen. There were signs of purple bruising appearing on one cheek.

Molly burst into tears as soon as she saw them. Lucy went straight to her daughter, sitting down and trying to soothe her.

'Is it okay if I ask you a couple of questions, Lucy?' Allie checked. When the woman nodded, Allie pulled up a chair from the table and continued. 'Are there only the three of you in the family?'

'Yes.'

'And have you lived in Sampson Street long?'

'Nearly twenty years, and there has never been trouble of this magnitude.'

Phil came in with a tray of hot drinks. Grace took one; knew the likelihood was that it would go cold.

'I'm going to ask you some questions too now, Molly,' Allie said once it was just the women again. 'Grace is going to write down what you say. Any detail – no matter how small – you can think of, please tell us. Okay?'

There was a slight nod from Molly.

Grace sat down on a chair next to Allie and pulled out her notebook.

'What do you remember, Molly?' Allie encouraged the young girl to speak.

'We were walking home and this man jumped out in front of us.'

'What time was this exactly?'

'About half past nine.'

14

'And where had you been?'

'Hanging around at the shops on Leek Road,' Molly said, looking down as she picked at the skin around her fingernails. 'We were just having chips in Potteries Takeaway.'

'They're always in that chippie,' Lucy admonished. 'I don't know why as Molly has something to eat before she goes out.'

Allie nodded, but kept her eyes on Molly. 'Did anyone see you there?'

'Not really.'

'Were you with friends?'

'We went in on our own, but Ethan and Chris came in and sat with us.'

'Ethan and Chris?'

'Boys from school. Ethan Farrington and Christian Knight.'

Grace noted down the names, underlining them so she could reference back to them later.

'And did you leave there to come straight home?' Allie continued.

Molly nodded. 'Erin had to be back by half past nine and it was a wet night, so not many people were out.'

'Was that the time Erin normally had to be in by?'

Molly clammed up so Lucy took over.

'Erin was grounded for coming in late twice last month,' she explained.

'Is that unusual for her?'

Lucy nodded.

'So you go to Potteries Takeaway to meet friends, Molly?' Allie turned her attention back to the girl.

'Mostly when the weather is bad. Jeff lets us hang around if there aren't too many of us and we don't make a lot of noise.'

'Jeff? Does he work at the takeaway?'

'Yeah. He's the owner.'

'Who would you usually meet there?'

'Kids from around here mostly.' Molly burst into tears and looked up at her mum. 'Do I have to do this now?'

Lucy hugged her, rubbing her hand up and down her daughter's arm. 'Does she?' she asked. 'Can't this wait until the morning?'

'Things won't be any clearer then and it's imperative we get the first statement down now, while the memory is fresh. The smallest details can help so much in cases like this.' Allie turned her attention back to Molly. 'I know this is hard, but we need to find out as much as we can about what happened. Are you sure there is nothing else you can tell me?'

FOUR

'Molly?' Grace urged as the girl sat still.

'We didn't have time to run or scream, or anything. I didn't even know she'd been stabbed at first. I just thought he'd hit her.' Molly took in a deep breath.

'Are you sure it was a he?'

Molly nodded.

'Okay, thanks. That's really good information for us to know. And can you tell us what he did then?'

'I told him to stop and he punched me in the face.' She pointed to her cheek. 'Then he ran away, into our street. I wasn't really watching because Erin went all floppy. I was crying, trying to hold her up but she was too heavy. She dropped to the path and then I saw my hands were covered in blood. Erin's were too. She was clutching her chest. I panicked then. I didn't know what to do.'

'Did you see where he came from?' Grace asked.

Molly shook her head.

'Do you have a phone?'

'Yes, but it was at home on charge. I ran to get Sara, Erin's mum.' Molly looked up for a moment. 'If I'd had my phone I could have called an ambulance. And then maybe—' She burst into tears again. 'Is she going to be okay?'

'She lost a lot of blood at the scene. I'm sure we'll have news soon,' Allie said.

Grace realised Allie was choosing her words carefully, just in case Erin's injuries were fatal. Allie's radio crackled as news came over the waves, but there were no messages for either of them yet.

'Can you describe this man to me?' Allie picked up where Grace had left off.

'He was white, quite small – maybe a bit taller than me.'

'She's five foot four,' Lucy volunteered.

'He was wearing gloves and all of his clothes were dark. He had a tattoo on his neck and the side of his face. Like a flame coming over the collar of his coat. And he had a large earring in. You know, one of those that leave a big hole if you take it out.'

'That's good, Molly. Could you say how old he was?'

'About twenty.' Her face creased in pain again. 'I didn't get a good look. It all happened so quickly.'

'And he ran away in the direction of Sampson Street, you say?'

'I think so. I was too busy trying to help Erin.' Molly burst into tears again, her sobs raw.

A glance from her boss and Grace closed her notebook.

'Okay, that's all we need for now.' Allie looked at mother and daughter on the settee. 'Thank you, Molly. We know Erin is a good friend of yours and we will do our best to find the man who did this to her.' She took out a contact card. 'We'll need to speak to you again but if there is anything else you can remember, please call me and one of us will come straight to see you.'

Lucy took the card from her as Grace stood up.

'I have one more thing I need you to do before we leave, Molly.' Allie pointed to the girl's clothes, blood speckles all over them. 'I need to take what you're wearing, your clothes and shoes and—'

'What on earth for?' Lucy sat up a little straighter.

'There may be evidence on them. There will also more than likely be footprints on the path that will have been made by Molly, so we'll need her shoes for comparison.' Allie looked at Molly. 'Can you change for us? I promise we'll look after everything and have it all back to you as soon as possible.'

Molly nodded.

Grace went to fetch some evidence bags and by the time she'd arrived back, Allie had collected what she needed. They took a few bags each and left the house in silence, promising to keep the family updated.

Outside, more police vehicles had responded; cars and vans with their lights flashing as they cordoned off the main entrance to the cul-de-sac. More of the support teams had arrived to coordinate things. Neighbours were still standing on their drives in groups of two, three and four. A couple in their fifties were sitting on their garden wall talking to an officer. Houses that might usually be in darkness by now were lit up at every window. A man with a dog patiently sitting at his feet leaned on a gate talking to an elderly woman. Children who were supposed to be in bed were hanging out of first-floor windows.

In the distance, Grace noticed Dave Barnett's vehicle. The senior CSI had parked in front of Simon's car. She rolled her eyes discreetly. She'd been right; Simon hadn't stayed away. She couldn't blame him though. This would be front page news, and would go national almost overnight, and he was the best person to help report it.

'They'll be able to see the place where it happened every single day,' Grace said to Allie once they were on the pavement.

19

To their left was the pathway, officers in forensic gear going about their jobs of searching for evidence. 'She was metres from her home.'

'So we have to nail the bastard who did this and make sure it won't happen again,' Allie told her. 'Can you act in family liaison capacity, let the Ellis family know what's going on, please? Actually, can you try and get close to both families as they live so near and seem to know each other well?'

Grace nodded. That sounded like a plan.

Allie's phone rang. The change in her features once she'd answered it made Grace assume the worst.

'Erin Ellis has died,' Allie said, with a heartfelt sigh. 'Let's seal everything off further down the road. This is a murder enquiry now.'

FIVE

One year ago

Erin glanced in the wardrobe mirror one more time before pouting and blowing herself a kiss. She picked up her phone, sent a message to Molly, and then slid it into the back pocket of her jeans.

Once she was downstairs, she pulled on her denim jacket and shouted through to the living room.

'I'm off out, Mum. See you later.'

'Is Molly with you?'

'I'm going across for her now.'

'Okay, don't be in too late. And I want some change from that note.'

Erin wrapped her scarf tightly around her neck and went out into the autumn evening. There had been plenty of rain but, even though the night was dark and cold, it was dry now.

She crossed the road to meet Molly. They had known each other since birth. Wherever Erin went, it was hardly ever without Molly, except when boyfriends had come on the scene and they'd spent the odd evening apart. It was only natural, a

21

part of growing up, and they had each other for when anything went wrong, and to discuss all the milestones of their first forays into relationships. Neither of them were virgins, having both tried sex out.

Molly was already halfway down the drive when Erin hit the pavement on the other side of the road. They linked arms as usual and headed along the path at the top of their cul-de-sac that would take them to the main road.

'Do you think Max will be out this evening?' Erin asked as they walked. 'I haven't seen him for a couple of nights. Wonder what he's up to?'

'Not sure. Has he WhatsApped you?'

'Not since the weekend.'

'Maybe he'll be there tonight then.'

Erin wondered if Molly knew how much she wanted to see Max. She'd spoken about him enough, although tried to keep it casual as he was so much older than them. He often came to the takeaway in the row of shops where they hung around. They'd both been impressed by his car, some kind of 4x4. He'd taken them out for a spin in it last week, tearing up the A500 with them laughing in the back.

Erin knew she didn't stand a chance with him, though. Max was too sophisticated for the likes of a schoolgirl. And she did look more girl than woman so far as her breasts were being slow to grow and her skin wasn't as clear as she'd like. However, she'd made the most of herself for Max: her eyes, easily her best feature, were coated heavily with mascara and her hair was clean and straightened. She'd pop more lipstick on before going inside, red lips inviting him to kiss her.

'I wonder if he has any mates,' Molly said. 'We haven't been on a double date in ages.'

Erin flicked her hair back as the wind swept it across her face.

They were still chatting as they turned onto Leek Road. Both girls had lived in Baddeley Green all of their lives, so knew the area and most of the teens extremely well.

Potteries Takeaway stood back off the main road, Steele's Gym only a ten-minute walk away. Lots of the boys who took boxing classes at the gym often called in for something to eat after, despite being teased that their bodies were temples. Max usually came in around seven if he was popping in at all. Erin had been keeping tabs on his comings and goings.

She pointed with glee when she spotted his car parked near the back of the takeaway.

'He's here!' She turned to Molly. 'Do I look okay?'

'Of course you do. You're a babe.'

Potteries Takeaway had been there nearly as long as the two of them had been alive. The owner, Jeff, always let them shelter when the weather was bad as long as they ordered food or drink.

There was a counter across the far wall with fryers behind it, windowed compartments showing the fish, sausages and pies that were ready to be bought. Behind, a large menu took up most of the wall, and there was a door that led through to the back.

Several tables were already full: two groups of teens, a couple in their late fifties, and an older man eating a fish supper alone. Erin sniffed. The smell was divine.

Max was standing at the counter with his back towards them but turned as they entered.

'My favourite ladies!' He grinned at them. 'Perfect timing. I'm putting my order in. Do you fancy anything?'

Erin turned crimson when he mentioned fancy.

'I'll have a portion of chips, please,' Molly said, taking the lead. 'I'm starving.'

'Me too, thanks,' Erin spoke eventually. Max always made her tongue-tied.

23

Max was twenty-four. He had black hair, left longer above his ears, strong features and a sleeve tattoo that wasn't visible right now. He wore grey jogging bottoms and white trainers below a navy blue hoodie with the number 17 on its back.

Brown eyes stared into her blue ones as he winked at her. He was taller than Erin. She'd always cursed being little more than five foot three, especially with the current fashion for flat shoes.

'Two more portions of chips, Jeff, when you're ready.' Max turned back to them again. 'Anything to drink?'

'Coke please,' they spoke in unison.

'Grab a table and I'll bring them to you.'

He was over a minute later with two trays of steaming chips, plastic forks sticking out of each one.

'There you go, tuck in.'

He sat down across from them. Erin did her best not to blush again but his presence was so intoxicating. She glanced at him as he tucked into his food. He had such long eyelashes. When he looked up, he caught her eye and smiled. She smiled back.

He seemed to like her.

They ate their food and chatted for a few minutes.

'What are you two doing on Friday night?' he asked. 'It's my friend Trevor's birthday, and he's having a party at his house. You should see it, it's huge. So posh.'

'We're not doing anything, are we?' Molly nudged Erin.

'No, we're free.'

'Wanna come?'

'Sure, where is it?'

'Over in Trentham. Are you able to get there or do you want a lift?'

'What time will it finish?' Erin didn't want to get grounded again. Her mum hadn't stopped moaning about last week when she hadn't got home until eleven after he'd taken them out in his car.

'I can drop you off whatever time you like. Don't worry if it's earlier than planned. I can always go back again afterwards.'

Erin looked at Molly, willing her to say yes.

Molly nodded. 'Okay, cool.'

'Great, I'll pick you up . . . outside here at seven?'

Both girls nodded and they continued to eat their food and talk among themselves.

'What are you lot chatting about?' Jeff, the owner of the takeaway, came across to them. 'Don't you have homes to go to?'

'You know we prefer it in here,' Molly grinned.

'You're only sheltering in case it rains again.' Jeff tutted. 'I know you don't come in here to see me.'

'Of course we do,' Erin replied. 'You're our favourite takeaway owner.'

'I'm the only one around here, you mean.'

'Well . . .'

They all laughed. The teasing was good banter. Erin liked how Jeff looked out for her and her friends. He was always there to talk to; could always sense if something was wrong. Not that she ever told him much. But it was nice that he cared. She missed having her dad to talk to, in that respect.

Twenty minutes later, Max drained the last of his drink. 'I'll be off then.' He stood up. 'See you on Friday, ladies. You'll have a blast, I promise.'

The girls waited for him to leave before looking at each other and bursting into excited laughter.

'We're going to a party with Max,' Erin exclaimed. 'I hope I get to spend some time with him alone.'

'You'd better pack the Durex if you do,' Molly said, raising her eyebrows. 'At his age, he'll expect a lot more than a long snog.'

'I would if he asked me.'

'He's twenty-four.'

'I'd like to try out an older man.'

'You sound like you've been shagging around. And you haven't!'

'You know what I mean. It might be fun. He's had far more experience.'

Molly nodded. 'At least I get to see if he has any hot friends now. Win-win.'

They high-fived each other and giggled at Jeff, who was now behind the counter and rolling his eyes at them. If he'd heard where they were going, he'd probably be annoyed they wouldn't be there with the usual crowd on Friday. Still, a party with Max beat hanging around with a bunch of teenagers.

And hopefully by the end of the night, Erin would find out if Max was into her or not.

SIX

Molly had changed into her pyjamas after the police had taken her clothes. She threw herself down on her bed and sobbed. She wished someone would tell her what was happening with Erin.

What was she going to do now? She couldn't say anything to anyone or she'd be in big trouble. She was on her own now. How had it all gone so horribly wrong?

She wanted to speak to someone, explain to them what had happened, even though the police had told her not to. But there was no one she was close enough to, except him.

She checked on social media. It was all over her Twitter feed and her Facebook page already. She had seven messages from friends trying to find out what had happened.

I've heard someone was stabbed in your walkway. I can't get in touch with Erin. Are you both okay?

Do you know what's going on in your street? Jaden says he spoke to a cop who's blocking the pathway to Sampson Street. He says someone got attacked. Is this true?

Are you okay? I can't get in touch with either of you?

What the hell is going on? Call me.

She quickly replied to the last message but the others, she ignored. Everyone just wanted to know who it was, rather than show any concern for her or Erin. She supposed she would have been the same, trying to figure out what was going on, perhaps sensationalising it as she sent messages to other people. But they would get nothing from her.

She wiped her eyes, spying the photos of her and Erin attached to the mirror on her wardrobe door. There was one where Erin had come to Ibiza with her. They were lying on sun loungers, a glass of lemonade apiece but the barman had made them look like cocktails with umbrellas and fruit around the rim. Molly recalled how grown-up the two of them had felt when really, they were nothing of the sort.

The next photo along showed them wearing large hats and silly sunglasses. It was taken in Erin's back garden, when they'd been thirteen. That summer had been glorious and they'd spent the whole school holiday in shorts and vests.

The one below that was of the two of them in school uniform. Another one had been taken at their joint sixteenth birthday party. Molly blinked back tears as she thought that all Erin's dreams might now be dashed.

There was a knock on the door. She turned to see her mum standing in the doorway.

'Can I come in?'

Molly nodded. She sniffed as Lucy hugged her again. It was good to feel her mum's arms around her and she savoured the moment because she knew her mum wasn't going to be happy when she found out what had been going on.

'I want you to know that I'm always here if you need to talk,' Lucy said. 'If there's anything worrying you, or if you remember something you're not comfortable telling the police, you're not on your own.'

'I know.'

They sat together for a minute and then her mum stood up.

'Try and get some sleep,' Lucy added. 'It's going to be a long day tomorrow.'

Molly nodded, wiping at her cheeks. She got into bed and pulled the duvet around herself, comforted by its closeness. Her eyes were so sore she could hardly keep them open.

Minutes later, Molly heard her mum's mobile phone ring. Lucy had been carrying it around, waiting for news of Erin. Molly rushed out of bed and onto the landing.

Lucy had sat down on the middle step, as if her legs wouldn't carry her any further, and she was crying.

'Mum?' Molly enquired. Her dad had come in to listen to the news too.

Lucy looked up at her, shaking her head. Tears rolled down her cheeks.

Even though she knew it would be bad news, Molly couldn't move. But she had to know.

'What's happened? Is Erin okay?' she asked once Lucy had disconnected the call.

She watched as tears poured down her mum's face.

'I'm so sorry, Mol. They tried to resuscitate her – they spent forty minutes trying to get her heart beating again – but she was bleeding internally. There was nothing they could do to save her.'

'No!' Molly's screams pierced the air. Erin couldn't be dead.

This wasn't happening. Erin was her best friend. Molly wouldn't be able to live without her.

SEVEN

Grace and Allie headed to the Royal Stoke, chatting about the case as Allie went through a checklist of things she needed to do.

'Have you any ideas who the suspect might be yet?' Grace asked. 'You've been on the job, so to speak, a lot longer than me. Anyone spring to mind?'

'It's that tattoo that will be the giveaway, I think. I'll get Sam to check our system to see what we have. I'm sure I've seen something like that on someone but I can't recall it at the moment.'

'Sleep on it. It might come back to you.'

'That depends on whether or not we get any opportunity to sleep tonight.'

'I hate doing this bit.' Grace sighed as they turned into the main car park of the hospital. 'Technically, this isn't the death knock but it still never gets easier.'

'Unfortunately death is part of our lives. Justice is too, though.'

'Absolutely.'

The two officers might have been mistaken for sisters as they walked into the hospital. Both had long dark hair, were of medium build and wearing thick black coats.

They were shown into a side room where Sara Ellis sat quietly.

'Mrs Ellis?' Allie asked.

The woman sitting in front of them sported a short bob, brunette with caramel highlights. A heavy fringe hung over puffed-up eyes, the woman's face red from her constant flow of tears. There was blood on her jumper, and under her nails.

Grace's heart went out to her. This was one of the differences between her and Allie. Allie kept her emotions to herself, making her seem much tougher than Grace could ever be. Grace often took victims' pain home at the end of her shift, the ghosts of the crime scenes following her.

She took a deep breath before moving further into the room.

'I'm DI Allie Shenton and this is DS Grace Allendale.' Allie showed her warrant card as she introduced them both. 'I'm so sorry for your loss. May we sit down with you?'

Sara nodded. 'My sister is with me. She's gone to fetch drinks.' She gave a half-snigger, half-snort. 'She thinks tea is the answer to everything.'

Grace sat down next to Allie, across from Sara, on a chair that reminded her of the days, weeks, months she had sat in something similar when she'd visited her late husband. Watching him wither away, waiting for him to die. Some memories never faded. She shook away the melancholy and got on with her job.

'I wanted to have a chat to you about Erin,' Allie began. 'More details will emerge over the next few days, I'm sure, but I'd like to hear from you, too.'

Grace saw the woman flinch at the mention of her daughter's name, as if she didn't want to hear it.

'What was she like?' Allie continued.

'She was a lovely girl. She was sweet, bright, happy-go-lucky for the most part.'

'Do you have a photograph of her with you?' Grace asked.

Sara reached into the handbag on the floor next to her feet. She found her purse, flicked it open and handed it to Grace.

Grace could see a pretty teenager, long brown hair with piercing blue eyes and a smile to light up a room. The young boy Grace had seen earlier at the Redferns' was sitting next to Erin.

'It would be great to get an image of Erin by herself that we can share with the press,' Allie said. 'I'm sure you have lots of those at home.'

Sara nodded in understanding and Allie passed the purse back to her after taking it from Grace. 'Erin was really good friends with Molly Redfern, I believe?'

'Yes, she's going to be so upset when she finds out.' Tears dripped from Sara's eyes again.

'And how was their friendship lately? The same as always?'

There was a slight pause before Sara replied with a nod.

'So there's nothing you've been worrying about?'

Sara looked at Grace. 'Erin was like any other sixteen-year-old. Great at times; stroppy at others. Helpful one minute; pushing her luck the next.'

'Have the girls always been best friends?' Allie questioned.

'Yes. They went everywhere together, did everything together.' Sara smiled, her eyes brimming with tears. 'They wore similar clothes, had the same hair styles, liked the same music and food. They were more like twins than friends.' She sniffed and wiped at her nose.

'And you and Lucy Redfern? I believe you're good friends too?'

'Yes, since we were at junior school. We got pregnant almost at the same time, and the girls were born two weeks apart. It's nice to see them growing up as friends, like us.' This time she wiped at her eyes. 'It *was* nice.'

'Did Molly and Erin always hang out near to home?'

'They went over to the Bennett Estate a lot. They have school friends who live there. Although they were a pair, they had lots of other friends as well. Erin was very well liked.'

'Did she always come home on time?' Grace remembered what Lucy Redfern had mentioned about Erin being late in.

'Mostly, yes.'

'And apart from the Bennett Estate, is there anywhere else she used to go frequently?'

'It would either be across the road to Molly's house, or they'd hang around at the shops on the estate. She was like me when I was her age. There's nothing much to do around here. But she wasn't a troublemaker. She never vandalised anything, nor got into trouble. Occasionally she'd come home a bit worse for wear having had a sneaky drink, but nothing I was worried about.'

The door opened and a woman with almost identical features to Sara's came in. She wore jeans and a jumper, no make-up, her hair tied back with a band. Her eyes seemed puffy from crying. She was carrying two plastic cups, steam coming out of them.

'Oh, sorry. I went to fetch drinks. Do you need me to leave?'

'No, of course not.' Allie introduced herself and Grace again.

'I'm Anna Grocott, Sara's sister.' Anna passed a drink to Sara and then sat down next to her.

'The police were asking about Erin,' Sara told her.

'She was a beautiful young woman and we're going to miss her so much.' Anna sniffed.

As Anna bravely tried to hold in her tears, Sara started crying. Anna held her until she was settled again.

Grace knew they were done before Allie even looked at her to nod. There was nothing to be gained by talking to Sara tonight.

'Can I give you a lift home?' Allie offered. 'Grace will be acting as your family liaison officer. But for now, you need to get some rest. Tomorrow will be a long day for you, no matter what.'

'When can I see Erin?'

'As soon as the necessary tests have been carried out.'

Grace saw Sara flinch again.

'You need to find this bastard, before he mugs someone else and causes more pain.' Anna's facade broke and tears rolled down her cheeks. 'It beggars belief how many random knife attacks there are nowadays. All over a stupid phone.'

'We'll do everything we can to bring this to a close for you,' Allie said. 'Now, I just need to make a call. I'll leave you with Grace for a moment.'

Grace gave a half-smile. Anna was entitled to her opinion, to let off steam after the death of her niece, but it was hard enough to police the people they knew who could prove to be a danger to society, never mind those who woke up one morning and went on a killing spree.

'I wanted to mention something to you while it's quiet,' she said to Sara. 'I'm afraid this is going to make the national news soon. You're going to get a lot of local and wider news reporters and journalists wanting to hear your side of the story.'

'Like bloody vultures, if you ask me,' Anna pouted.

'I'm just warning you. Things might become a little invasive. If anyone asks to speak to you, or indeed you want to give a statement, would you let us know? We can do our best to make things more comfortable. The last thing you need now, Mrs Ellis, is someone hassling you and your family.'

'Would they do that?'

'Most press representatives are good at what they do. But there are some less scrupulous ones too. We don't want you speaking to the wrong people and getting hurt. So if you could field all enquiries through me, that would be great.'

'I don't want to talk to anyone,' Sara said, her head bowed again. 'It won't bring my little girl back.'

Grace gnawed at her lip, unsure what to say. Nothing would help with the situation anyway. The family and the community had suffered a terrible loss.

EIGHT

Grace opened her front door with a heavy load on her shoulders, but the feeling of safety enveloped her as soon as she stepped inside the house. She couldn't begin to imagine how Sara Ellis, or Molly Redfern and her parents, were feeling right now. Their grief was rubbing off on her and she needed to compartmentalise it before going back into work. She couldn't help being emotional; would never apologise for it, but she didn't like showing it.

She made a cup of strong coffee and sat in the conservatory while she tried to let the events of the past few hours go. Grace had accompanied Sara Ellis to collect Nat from the Redferns', and the pain etched on Sara's face was almost unbearable to see. Nat had clung on to her as they'd walked across the road to their own home, and Grace was glad it was too dark for any late-night snappers to catch a shot. It would be what everyone wanted to see, the grieving family. Although personal images often did the trick to sell more papers, they always felt intrusive to her.

Once she'd left the Ellises in their home, she had dressed in forensic gear and walked along the pathway to look at the crime scene. She'd chatted to Dave Barnett, who was packing up to leave. His team would resume their work at first light.

Standing in the dark while it was mostly quiet around her had felt eerie but she'd wanted to walk the path that had led Erin to her death. It helped her connect with the girl, imagine what she had been going through; make her think of things that she could ask Molly about.

As she'd tried to put herself in the victim's head, she'd looked around. There was a house to her right, but to her left an open field. The hedges each side were thick and at least two metres tall. As she stepped along the path in shoe covers, she frowned at the tarmac. It was unlikely they'd get any footprints.

She took a final sip of her coffee while she made a mental list of what she wanted to discuss or follow up on the following morning – or rather, today – before going upstairs.

Ten minutes later, after a quick shower, she climbed into bed next to Simon. Even though it was three a.m., she knew he wouldn't have been asleep long.

'Hey,' he said, a yawn following.

'Hey. What time did you get in?'

'About one, but I couldn't settle.' He put an arm around her. 'How are things?'

'Nothing new yet.' She snuggled in close to him. 'Obviously it's dark, so we'll know more in the morning. I hope we find out what happened soon, for the family's sake.'

'Me too. Teagan sends her love. Says she'll never get used to the things you work on.'

'Tell me about it,' Grace humoured.

He drew her nearer. 'I'd like to take advantage of you right now but I'm too tired.'

She pinched him playfully. 'I'm drained of all emotion anyway.'

'Yeah, kids get to you more, don't they? There were a lot of teens hanging around. I spoke to a few of them.'

'Did any of them say they'd seen either girl that evening?'

'No. Some would have been waiting to hear so they can spread the gory news first, but I reckon a lot of them would have been friends with the victim.' He paused. 'Am I allowed to know which girl it is?'

'Yes, tomorrow morning. There'll be a press release about it first thing.'

She heard him chuckle, and was glad he didn't push her to say more. She could tip him off, and had he not been her partner she may very well have done because as a journalist she trusted him implicitly. But there was no way she was chancing anything getting in the way of their personal lives. She had settled in Stoke-on-Trent now and didn't want to move on again.

They said goodnight to each other; Grace yawned and closed her eyes. She had about three hours before she would have to be up. Time to switch off and get some rest.

Because she knew she was in for a few late nights.

THURSDAY

NINE

Sara was sitting on the settee, a blanket wrapped around her shoulders. The curtains were closed and Nat was asleep upstairs. Lucy had offered to keep him overnight but Sara had wanted him near. Besides, she knew he'd never get to sleep unless he was at home. Not after she'd broken the news to him.

During the journey to the Royal Stoke, the ambulance had pulled over at the side of a road to start resuscitation. When it was becoming apparent there was no pulse, and Erin continued to lose blood, they started on their way again. Sara had sat at the side, holding her child's hand, feeling how cold she was as her life seemed to be slipping away. She prayed to any God that would listen, but knew in the back of her mind that Erin was losing the fight for her life. Her daughter hadn't spoken; hadn't shown any signs of reaction – not even when the paramedic shone light into her eyes.

At the hospital, she'd been shown to a side room while they continued to work on Erin. A doctor had then told her that despite their best efforts, Erin had been pronounced dead.

She'd stayed in the same room until the detectives came to her. They had been nice, especially Grace. She seemed a woman who understood how important it was for her to slot together all the missing pieces to the puzzle.

When Sara had been dropped off by the police in Sampson Street, she'd gone to collect Nat. Almost as soon as Lucy had opened her front door, she'd run into Sara's arms, bringing more tears. Lucy had insisted on coming across to her house as she'd half-walked, half-carried Nat up to his bed. He was inconsolable but worn out, crying himself to sleep eventually.

Once everyone had left, it had been nearly three a.m. Sara hadn't gone to bed herself. She knew she wouldn't sleep, and once she was all alone she had cried, letting it all out.

Now here she was, three hours later. It was early morning and the birds were singing, but Sara still hadn't slept. She was as wired as if she'd taken drugs. Her mind refused to switch off. Besides, waking up and realising that Erin was dead would be torture. She still couldn't believe her beautiful girl had gone. How had she walked out of the door at seven o'clock and not returned?

She wished the day would never start. It would be full of telling people, news spreading, Erin's name everywhere as it hit the headlines. *Teenager stabbed to death in walkway.* She hoped the press wouldn't be too intrusive. Of course they would need their help but her family needed to grieve.

She recalled the times she had watched press conferences when someone had been murdered; police trying to put together victims' last known movements, hoping to jog the memory of someone who might have seen something. She hadn't given the families a thought once the clip had moved on to other news. Now she was standing in the shoes of every one of those families. She, too, was the parent of a murdered child. A child killed in Sampson Street, where neighbours were friendly and wouldn't dream this sort of thing could happen on their doorstep.

Sara remembered what her last words to Erin had been as she was leaving the house; the final words she would ever say to her. She'd given her five pounds and told her not to ask for any more money that week. Erin would often run errands for her but she hardly ever saw the change if she gave her a note. She knew she spent a lot of money in the chippie on the main road. She could never understand where it all went on her tiny frame. She was such a thin girl.

Now she was a dead girl.

Sara was glad her sister had come to the hospital after she'd rung her, sobbing down the phone as she relayed what had happened. Anna and Sara had always been close. She and Sara's brother-in-law, Mike, lived a few minutes' drive from them and had looked after them when she and Rob had divorced. It had been hard not to have a man around the home, especially to discipline Nat, but Mike had been there for her. She wasn't sure what she'd do without the two of them.

Usually she would look to Lucy for support but she didn't know what to say to her. She couldn't blame her. Tomorrow she would tell her that it was okay; that she shouldn't feel guilty. Sara felt remorseful herself at wishing it had been Molly who had been attacked instead of Erin.

This shouldn't affect their friendship, but Sara knew instinctively that it would drastically change *everything*. There would be no more Molly popping round, no more noise from Erin's bedroom as she told them to be quiet. There would be no more trips to the cinema, afternoon tea with her and Lucy. No more foursome, mothers and daughters. No more moaning about their daughters; no more asking what they were up to, dreaming about what they would become. Molly would go on to fulfil all Lucy's hopes and dreams. Sara only had Nat to wish and hope for now. There would always be an Erin-shaped hole that could never be filled.

Now the morning had arrived, it was going to be hard telling people what had happened. First she would have to phone work and let them know. Anna had rung Rob and he'd said he'd be there as soon as he could. She was dreading seeing him, hoping they could be civil to each other.

She went upstairs to check on Nat. He was sitting up in bed, tears pouring down his face as he looked at his iPad. Sara went to him and pulled him into her arms, letting him sob.

The screen was showing a photo of Erin messing around with Nat. It was a selfie and they were both doing exaggerated trout pouts. Despite the age difference, they had become close since the divorce. Nat was going to be lost without her.

They were *all* going to be lost without her.

She hoped they got Erin's attacker soon, so they could bury her. Take care of her little girl the only way she could now: put her safely in a box, six feet under.

A loud sob escaped and Nat clung to her even harder.

She had to be brave, get through this for his sake. She could save the tears for when she was alone, hide her grief from Nat. He needed her support.

'Why did someone do that to her, Mum?' He spoke so softly she almost missed it.

'I don't know, Nat. But I'm sure the police will catch whoever it was soon.'

'I hope he doesn't do it to anyone else.'

The thought hadn't struck her until then, that it might not be a one-off attack. Whoever was out there could kill another person, another young woman. She closed her eyes to rid herself of the images that thought created. She wouldn't wish this on any parent.

There was a knock at the front door.

'That'll probably be Auntie Anna.' Sara wiped at her eyes. 'Why don't you go and take a shower if you're not able to sleep? I think it's going to be a long day today. You could have a nap this afternoon.'

Nat nodded and she went downstairs to face the day with dread.

TEN

One year ago

Molly stood by the side of the road. She checked her watch – it was ten past seven. Max had said he'd pick them up at seven.

'I hope he isn't going to stand us up and make us look stupid,' she said, as she looked at the oncoming traffic, trying to spot his car.

'Max isn't like that,' Erin replied. 'He won't let us down.'

'He won't let *you* down. I can tell he fancies you.'

'Can you?'

'He can't take his eyes off you.'

'He is rather dreamy.' Erin turned to her with a smile. 'I can't stop thinking about him.'

'I hope I'm not going to be a gooseberry tonight.' Molly nudged Erin playfully.

'You won't be. He's invited us *both* to the party.'

'Yeah, so he can get you all to himself.' Molly rolled her eyes. 'He's into you, not me.'

'He is, isn't he?' Erin giggled.

A few minutes later there was a beep of a horn and Max pulled up by the kerb. The window went down.

'Hop in, girls. Sorry I'm late.'

They climbed into the back of the vehicle and he sped off. Aftershave and the smell of new leather filled the air. It was a comforting combination. Rap music was playing quietly.

'What do you know, girls?' Max looked at them through the rear-view mirror. 'You ready to party?'

'We sure are,' Molly replied confidently, while Erin giggled.

Of the two of them, Molly had always been the more self-assured. From their early days she had been the leader and Erin had followed. Molly liked it that way; that she had someone to look after, and someone to look up to her. Erin would do anything for her. She was a true friend.

They drove through Hanley and Stoke, and were on the outskirts of Trentham within fifteen minutes. Just before they reached the Trentham Estates, Max turned off and drove along a road where the houses were twice the size of the girls' homes in Sampson Street. Each one had a sweeping driveway, with the buildings set back quite a way from the road. Molly gazed at what she could see of them as they passed, longing to live in one of them and to be rich enough to afford that lifestyle. She was determined to make something of herself when she left school – she wasn't going to be the one in her class who did nothing and expected everything for free. She wasn't into handouts. She wanted to pay her own way.

It seemed so inviting. And quiet, not like their street. Something noisy was always going on there, often including her and Erin.

Max pulled into a driveway and Molly looked up at the house as it came into view. It was an older property which had been extended to twice its original size. A large double-doored entrance stood to the right, a triple garage to one side and at least eight windows to the other. There were several expensive-looking cars parked in front of it already. Max squeezed his in where he could.

'Come on, girls.' Max beckoned as he got out of the car. 'What are you waiting for?'

They quickly followed him.

He opened the front door, the music getting louder as they all went inside. Molly tried not to stand there with her mouth open. The house was beautiful, and so grand. They'd stepped into a large hallway with several sets of doors leading off it and a staircase up to a galleried landing. Erin's heeled shoes tapped across the marble tiles. Molly nudged her.

'This room is bigger than our bedrooms combined,' she whispered.

One of the doors opened and the music became louder again. The man who came out of the room was fifty at a push, with a round stomach bursting out from a white shirt, wearing a red tie and black trousers. His hair was fair and there wasn't much of it. He was laughing at something someone else had said and then he saw them. His eyes lit up and he gave the girls a wide smile, showing a perfect set of white teeth.

'Max,' he cried. 'So good to see you. And,' he looked at them both in turn, 'you must be Erin and Molly. Which one is which?'

'I'm Molly.' She pointed to herself. 'And she's Erin.' Molly nodded towards her friend. 'Is it *your* birthday then?'

A glance crossed between the two men. 'Yes,' he said. 'I'm Trevor. Come, let's get you a drink and there's plenty of food.'

They were shown into a sumptuous room three times as big as the hallway. White walls, black leather settees, grey rugs. A glass window from floor to ceiling took over the back of the room, lights illuminating an impressive landscaped garden outside. About twenty people were dotted around, some sitting, some standing up. Men in suits, ties hanging loose. Women in short dresses and high heels. The room temperature was set to high, the laughter tinkling as much as the glasses that were being filled.

'I'm glad we dressed up now,' Erin whispered.

'Me too,' Molly whispered back. They'd discussed what to wear in great detail since the moment Max had invited them. She had told her parents there was a school disco, and Erin had followed suit. Usually they wore casual clothes and Converse trainers but Erin had insisted it had to be more than just wearing jeans if it was a birthday party.

Molly was wearing a red woollen dress that came just above the knee with three-quarter-length sleeves, and ankle boots with a block heel. Erin wore a black shift dress and a purple woollen bolero-style jacket. Her shoes had quite a high heel; Molly thought she'd never be able to walk in them, but knew Erin was after dazzling Max with her youth and beauty. Molly hadn't seen anyone who she wanted to impress yet.

A few minutes later, they moved into another room, the colour scheme following through. Trevor had been true to his word and they were each holding a glass of wine. A woman was circling the room topping up drinks whenever someone emptied theirs.

'What shall we do?' Erin asked Molly as they hung around the edge of the room.

'I don't know.'

'There are lots of people here.'

'Everyone seems so much older than us.'

'So you might get an older man too,' Erin giggled. 'Any of them take your fancy?'

Molly glanced around the room. 'Not really. Where did Max go?'

'He said he had to speak to someone and then he'd be right back.'

'Do come and mingle a little, ladies,' Trevor said, beckoning them over. 'I know you're shy but we don't bite.'

They sat down either side of him and he put an arm around each of them. Molly wasn't particularly comfortable with it; she could sense that Erin had her doubts too. But Trevor removed his arms after a few seconds as someone brought him over a drink.

Molly glanced around the room. Erin was right about the men being older but most of the women were a lot younger, like them.

Max came over with a plate of food. 'Anything?' he asked, handing it to them.

Molly took a piece of ciabatta bread and scooped up some of the tomato dip. Erin did the same.

When someone shouted Trevor over, they sank down in the gap he left. They giggled.

'Lovely house, isn't it?' Max perched himself on the arm of the settee. 'Want me to show you around?'

Molly took this as her cue to help her friend. 'I'm fine here. Why don't you go, Erin?'

'Okay,' Erin smiled up at Max.

Max extended a hand and helped Erin off the settee, then led her through the crowded room. Erin secretly threw Molly a thumbs up with her free hand, and Molly stifled laughter. Earlier on Erin had been nervous about Max not turning up and now she was eager to get him alone. She watched as they left the room, only then feeling a hint of envy.

'Would you like a top up?' The woman handing out the drinks appeared by her side. Up close, she didn't look much older than Molly. She was tall and thin, wearing a black tube dress with her blonde hair tied in a chignon. Red lips smiled at her; sultry eyes too.

'I'm fine, thanks.'

'Where's your friend gone?'

'She's with Max. He's giving her a tour of the house.'

The woman nodded. 'Well, I'm Rachel. I can introduce you to a few people, if you like?' She topped up Molly's glass regardless of her polite refusal. 'Here, drink some more of this and I'll be right back.'

Molly smiled at her and took a sip of the wine. She glanced around the room again and decided to let herself go and see where the evening took her.

If Erin could play, so could she.

ELEVEN

Lucy was sitting at the table. They'd recently had a new kitchen fitted, lots of tall units with handle-less panels in a glossy cream finish and an island that Molly always sat at. They had also opened out the room with an extension, bi-folding doors creating a sense of the outside coming in.

Today she couldn't feel any excitement at its newness. She'd barely had an hour's sleep and her eyes were swollen from crying. After waiting for Sara to come home, she hadn't wanted to leave her side. Once the police had left and Molly was upstairs exhausted and asleep, Lucy had thought that Sara shouldn't be alone. But Sara said she needed space to deal with things on her own for a while. It stung Lucy to know that she couldn't comfort her friend; she could certainly tell that Sara's sister Anna was hurt too as they both made their way out of the house.

She shook the thought away and took a deep breath. Poor Erin. Lucy couldn't even say the words in her head without tears appearing. Erin had been such a huge part of their family life. In some ways it had been like having two daughters. Erin and Molly had been inseparable for so long.

52

And poor Molly. She had to think of her own child too. It would affect her deeply, now that Erin was gone. Lucy couldn't help but feel guilt as well as relief about Molly coming home and not Erin. Molly was the only child they had – but how could she explain to Sara that at least she still had Nat, without it sounding appalling? If anything happened to Molly, their family would be devastated. There would only be her and Phil. Lucy hadn't been able to get pregnant again, despite them trying for a second baby. In the end, they'd given up. They spoiled Molly as a result – a little too much at times.

Suddenly, Lucy took a sharp breath. Could Molly identify the killer, but be keeping it to herself because she was afraid for her own life? No, no one would come after Molly. The two girls had been in the wrong place at the wrong time, that was all. It wasn't going to happen again.

Feeling the need to see her child, she checked on Molly. She was in her room, curled up in a ball on her bed, hugging her teddy, just as she had been when Lucy had gone across to see Sara.

She knocked lightly on the bedroom door before stepping in. Molly turned her head but didn't say anything.

Lucy sat down on the side of the bed. 'Have you managed to get any sleep?'

'A little but I kept having horrible dreams.'

'Would you like to come downstairs and I'll make you some toast?'

'I'm not hungry.'

'Okay. Well, I'll ring the college later. There's no way you can go in for the next few days.'

'I don't want to go ever again. How can I, without Erin?'

Lucy held back her tears as she placed a hand on Molly's arm. 'Things aren't ever going to be the same, duck. You're on a new path now. But you can do it. I have every faith in you.'

'I can't think of anything like that while Erin is dead.' Molly seemed mortified at the thought.

'I know this isn't really relevant but when I was seventeen, I lost a cousin. She was like my best friend and I thought my world had ended.'

'You mean Susan?'

Lucy nodded. Molly had only known her from photos, having not been born until seven years later.

'I wasn't sure I'd ever get over it at the time. I felt as if my life was finished, like my heart had split in two and would never recover. But gradually, it got better.' She pressed a hand on her chest. 'I never forgot her. She was, and is, always close by. I feel her presence at times when I need it. I can't explain it, and I know it sounds weird, but I do.'

'Erin was murdered, Mum. I saw it happen.'

Lucy pulled Molly into her embrace. 'I know you did and I'm sure that will take time to fade as it's a horrible memory. It's not going to be easy while the police find whoever did this. I guess what I'm trying to say is remember all the good times that you and Erin shared while all the bad stuff is happening. But I also want you to know that I don't hold you responsible in any way. Because I know you might be feeling that it's your fault and it isn't, Molly. It isn't.'

'But everyone is going to blame me,' Molly replied, breaking into a sob.

'No, they're not. I won't let them.' She paused. 'This sounds terrible but I'm so glad it wasn't you.'

They sat in silence for a while.

Molly pulled away. 'They'll all think I'm terrible for leaving her, won't they?'

'Of course not. You went to get help.'

'I just panicked. She was making such a funny noise.'

'You did the right thing.' Lucy paused. 'Before I go back downstairs, is there anything you need to tell me?'

Molly wiped at her eyes. 'What do you mean?'

'Is there anything else you've remembered since last night?'

'No.' Molly shook her head vehemently.

'You can trust me, if there's something worrying you.'

Molly dropped down in bed again and pulled the covers closer to her neck. 'I'd like to be alone for a while, please.'

Lucy left her then. Downstairs, she put on her coat, reached for her keys and let herself out through the front door. Outside it was cold, a bit of drizzle in the air, and people were starting to wake up for the day. There were a few lights on in the houses around her.

She padded across the road in the dark with an eerie feeling that someone was watching her. Of course no one would be, but it didn't make her feel any better. Her senses were obviously heightened.

At the Ellises' house, the lights were on upstairs and downstairs. Lucy wondered if either Sara or Nat had got any sleep last night. She glanced across to the entrance of the walkway, where there were two uniformed officers on guard. One of them came across when he saw her, stopping level with Sara's gate. But once Lucy told him who she was, he let her go on her way.

She almost ran up the path to knock on the door, hoping it would be answered soon. Seconds felt like minutes as she waited to see her best friend.

Molly got off the bed and moved to stand at the window. As soon as she saw her mum go into Erin's house, she picked up her phone and tapped out a message.

At half past six, there wasn't much happening on the street

55

right now. It was dark and would be for another hour. Then Molly reckoned it would be chaos again – more questioning, more upset.

She looked down at the note she had written in memory of her best friend. Later, she would take some flowers to the top of the cul-de-sac. More tears came as she remembered that Erin was dead. She would never see her again, how could that be right? How could so much have changed in a matter of hours? One minute, they'd been talking; the next, Erin was falling to the floor. All she could think of was Erin's face as the colour drained from it and she fought for her breath.

She'd have to leave home sometime today, perhaps on the pretence of getting some fresh air. She had to see him. He hadn't replied to her message yet, but it was early. He would know what to do to make things better.

Two doors down, one of the neighbours was going out to work. Fred looked up at Molly's window and she moved away. She couldn't understand why he would do that. She bet he never usually did. Or maybe she'd never noticed until now. Perhaps he was a pervert and always looking her way. She laughed a little manically.

Then she burst into tears. Erin would have found that funny. Now she couldn't share anything with her. She was gone for good.

She got back into bed, ignoring the rumbling in her stomach. She didn't care if she never ate anything again. She wasn't getting up until she was forced to. The day was going to be horrible – she knew she would have to face more questioning from the police, and everyone outside the family would start to learn what had happened. They'd all be talking about her.

Would they all blame her too, she wondered? Would people say she should have acted faster in going to get help, or tried harder to save her friend's life?

Molly vowed not to return to college for a long time. No one could make her, and she had somewhere to go if she had to skive off.

She picked up her phone and tried to call him this time, but still it went unanswered. She threw it down and curled up on the bed, hugging her knees for comfort as she felt so alone.

Already, she was lost without Erin. She wasn't sure she wanted to go on without her after what had happened.

TWELVE

'How are you feeling?' Lucy said to Sara as soon as she answered the door. Then she shook her head and burst into tears. 'What a stupid thing to say. I can't stop thinking about Erin and I can't imagine what you're going through.'

And then she was in Sara's arms as they cried together.

Afterwards they went into the living room and sat down on the settee. Sara's house always had a lived-in feeling, without being too messy. Lucy could see Nat's trainers by the side of the armchair, and an iPad on the chair. Yesterday's newspaper was on the coffee table.

Despite the clutter, it was always clean, with a tang of an air freshener in the air. The kitchen hardly ever smelt of stale food, but there would be things left out on the worktops that would drive Lucy mad. She and Sara always joked about Lucy's OCD tendencies and Sara's relaxed approach to cleaning – Lucy was the polar opposite of Sara and couldn't go to bed until all the cushions had been fluffed up again, and everything was cleared away and put back in its right place.

Though Sara may have been a little untidy, she was a good mum. There was never any doubt about that.

'How's Molly?' Sara asked.

'Devastated, as are we all. She's in her room, trying to get some rest so I thought I'd come round. We barely had time to speak last night and I know the police will be here today. I needed to see you, see how you were. I can't stop thinking about it.'

Sara sat back in the settee and wiped away tears. 'I don't know what I'm going to do without her. I keep thinking it's a nightmare and I'll wake up and she'll come through the door and ask what's for tea. I keep thinking she's over at your house with Molly. I keep thinking . . . well, anything but the truth, because it's so hard to bear.'

'Don't upset yourself,' Lucy soothed. 'How is Nat?'

'Trying to act all grown up but failing.' She gave a faint smile.

'Does everyone know now? Your family? Rob? Do you need a hand ringing around people? I can take some of the onus for that, if you like.'

'Thanks. Anna did some of it last night. You know, the important people. You, my parents, Rob and his parents. It was too late to call anyone else but would you do our mutual friends?'

'Yes, of course. I'll do that this morning.'

'Thanks. I'll ring a few people – Erin's college, my work and the like, as soon as they are open, and Anna will be around this morning to do some more too.' She shrugged. 'I still don't know what she'll be able to do here beyond that though.'

'I can stay as long as you want.'

'It's okay. You need to look after Molly. She's going to be broken.' Sara looked away for a moment. 'I can't believe I'll never hear them coming through the front door like whirlwinds. That I won't hear them running up the stairs to her room. That I won't have to tell them to bring the noise down or stop squealing. Our homes are going to be so quiet without her, aren't they?'

Lucy's eyes welled with tears again and she patted Sara's arm to comfort herself as much as her friend.

'Have they said anything about when you can go and see her? Or when they will give out her name?'

'I identified her at the scene, so it's being released to the general public this morning. I'm going to see her again this afternoon though. I need to.' She paused. 'They want us to speak on camera, appeal to the general public. I'm not sure I can do that.'

'You can.' Lucy nodded. 'I can help you if necessary. You're not going to be alone to face this. And you have Anna and Mike too.'

'All those times we've watched press conferences and said that one of the people speaking out were the murderers.' Sara shook her head. 'How could we have said that? Are people going to think that of us? Will—'

Lucy shook her head but knew she could do nothing to stop anyone thinking those thoughts.

'Do you think it's what we've been worrying about, though? Perhaps we should mention that to the police?'

Lucy grimaced. She and Sara had been concerned about the girls for a few months now. Yet each time they had tried to talk to either of them, they'd clammed up. Said there was nothing worrying them. That they were okay, everything was fine.

But they'd both come home drunk on several occasions, and one night, Molly had been so wired that Lucy had asked her if she'd been experimenting with drugs. Molly had flatly denied it.

'I think we might have to.' Sara wrung her hands. 'Although we don't have anything concrete.'

Lucy nodded. 'I just hope they weren't delivering things for other people.'

They had also been discussing the girls' behaviour. They had both changed significantly over the past few months, but equally that could be down to teenage hormones. Lucy was forever arguing with Molly, but she could remember doing the same with her own mother. It seemed a rite of passage at sixteen.

'Should I speak to the detective, Grace?' Sara suggested. 'She's my family liaison officer. I could tell her what we know.'

'Let's tell her together then. I don't want the burden on you alone. Did she say what time she'd be here?'

'No, just that she'll see me this morning.'

'Will you text me when she arrives?'

Sara nodded. Eventually, after a silence, both women stood up.

'If there's anything I can do for you, or if you need to speak to someone,' Lucy reiterated, 'you can call me anytime. Or come across. You know that, don't you?'

Sara nodded. They embraced again and then walked through to the hallway. Lucy didn't want to leave but didn't know how to be any more useful. She would pop across later in the morning.

She'd speak to Molly again too. She wanted to; needed to. Maybe Molly might volunteer a little more information. She and Phil would have to be firm with her if she was scared. Show her that they would deal with whatever she told them and then they would protect her if necessary.

Sara stood on her doorstep as she watched Lucy go into her house. Apart from the police officers and the crime scene tape she could see flapping in the wind, the street was mostly quiet. Lights on in the windows of the homes around her. Neighbours would be getting ready for work, heading off over the next hour or so. Luckily for them their lives hadn't changed much. They could go about their business as usual.

As she turned to go back inside, a car drew up a few doors

away and she heard someone shout her name. Sara narrowed her eyes to see who it was in the dark, then a sob broke through as she recognised it was Rob.

He got out and ran towards her. Although Sara hadn't seen her ex-husband much during the year since he'd moved to Dorset, his familiarity comforted her. They were Erin's parents. Between them they had created a loving and wonderful daughter. All the years of betrayal, fighting and acrimony between them evaporated in that moment as they mourned the loss of their daughter.

'I came as soon as I could.' Tears were pouring down his face. 'Please tell me it's not true.'

'She's dead, Rob, and I don't know what to do.'

She rushed into his arms and they clung to each other as they sobbed.

Afterwards, they went inside and she told him what had happened the night before; finding Erin on the path, going to the hospital, the police bringing her home when there was nothing more anyone could do for their little girl.

'Did she suffer?' he asked.

'If she did it wouldn't have been for long. She was unconscious when I got to her and she . . . she never opened her eyes again. I didn't get to say goodbye to her either.'

The noise of their voices brought Nat downstairs. When he saw his dad, he ran into his arms. Sara was going to leave them to it but Rob reached for her again.

They stood in a triangle of grief, supporting each other as they tried to take in the enormity of what had happened. Of how different their lives were about to become. Of how much Erin missing from their family would affect them all.

How they had lost a daughter and a sister before her seventeenth birthday at the hands of a killer.

THIRTEEN

Molly held the phone close to her mouth as she spoke to him. She'd been warned by the police not to communicate with anyone outside her family, or to release any details, but she wasn't about to do that anyway. She just wanted to see him.

It was hard not to be with him. Their relationship had always been on the quiet but now they would have to be even more careful they weren't caught. No one had known about them except Erin, and she couldn't say anything now.

'I can't believe she's dead,' she said.

'What are the police saying? Have they found anything out?'

'I don't really know.'

'What were they asking you?'

'Just what happened to Erin. I didn't tell them anything else.'

'Do you know who attacked her?'

'I didn't see.'

Even though they weren't together, as she explained everything, she could almost imagine his features getting darker.

'You're sure you didn't see who it was?' he asked afterwards.

'I swear.'

'You're not afraid to tell me?'

'No. The police said they'll be checking CCTV, looking at who had gone in and out of the walkway.'

'You need to keep me informed of what's going on,' he said. 'Can you do that for me?'

'Yes, I'll ring you as soon as—'

'No phone contact.'

She flinched as he bellowed down the line. 'Don't be mad,' she whispered.

'Sorry, Mols. I didn't mean to scare you.'

'It's okay.' It wasn't, really, but she wanted to keep him on the phone.

'All right, then. It's best if I ring you now, unless you have something to tell me. Are you clear on that?'

'I'm not a child!'

'I know.' A sigh. 'I'm just watching out for us both, that's all. It would be hard if we couldn't be together, wouldn't it?'

Molly would rather kill herself than not see him again. Without him and without Erin, she'd be totally alone. 'Yes, I'd hate that.'

'Me too. So for now, for the next few days, we'll stay in touch over the phone. We can't be seen together, do you understand?'

'But I need to see you soon.'

'I'll be in touch.'

'When?'

The phone went dead just as Molly heard the front door open. She dived back into bed before it had closed, prepared to feign sleep if necessary. She needed to think about what to do next.

And she had to see him soon. It wasn't enough to hear

his voice. She wanted to be held in his arms, soothed by his words.

She had to find a way.

He cursed, banging the palm of his hand on the steering wheel of his car. This was too close to home again.

He needed to get out, but he was sure they wouldn't let him. Once you're in, you're in, they had told him.

He hadn't had much choice in the first instance after they said he owed them. In a way he did, but in others, he had paid his dues several times over now.

One thing was certain, Eddie wasn't going to be too pleased. A smile played on his lips. Maybe he could use that to his advantage.

He picked up his phone and dialled Eddie's number.

FOURTEEN

One year ago

At the party, the two men Molly had been talking to with Rachel had disappeared, leaving her alone. It was less than a minute before someone else joined her. This time it was an older woman. At a guess, she was in her mid-forties with a Botoxed face that tried and failed to lose her ten years. The dress she was wearing looked expensive and her heels were higher than Erin's. Molly had recognised the red soles synonymous with Christian Louboutin when she'd seen her earlier.

'Hi.' The woman held out her hand. 'I'm Angela. I don't think I've met you before.'

'Molly. Max invited me and my friend.'

'Where have they gone?'

'Max wanted to show us around. I stayed here and Erin went with him.'

'Ah, Max.' Angela purred. 'He's such a lovely guy. Have you known him long?'

'A few months.'

'He works for my husband, Trevor.'

'I thought Max worked at Steele's Gym.'

'He does that as well. Trevor runs a security company.'

'You mean, like bouncers on the doors?'

'A little.'

'Do you work for the company too?'

Angela tipped back her head and laughed. 'Not me, darling. I let the men do the heavy lifting.'

Molly smiled, a little confused but not wanting to show it. It must be amazing to live such a lifestyle. It seemed obvious to her they had no money worries at all. The wine she was drinking was good stuff. Already she was feeling more than tipsy.

'Why don't you come into the main room for a while?' Before Molly had time to say she was fine where she was, Angela had pulled her to her feet. 'There are lots of people I can introduce you to while you wait for your friend to come back.'

An hour later, Molly was laughing with a group of men as they told her some anecdotes about working for Trevor. She found out that he also ran several beauty parlours around Stoke-on-Trent.

'Everything is above board, legit,' Angela explained as she rescued Molly from the group. 'We're not into anything kinky.' She stared pointedly at Molly. 'Unless you are, of course.'

Molly had no idea what she meant and felt too stupid to ask so she nodded. 'Oh, I'm fine with it,' she replied.

'Good.' Angela smiled. 'Then I think we're going to get along just fine.'

Angela was called away then, leaving her standing alone. She looked around the room, feeling a little more confident. One man kept looking over at her and smiling. He was very distinguished, Molly's version of tall, dark and handsome. He flashed an expensive watch as he drank his drink, laughing with the crowd he was chatting to.

She'd noticed him earlier. He'd been talking to a couple of men until they had been joined by two women and gone to get drinks with them, she presumed. Angela had called out to him, letting Molly know his name was Chad.

He looked at her again, smiling. She smiled back shyly. Then she lowered her eyes to the floor momentarily as she saw him start to walk towards her.

'Hi there. I know this sounds a bit corny, but I haven't seen you here before.'

'I came with my friend, Erin, and Max.'

'Ah.' He nodded in recognition. 'Can I get you a drink . . . ?'

'Molly.' She shook her head. 'I'm fine, thanks.'

She knew if she had any more fluid, she'd have to nip to the bathroom and she didn't want to leave Chad now he had come over to her. Up close, he could be as old as her dad, but he certainly looked after himself. He was clean-shaven with short hair, neat and tidy, and strong features. His white shirt had a familiar designer logo on its pocket, his jeans the cut of expensive denim. He looked . . . rich. She liked that.

'So how are you enjoying the party?' he asked.

'I've had a great time. Angela and Trevor seem nice.'

'They're friends of mine. I've known them quite a while. They're a good sort. How about you?'

'How about me what?'

'How do you know Max?'

'We go to the same gym.'

His face seemed to darken for a moment, but then his smile returned. 'A gym bunny?'

She laughed, aware her lie might come back to bite her. But she couldn't very well say that she had met him at the local takeaway joint. How very immature.

They chatted for a while and before she knew it, Max had come back with Erin and it was half past ten.

'Time to get you two home,' he said, still holding on to Erin's hand.

Erin stood beside him with a grin.

Molly could see she had no lipstick left on. Well, at least one of them seemed to have had a successful evening on the man front.

'Bye, Molly,' Chad said. 'Hope to see you again soon.'

Molly gave him a quick wave before she and Erin left the house all of a giggle.

In no time at all, they were home. Max parked at the end of Sampson Street, killed the engine and turned to them sitting in the back.

'Did you have fun, ladies?'

Both nodded, smiling at each other.

'Fancy going to a party next month?'

'It can't be Trevor's birthday again.' Erin giggled.

'No, but they have regular parties. He's a good boss, is Trevor. Treats his employees well.'

'We'll think about it.' Molly grabbed the door handle and shimmied across the seat. She needed some fresh air. If she went in like this, her parents would ground her. It was clear she'd been drinking.

'Well, I'll see you in the week, no doubt?' He was looking at Erin rather than both of them. Molly felt a pang of jealousy.

They said goodbye and watched him drive away.

'I've had a great night,' Erin said.

'You were gone ages!'

Erin's hand went to her mouth. 'Oh, I'm sorry. Max got me another glass of wine and I didn't realise the time after that.'

Molly waved away her comment. 'I want to know if you're seeing him again, on your own.'

Erin sighed. 'I'm not sure. He didn't say. So whatever happens, we're both going to the party next month, okay?'

'I was a bit bored by myself.'

'You weren't on your own. You were with that man.'

'Chad? He was dull.'

'Oh.'

Molly nudged her. 'I'm joking. He was nice to talk to. So yes, we'll go again next month.'

'Cool!' Erin beamed.

They linked arms and walked the last few metres home.

'Are you okay with me seeing Max, if he asks me?' Erin questioned as Molly got to her front gate.

'Of course I am.' She gave her friend a hug. 'I think you should go for it. He seems really nice.'

'Yeah, he does.' Erin staggered around a bit and then stopped. 'I'm a little drunk. Have you got any mints?'

'You'll be lucky to hide it with a sweet.' Molly rummaged in her bag until she found a packet. 'Here you go. Blame me if your mum says anything. Say it was me who wanted to go.'

'But they'll both go mad then and you'll be in trouble too.'

'It's better than her grounding you. Let's hope my mum and dad are both asleep on the sofa when I get in, so I can pop my head around the door and then sneak off to bed.'

'I suppose.' Erin flung her arms around her neck again. 'Oh, Molly, what a great night. I feel like I could fly!'

'Best get you into bed then before you do yourself an injury.'

'Yes sirree. G'night.'

Molly waited at her gate until she could see that Erin had gone into her own garden. They waved to each other and she went inside.

How she wished she was as pretty as Erin. Sometimes having ample confidence for the two of them wasn't enough. Because no matter what she had said to Erin, she couldn't stop thinking about Chad.

At least she would have sweet dreams that night; that is, if the room would stop spinning.

Awake early the next morning, Erin thought about the night before. She stretched out in her bed, her smile wide as she recalled everything about Max. The way he winked at her to reassure her, the curve of his lips, the sultriness in his eyes.

She hoped he didn't think she was too young for him. His kisses had been keen when they'd been alone, but he hadn't given her one at the end of the night, like she'd hoped. She'd wanted him to. Maybe it was because she was with Molly. They had both been in the car. But he could have shouted her back.

She knew she would always be second best to Molly. She didn't mind though. Molly was outgoing to her shy; extrovert to her introvert, daring to her scaredy-cat.

She knew she wouldn't have as much fun in her life if it weren't for Molly. When Max had invited them to Trevor's party, she never would have gone unless Molly had agreed to go as well.

Even though they were only fifteen, it was Molly's encouragement that had made Erin that little bit bolder. Going for a walk around the house with Max had been daring for her, and she wouldn't have done it if Molly wasn't there to rescue her if things got heavy.

They'd been lucky growing up together and becoming good friends. Erin remembered her mum saying something like 'You can choose your friends but you can't pick your family.'

Yet, as they grew older, both of them realised that things would change. Boys would come on the scene, serious boyfriends and then perhaps marriage. Their bonds would either be broken or strengthened, and only time would tell. But for now, Erin knew she was lucky to have Molly to look out for her.

When Molly had said she wanted to go to the next party,

Erin had been relieved. Max had taken her phone number but she wasn't sure if he would call. He was nine years older than her and at fifteen that was a massive age gap. But she and Molly were mature for their age, both well developed and level-headed.

She couldn't wait for the next party to come around, was looking forward to it so much. But first she would hang around at the chippie to see if Max came in again.

'Erin, are you getting up this morning?' Mum shouted from downstairs. 'The hoover will be on in five minutes whether you're out of bed or not.'

'I'm up!' Erin pulled the duvet back with a sigh. She was glad there was no school today. She couldn't wait until next May when she was done with it for good. She had a life waiting for her outside of Stoke.

She and Molly were planning on going to Spain after school finished. They were going to work there through summer.

But for now, she hopped into the shower. She couldn't wait to see Molly and talk about it all.

FIFTEEN

The mood was sombre as everyone gathered for a team briefing a few minutes after eight a.m. DCI Jenny Brindley was present and she'd asked Allie to update everyone. Although Jenny was the one who got her knuckles rapped if their team didn't come up with the goods quick enough, she was always one to stay on the periphery. She believed the team worked well without her, so she let them get on with it and only ever interfered when absolutely necessary.

'Welcome to Operation Doulton,' Allie started.

When Grace had started to work in Stoke-on-Trent, the first operation had been named Wedgwood. She knew of Josiah Wedgwood, but it wasn't until she'd found out the fourth operation name that she'd queried the other cases she'd worked on and discovered that Middleport, Spode and Doulton had also been known names in the pottery industry.

Allie relayed the findings from the previous night and then got everyone up to speed with what had happened since.

'Molly Redfern identified the mugger as a white male of medium build and height. It doesn't give us much to go on. The description could match a lot of men, but she did mention seeing a tattoo. She said it was like a flame rising up the right side of his neck and cheek. Does anyone come to mind?'

There were a few murmurs around the room, lots of shaking heads.

'Okay, let's search the usual intel to find anything that might be useful – personal sources, suspects we have on record, anyone who might know something, that kind of thing. We also found a mobile phone in a black leather case at the bottom of a hedge. Sara Ellis has confirmed it belonged to Erin so that's gone off to the tech team for analysis.'

'So the mugger left the phone behind?' Grace questioned.

'Perhaps he panicked after he saw what he'd done and threw it?' Perry suggested.

'That's possible. What's next?' Allie checked her list. 'Molly mentioned a chip shop – Potteries Takeaway. Perry, can you go and speak to the owner? See if he has any knowledge of them, what they were doing in there last night?'

'Yes, boss.'

'We'll also need to search the house this morning. I'd like you to help with that, Grace. Can you see what you can find in Erin's room, leave the team to do the rest? It will make it a little less intrusive.' Allie paused. 'The press release goes out this morning at nine. Speculation is already rife and I don't want to put pressure on Molly Redfern, so I authorised it to go out as soon as possible. Everyone will be asking her what's gone on, I assume.' She glanced at Sam. 'Anything from CCTV yet?'

DC Sam Markham had been looking through the footage in Leek Road last night and again as soon as she'd got in that morning.

'I've already gone through who went in and out of the walkway around the time Erin Ellis was murdered,' Sam replied. 'I've followed the two girls from Potteries Takeaway, which is

74

a few minutes' walk from their homes. They go into the walkway and between that time and when the ambulance goes past to get to Sampson Street, no one else has entered to follow them, nor come out afterwards. CCTV doesn't cover the other end of the path so I'm hoping there will be home security footage on one of the houses. I've also got stills of anyone seen going into the walkway from Leek Road from up to two hours earlier. There are three lone males, and I'll be sharing the images on social media in the hope people can rule themselves out soon. It's a busy main road with a lot of footfall.'

'Do you think someone was already waiting for them?' Perry asked.

'There are hedges either side,' Grace said. 'What's behind them?'

'One is a border to a residential property and the other is next to a spare plot of land,' Sam added.

Allie paused. 'That's interesting.'

'So is a bit of footage I've picked up nearby too from a business opposite.' Sam glanced over at Grace quickly. 'It's of Leon Steele.'

Grace moaned. 'What's he been up to now?'

'He's seen talking to Erin outside Potteries Takeaway.'

'For a long time?'

'A minute at the most. You can see them laughing about something and then he goes into the back of the shop.'

'I wonder what they discussed?'

'We all know the influence the Steele family have around here, and Erin Ellis can be linked to him because of the takeaway,' Allie said. 'Someone needs to go and speak to him.'

'But it's near to where he works,' Perry said. 'Surely we can't question him just for being there?'

'We can't, but let's see if he knows anyone that uses the gym who has a flame tattoo. That should cover us. And it won't hurt to keep him on his toes. Leon Steele is never far from trouble.'

'I'll go, boss,' Perry said.

Allie nodded and then looked at DCI Brindley. 'Anything else to add, ma'am?'

'No, I think you have everything covered,' Jenny said. 'Just keep me informed of developments as they happen.'

'Thanks.' Allie turned back to the team. 'For now, I'll get the house-to-house gang looking for any further camera shots too.' She swept her eyes around the room. 'Let's crack on then.'

SIXTEEN

Fifteen minutes later, Grace followed Perry down the stairs to the ground floor of the station, deep in thought.

What was Leon doing at the takeaway? She supposed he could be buying food but even as she thought it, she doubted as much. Leon's body was his pride and joy, a little too much in her opinion. He was narcissistic to a tee, flexing tanned muscles at every opportunity.

And she knew from a previous case that he had a thing for young girls. Two years back, they'd busted a sex grooming ring. A group of men had been exploiting young girls and taking them to parties, where they were handed around like sweets. Their team had put a stop to it but she wondered if it had started up again.

Eddie's words of warning came back to her from the year before. Even then he'd been worried that his brother Leon was up to his old tricks. Grace had been on the lookout but hadn't heard or seen anything to suggest he was. Having said that, Leon was cunning. If he was doing it again, he would be certain to use methods where he wouldn't be implicated, like he had before. He was a tough nut to crack, covering his back implicitly.

They made their way across the city, the morning rush-hour just abating. Frankie had joined them too; Allie had thought he'd be good to have on the ground.

Perry dropped them off near to the crime scene. 'I'll come around to you once I'm done,' he said.

Grace nodded to him and closed the car door. She turned to Frankie.

'Right, all you need to do is keep an ear out for anything you feel would be useful for us to know, and then field intel from us to them. Try and build up a rapport while I check Erin's room. Some families let you; others don't.'

'If in doubt, I make a good cup of tea. It's the best remedy.'

'You see, you do have the right skills,' Grace teased. 'All the better to keep the riffraff of Stoke under control.'

In Sampson Street, extra officers meant they could get to work more thoroughly. Grace spoke to a few people in various modes of policing before leaving Frankie going house-to-house while she made her way across to the Ellis household. Just before she crossed the road, she spotted a man heading towards the Redferns' house. She hotfooted it over to him, hoping to intercept before he got to their front door.

'Can I help you, sir?' she asked as she reached the gate.

The man turned abruptly. 'My wife saw on social media this morning that it was either Erin or Molly who had been attacked. I – my wife and I – wanted to know. We live next door but one, you see. We go to bed early and, you probably won't believe this, but we never heard a thing. And now—'

'We can't tell you anything yet.' Grace walked towards him. 'Let's leave the family for now, shall we?'

She beckoned him away but he stood his ground.

'I only want to be sure they're okay. I've known both girls since they were born. Is it true, what they are saying?'

'What have you heard?'

'Of course I don't believe a word of it, but it's on Facebook that one of them has murdered the other.' He pointed. 'On the pathway, over there . . .'

Grace cursed inwardly. Social media. The downside of every investigation. In policing it had its moments, allowing them to quickly put out appeals for witnesses of crimes, but it often caused a lot of unnecessary stress for the victims' families, not to mention making it difficult for them to police cases every now and then. There was nothing worse than a hostile crowd, buoyed up by a comment on Twitter or a video on Facebook. It made the police's job hard, and the families of the deceased suffered too.

People couldn't help guessing, especially when they saw a walkway cordoned off with crime scene tape and a house across the road with numerous officers going in and out.

'It's all speculation for now,' Grace appeased. 'Did you see anything last night before you went to bed? Anyone running from the path into this street?'

'No, we had the curtains drawn.'

'Well, for now, that's all we're interested in. Witnesses coming forward to help us with our investigations.' She paused. 'Let the families have a bit of breathing space, sir. You'll find out soon, but we have to put them first, not their neighbours.'

Her words finally did the trick. He hung his head down a little. No matter what he was thinking, when put like that, it made sense to back off.

'This is DC Higgins,' she introduced Frankie, as he joined her at the Redferns' gate. 'Why doesn't he come and speak to you and your wife?'

'Yes, boss.' Frankie nodded, not a hint of a change of plan in his expression.

'And make sure you get as many details as you can from

them about the girls' home lives too,' she muttered. 'You can tell them it was Erin who was killed, as her name is going to be released any minute now. Might as well use that to get some useful information from them.'

SEVENTEEN

Potteries Takeaway was set back off Leek Road, with enough parking space for several cars. The frontage was largely a glass window with a door to its side. The name of the business was written across the window along with images of burgers, kebabs and milkshakes. Red paint around the frames was coming away, the wood rotting underneath.

At first impression, Perry wondered if it had been passed by environmental health. Kids these days would eat anything though. He smirked to himself; he'd been known to do the same after downing a few pints on a night out and getting the munchies.

The sign on the door said closed but he'd rung ahead to speak to the owner. The takeaway didn't open until five p.m. but Jeff Harvey had said he'd be there early to speak to him.

Through the glass window in the door, he could see a man behind the counter. He knocked to get his attention.

'Mr Harvey? DS Wright, Staffordshire Police.' Perry held up his warrant card as the door was opened. 'We spoke on the phone.'

'Come on in.'

Jeff Harvey was in his late forties, with thinning grey hair and pockmarked greasy skin. He was round, looking as if he ate as much food as he served and his eyes seemed friendly, if a little wary, at Perry's presence.

'I was wondering what was going on last night,' Jeff said after they'd both sat down at one of the tables. 'The kids were coming in saying someone had been stabbed. Is that right?'

'Yes, I'm afraid so. The victim is Erin Ellis.'

'Erin? Ah, hell.' The man seemed to pale before his eyes. 'That's terrible news. I've known her and her friend Molly for years. They've been coming here since their early teens. Do you know who did it?'

'We're looking into several leads at the moment.' Perry got out his notebook and flicked it open to a new page. 'The incident happened at around 21.30 last night. According to our witness, Erin was in here with Molly Redfern before the attack. We need you to confirm this for us.'

'Yes, they were here. They came in about half past eight. There were only the two of them. They ordered chips each and sat down to eat over there.' He pointed over Perry's shoulder to a table in the far corner. 'That's where they sit if it's free. It's a good seat, you can see what's going on.' He paused as an articulated lorry rumbled past. 'There was something about them, though. They weren't as friendly as usual, as if they'd been arguing. But when the boys joined them, they seemed to perk up.'

'Boys?' Perry's ears pricked up at the mention.

'Not boyfriends, I don't think. There are a crowd of teens who come in here regularly. You get to know them. Molly and Erin were part of a large group. The lads were too.'

'Their names?'

'Ethan and Christian. I don't know the surnames of any of them.'

82

'They live around here?'

He shrugged. 'I'm not sure, but they come in often. One of them has a car. A white Fiesta.'

'Do Molly and Erin ever go with them in it?'

'Not that I know of, but I can't see everything that goes on.'

'What about the other staff? Do you do deliveries?'

'No, we don't have the need really. I have two full-time staff, both women, and a lad who does me about twenty hours a week. We've been here for fifteen years, got a good reputation for the best fish and chips around.'

'I'll need a quick chat with them all. Will most of them be in work this evening?'

Jeff nodded. 'From half past four.'

Perry made a note of the time. 'So you mentioned the girls might have been arguing. Do you have CCTV?'

'Yes. The recordings are in the back office.'

Perry followed Jeff as he lifted the lid for them to go behind the counter. They went through into the kitchen area, the smell of grease making him grimace. The place wasn't filthy but there was a fair bit of uncleanliness present. He changed his mind about what he'd been thinking earlier, swore he'd never eat a dirty burger again.

Jeff pushed a door open and led Perry into a small, windowless office, no tidier than the kitchen. Papers were stacked up on top of cardboard boxes, hiding the desk until he was further in the room.

'The camera monitor is there.' Jeff pointed to a shelf behind his desk, pressing a few buttons as he reached it. Soon he had located the time just before the girls came in.

'How long does it cover?'

'Two days and then it records over.'

Perry watched as Jeff fast-forwarded through it. They did seem to be having some kind of disagreement about something

– one of them was waving her arms about as the other sat with hers folded – but when the two boys Jeff had mentioned came in and joined them, they stopped. They left together an hour later. The boys were still in the takeaway at the time of the murder.

'I'll take this with me.' Perry pointed to the disc. 'I'd like someone to analyse it further.'

'Sure. Any problems you see?'

'No, just routine stuff.' Perry wasn't about to tell him that he wanted to see the footage before the girls came into the takeaway too.

Jeff ejected the disc from the machine and handed it to him. 'I'm so sorry about Erin. The news will be out this morning, you say?'

'It's been on the nine a.m. bulletin.' Perry nodded. 'Thanks for your time. We'll be in touch if we need to speak to you again.'

'Happy to help, Sergeant.'

With those words ringing in his ears, Perry left. He sniggered to himself. He reckoned helping the police wasn't in Jeff Harvey's vocabulary.

Jeff watched as Perry walked across the forecourt towards his car. Once the police detective had moved far enough away, he got out his phone. He wasn't one to panic but this was a little too close for comfort.

'I've had the police sniffing around,' he said once the call connected. 'Erin has been murdered.'

'Say that again?'

'Yeah, you heard right. I couldn't believe it either. Stabbed on the way home and died soon after.'

'Did they catch who did it?'

'No. The girls were here last night.'

'I saw them too.'

'Do you know anything about it, then?'

'Of course I don't.'

'So what the hell is going on?' Jeff paced the room, running a hand over his head. 'This won't come back on me, will it? I'm not going to—'

'Leave it with me and I'll see what I can find out.'

The call was disconnected before he had the chance to reply. Jeff cursed loudly. He hoped everything wasn't about to come out.

Leon Steele stared into space as he thought about the phone call, wondering what repercussions it might have for him. He'd seen both girls the previous night when he'd popped in to see Jeff. The police were bound to check up on him. Shit.

'Who was that on the phone earlier?'

He looked at his brother, Eddie. 'Jeff Harvey. Some girl was murdered last night.'

'Anyone you know?' Eddie reached for his phone and began to scroll up the screen.

'Yeah. Erin – she's one of the kids who comes in to the takeaway. Police haven't given out a lot of details yet but she was stabbed on her way home. She lived in Sampson Street.'

Eddie paused. 'Where were you when it happened?'

'I was at home with Trudy. Where were *you*?'

'Don't give me that shit.'

Leon sighed. 'I know better than to hurt someone that young.'

'That's not what I've been hearing lately.'

'Fuck off, Ed. You don't get to tell me what to do.'

'I do when it brings the cops sniffing at our door.'

'Does that include our beloved half-sister?' Leon steepled his fingers and glared at Eddie across the desks. 'You're quite partial to Grace, as I know.'

'She's family.'

'Stop saying that. She isn't, nor will she ever be. You've tried for nearly two years to get her on side, and it hasn't happened. She won't help us.'

'We'll see.'

'What are you planning?'

'Nothing, I'm just thinking out loud.'

Eddie's phone rang and the conversation was over.

Leon left the room. Stuff Eddie – he didn't owe him anything. Leon may be the younger brother, but he didn't need anyone's help to defend himself. Eddie had better watch out.

First, he had things to check out and he needed a little privacy, not his nag of a brother earwigging his conversation.

He also wanted to listen to the news to see if there were any further details on the killer's identity.

Because the girl wasn't supposed to have died.

EIGHTEEN

Rob Ellis was sitting in the garden. He'd only been back in Stoke for a few hours and already it was getting to him, the oppressive atmosphere, the police calling in. People who he knew but hadn't seen in three years asking him questions. All he wanted to do was cry in peace. Everything was so hard to take in.

It had been bad enough coming back to the house, leaving his partner, Lyn, in Dorset. Lyn had wanted to come with him for support but he'd decided to make the journey by himself. He'd needed to see Sara alone at first, and deal with Nat. Now, he wasn't sure why. If they'd come together, he and Lyn could have booked into a hotel and had time away.

Yet, even though he felt like a stranger in the house, he couldn't let Sara deal with this on her own. Erin was *their* daughter. He'd shirked his responsibilities once; he wasn't going to do it again.

He'd be given time off work, plus he had a few days' holiday he could take. After that, he'd have to go back but he had faith in the police to get things sorted quickly. People knocked them all the time but they did a good job. They would find his daughter's killer.

A sob caught in his throat but he buried it as he got up. He walked down the garden to the place he'd once called his sanctuary. The morning air was cool but dry and he was glad he'd erected a six-foot fence either side so that the neighbours couldn't see him, perhaps stop him for a chat to find out if there was any news.

The door on the summer house was stiff but eventually he pulled it open. Inside, he searched for the light and switched it on. The place was a tip. It clearly hadn't been touched since he'd left.

It had always been his domain. 'Let's get a summer house so we can spend more time in the garden with the kids,' he'd said. He'd used the room as a shed in the end, rather than as it was intended. It should have been a family room, an extension of the house, but he'd been so busy and always working that it had ended up a storage unit.

And it was more so he could have somewhere to go on his own to get away from the noise and the arguments. He used to come and have a crafty smoke in there all the time before he'd given up.

All of a sudden, he felt compelled to clear it out. It had cost over five thousand pounds several years ago and had a high spec of everything. Now, it looked no more than a tip. If he got rid of the rubbish, Nat would have somewhere he could call his own. He'd probably like that; he could even camp out in it. The building was still structurally sound.

Rob went back into the house and then returned with a roll of black rubbish bags. Sara had looked at him as if he was mad when he'd told her what he was doing, but he needed to keep busy. It would give him something to do before they could go and see Erin. He couldn't sit and talk to people yet.

First, he made a start on the shelves he'd fitted the length of the far wall. Tins of leftover paint and hard paintbrushes that had been used and not washed out all went into the bag, followed by three roller trays and several rollers. Then boxes of screws, and tins of rawl plugs. Rob couldn't understand why he'd bought them all in the first place. He'd started doing a few odd jobs around the house but DIY wasn't his forte, really.

He'd been there half an hour or more when he spotted a pile of old car magazines. He reached for them but the glossy covers slipped between his fingers, dropping to the floor. In between them was a notebook, a thin exercise book like the ones he remembered using at school.

It seemed someone had been using the place after all.

But it wasn't an exercise book. It was a two-year diary, with one week spread across a page. Rob knew it was Erin's without her name written on the front. It pained him to see her hand-writing, even though a lot of it was scribbled hurriedly. Erin had kept a diary from a young age, ever since Sara had bought her one with a padlock and key for Christmas.

He flicked through it, seeing lots of entries. Some pages were completely empty, others full. Some talked about school, what her and Molly had been up to. The last entry was the day before Erin had died. He pulled a deck chair from the wall, unfolded it and placed it where he could see if someone was coming. Then he sat down and, after a deep breath, opened the book at the first page.

October 25 – First night meeting up with everyone. Me and Molly loved going to the house. It was huge and like nothing we'd ever seen before. There were four bathrooms! Imagine having a house like that.

He flicked on a few pages.

January 27. I couldn't believe that Max wanted me to go with Steve. At least he was gentle and kind. Max was there the whole time so it wasn't as if I was doing something I didn't want to do. Molly was in the next room with Dave.

I thought Max liked me as more than a friend but turns out he's paid to introduce girls to men. Still, it was fun in the end and I got a bit of money. I got too drunk though. Must be more careful at the next party or Mum won't let me go.

Rob closed his eyes momentarily. What the hell had Erin been up to before she was killed? Images of his daughter doing all sorts came rushing to his mind. Why hadn't Sara been taking better care of her?

But then again, he had left them so he was no better. And he knew no one could see what Erin was doing when she wasn't at home. They'd had to trust her as she grew up.

It seemed as though they had been wrong to do so. Their child had been exploited.

March 27. A huge party tonight. There were more girls than men this time, which was a relief, although I didn't like some of them. They can be right bitches at times, but once we'd had a drink, we didn't see them much anyway.

We split into couples. I got landed with dirty Derek again. He is such a leech and his breath is minging. I wanted someone younger but there weren't many young men there. It seemed like an older man's party this time. I hope this isn't something that's going to become the norm. Not sure I'm into all that.

Angela doesn't think so. She said it was a one-off. We'll see. We've been lied to before.

Rob wiped his eyes, unable to see for crying. If he could get his hands on the bastards he would kill them himself. The police were going to have a field day with this information.

His first reaction was to rush across to Molly's house and ask her what was going on. Tell Lucy and Phil what their daughters had been doing.

His second thought was that he wanted to keep it to himself, shield his daughter and his family from the inevitable press storm this would create.

But he knew they needed to see it, however hard it would be for him and Sara. After all, maybe it could lead to Erin's killer being found.

His shoulders slumped back and he gave in, letting his grief out in big, audible sobs. The last few months of Erin's life hadn't made for happy reading. Their daughter had been groomed and neither of them had known anything about it.

He wanted to read the diary from start to finish but knew it would be unbearable. Instead, he left the mess he'd created helping to tidy up and went into the house. He had to tell Sara but he was torn. He didn't have the words to tell his ex-wife what their little girl had been subjected to, but he knew it could help the police with their enquiries. If the man who had killed Erin was known at one of these parties, they could get him charged and off the streets so he wasn't able to do it again.

Erin needed to be at peace. She deserved that much, especially after all those terrible things she'd written about in her diary.

NINETEEN

Nine months ago

Erin could hardly keep her eyes open. Her head was flopping about so much but she knew she mustn't fall asleep. She turned to her right when she heard someone moan. There was a man sitting next to her, a girl she'd seen earlier sitting astride him. Oh, God. She turned away. They were having sex right next to her.

She pulled herself up from the settee and stepped across the room, going to find Max. She hadn't seen him in a while. There was a man and a woman in the doorway kissing. She squeezed past them, trying to avoid contact.

'Hey pretty one,' a man in the hallway said, leering at her. 'So you're awake now? You passed out earlier. Can't handle your booze.' He took her hand and pulled her into his arms. 'Want to play?'

She pushed him away. His breath smelt of beer and garlic. His shirt was half undone, showing his gross hairy chest above a protruding stomach. But the worst thing was, he was old enough to be her dad.

His demeanour changed and he grabbed her tightly by the forearm this time. 'Don't fuck around with me.' His lips curled in a snarl. 'You don't know who you're messing with.'

'Please, leave me alone.' The tears she was holding in began to fall. She hoped he would take pity on her. But it didn't work.

'You and I have unfinished business.' He opened a door and pushed her into a small bathroom. She heard the lock click into place before he turned to her.

It was then she remembered what she had been doing before the drink had taken its effect. She had been kissing him, running her hands all over him. Had she been thinking it was Max?

Oh, no, Max. Where was he? What would he think if he saw her with this fat toad?

Her back was against the sink and there was nowhere to go. He moved forward, undoing the zip on his trousers.

'The least you can do is relieve me,' he said, licking his top lip.

She swallowed. Even without the lecherous look on his face, the force with which he'd grabbed her and pushed her into the room was enough to scare her.

'I don't want to,' she told him, her voice timid.

'I don't really care.'

There was a knock on the door. 'What's going on in there? No locks, you know the score.'

The man fastened his trousers hurriedly and opened the door.

'Sorry about that,' he laughed. 'Force of habit to lock it.' He pushed past.

Erin slammed the door behind him and locked it again.

There was another knock at the door. 'Are you okay in there? You can come out. He's gone and I won't hurt you.'

'I'm fine,' she said, hoping whoever it was would go away. Then she sat down on the side of the bath and cried. She retched at the thought of what might have happened if he hadn't been stopped.

She waited a few moments while she calmed down. At least she was thinking a little better now that the alcohol was wearing off.

When she felt brave enough to open the door again, she stood up. She was going to look around the house until she found Molly and then she was going home.

Keeping her eyes to the ground as much as possible to avoid eye contact with anyone, she searched the rooms downstairs, appalled to find girls in with the men doing all kinds of things. Some of them were with more than one man.

Shock winded her as realisation began to sink in. She'd thought Max had brought her to this place because he liked her, not because he wanted her to do things with other men.

She knew there were seven bedrooms in this house, and she would need to search them all to find Molly. She opened the door to the first one but it was empty. In the next one she found two men sitting on a bed as a young girl danced for them. She was wearing nothing but a thong, throwing her arms up into the air, flicking her hair and running her hands over her body.

'Shut the door unless you want to join us,' one of the men shouted.

Erin closed it quickly. Her heart beating rapidly, she looked in to the next bedroom to find a man with his back towards her as he pressed himself into a girl. The girl turned to her with a vacant look. She closed that door too.

Finally, she found Molly.

Erin stood in the doorway, shocked to see her friend with hardly any clothes on. A man was having sex with her. In a chair beside the bed was another man. He was watching them.

Erin didn't know what to do. Should she cry out and get

Molly free of them? Or would they drag her into the room and make her have sex with them too?

She hated Max so much in that moment. He'd said he'd look after her, and Molly, but look at what they were doing. This didn't seem right at all. What kind of boyfriend would let this happen?

Not that he was even her boyfriend. He had told he cared about her when they went out together, but even those times were coming far and few between now.

Max said it was good to experiment too and that he was there for her when she needed him. Well, where was he now? She wanted to see him, be taken into his arms and reassured.

Because right now, she was scared and all she wanted was to go home.

TWENTY

After visiting Potteries Takeaway, Perry made the two-minute drive to Steele's Gym and parked in their car park. The business was in a single storey building that used to be a school. Once through a small lobby, there was a door into the gym itself.

When he opened it, the first thing he heard was the noise of fist on fist as two men sparred in the boxing ring to his right. To his left, rows of benches and stacks of weights dominated the far side of the room. There were about twenty men in total. Perry noticed no women, the reception being as empty as the last time he'd visited. The blinds were down on the window and door that had once been Posh Gloss Nail Bar.

The main offices were situated at the back. Perry ignored everyone as he walked through to them. Most people knew who he was in here, there was no need for formalities. He was surprised that no one thought to stop him, though. He wondered if someone would send a quick text message to alert the brothers. There was certainly time.

Perry knocked on the door.

'Yes?'

'Staffordshire Police.'

'Come on in.'

Inside, both Eddie and Leon were sitting at desks opposite each other. There was a settee and a low table in the other half of the room. Filing cabinets lined one wall, certificates and trophies adorning shelves on another.

A photo of Eddie with Josh Parker, who had been murdered in the car park in 2018, stood prominent above his head. Parker had been Eddie's right hand man, but he had been burnt alive.

'Perry.' Eddie smiled, his act of being pleased to see him fooling no one. 'What can we do for you?'

'I have a few questions I'd like to ask.'

Leon sighed and then threw down the pen he was holding. 'About what?'

'There was a young girl murdered last night and we're checking out her last known movements before she died.'

'Jeff Harvey rang me earlier, from Potteries Takeaway. I own the building. He told me Erin and her friend came in regularly, as do a group of teens.'

Perry kept in his annoyance, realising that owning the building gave Leon a legitimate reason to have been on the premises.

'Did you see them last night?' Perry asked.

'Yeah. I was in there for about twenty minutes. Jeff had a problem with one of the electric sockets so I went to check it out before arranging for someone to fix it.'

'And this would have been around what time?'

'About half eight. I'd finished my shift here at seven, had a workout and a shower before calling in on my way home.' He stood up and leaned his knuckles on the desk. 'What's with the questions?'

Perry said nothing. It wasn't necessary to elaborate and Leon knew it.

Leon shook his head. 'You have some nerve. Are you going to come to us every time someone in Stoke cops it?'

'If you're in the vicinity, which you often seem to be,' Perry challenged, 'then, yes.'

'I had nothing to do with it. The news bulletins said it happened around half nine last night. I was at home for nine. You can check with the other half, unless you value your life.'

Perry had met Trudy Steele a few times now. He'd never liked what he'd seen of her on any of the occasions.

'You didn't come here just to ask me that. Only, that's harassment if you did, and I've a good mind to complain to—'

'We're after a suspect with a distinctive tattoo, wondered if they were a member of the gym?'

'Hardly a plausible excuse.' Leon glared at him. 'What's the tatt?'

'Flames coming up the side of the neck and face.'

'Haddington,' both men said at the same time.

It surprised Perry that they would give his name up so readily.

Eddie shook his head. 'It won't be him. He's living in Spain with his mum. She went over a couple of years ago. He didn't want to go with her, so he sofa surfed for a while, but he was caught thieving from Picton's Warehouse and jailed for six months. As soon as he got out, he went overseas. I haven't heard he's come back.'

'Although he might have, I guess,' Leon added.

Perry cursed inwardly. Ah well, one suspect possibly ruled out, even with such a distinct tattoo, and it was looking likely that Leon wasn't involved after all.

'Now, if there isn't anything else, Sergeant,' Leon said. 'We have things to do, don't we, Ed?'

'Oh, I'm fine watching the show.' Eddie placed his hands behind his head and sat back in his chair. 'Would either of you like a coffee?'

Leon rolled his eyes, muttered some profanities and stormed out of the room.

'Peace at last.' Eddie sat forward again. 'Sorry about Leon, you know how tetchy he is. So how are you? And the wife and family?'

'That's none of your business.' Perry turned to leave. 'Whereas anything you say is mine.'

Eddie's face hardened. 'Grace and I might have a mutual agreement to share information at times but it doesn't extend to you.'

'Care to enlighten me?' he said.

Eddie stayed silent for a moment and then shook his head. 'I'll leave that to Grace.'

'Just get in touch if you hear anything,' he said before leaving the room.

Perry tried not to frown as he let himself out, pondering Eddie's words. Because that last comment about Grace didn't sit well with him.

TWENTY-ONE

Grace disliked looking in victims' homes for evidence, clues of what might have made one person kill another. It seemed so invasive to go through their belongings but the police learned so much about the life people were leading before their death.

It was particularly poignant when it was a teenager, like Erin. Seeing how she'd been living her life brought home to Grace that it had ended prematurely. Erin would never go on to love anyone, get married, start a family, have a career – whatever she'd dreamed about. It was hard to see someone cut down in their prime.

Erin's father had been upset when she'd asked if she could see their daughter's room, but Sara had soothed him, saying anything that could help needed to be done. Rob had gone out in the garden, unable to cope with anyone going through Erin's things. Grace would ask Sara more about the girls' relationship once she'd searched through Erin's room. She would choose her moment to see if there was something they were missing. Were Molly and Erin the close friends everyone was assuming?

She followed Sara upstairs, into one of the bedrooms at the

back of the house. It was a double bedroom but Erin just had a single bed pushed against the wall, giving lots of floor space. Pale pink striped wallpaper complemented the bedding. There was a messiness about it that reminded her of how she was in her teens. Clothes hanging on the back of a chair, make-up out on display; shoes pushed under the bed and in every corner.

'Erin loved this room.' Sara ran a hand over the wooden dressing table in front of the window. 'Until she was ten, she and Nat had shared, but we moved Nat into the box room then. He inherited Erin's cabin bed. She chose the wallpaper and soft furnishings. It's changed several times since that ten-year-old wanted unicorns all over it.'

Grace smiled, but knew she needed to be alone to do this. 'Thanks, Sara. I'll give you a shout once I'm done,' she said.

Sara nodded her understanding, reluctantly leaving the room.

Grace wore latex gloves as she searched through the teenager's belongings. She checked around the usual places; the drawers on the dressing table and underneath the bed and mattress.

She opened the wardrobe and had a quick search through the clothes hanging up. All the shades of the rainbow came at her, colours mingling together in no particular order. There were a few dresses, numerous tops and a pile of jeans and leggings next to several more pairs of shoes. She checked above and on top of the unit, underneath too.

There was nothing to indicate Erin was in any trouble. She seemed as if she'd been a well-loved young girl, with parents who cared for her, but Grace knew how looks could be deceiving. She'd had lots of family members lying to her over the years to cover up crimes, secrets and lies.

Maybe the wider search team might find something in the house but, for now, there were no immediate clues in this room.

She was about to go downstairs when she sensed someone watching her. She turned to see Nat in the doorway.

'Hi,' she said. 'Are you okay?'

'We used to share this room,' he said.

'Yes, your mum has been telling me. I believe you have the cabin bed now.'

He nodded. 'Want to see it?'

'Yes, please.' Grace knew it would unlikely be of any relevance to the investigation, but she didn't want to upset the boy by saying no. It wouldn't hurt her to give him a few minutes of her time. She followed him across the landing.

Nat was up and down the ladder on the bed before she had got to the room. He held out his iPad.

'I have a lot of photos.'

'Will you show me some?'

He popped a code into the tablet and it sprang to life. A few more clicks and he handed it to her. The first photo was of him and Erin. It seemed quite recent.

'That was taken at my Auntie Anna's birthday last month,' he told her. 'We went out for a meal. Erin didn't want to go because Molly wasn't invited. She was miserable but I made her smile.'

'That's a very important job for a brother to do,' Grace said matter-of-factly.

Nat scrolled through the iPad slow enough for her to get a sense of their relationship as brother and sister. It showed that they cared about each other, spent time together. Molly featured in a lot of the photos too, especially the selfies.

'My mum was always snapping us on her phone,' Nat added. 'She said when she was young, there was no such thing as a mobile phone, so she hasn't got many photos of herself. So she made up for it by taking lots of us. She must have hundreds.'

'Your sister looked very happy,' Grace said honestly. In many of the photos, Erin seemed as if she hadn't a care in the world. 'She and Molly were really good friends, weren't they?'

'Yes, they spent a lot of time together. They were always laughing.'

'They never argued?'

'Sometimes, but never for long.' He glanced at her sideways. 'Can you keep a secret?'

'Of course.'

He ran over to his wardrobe and pulled out an envelope. 'This was Erin's. She didn't know I knew it was there.'

Grace looked inside. There was a bundle of money. At a push, she'd guess there was a fair few hundred pounds.

'I have to keep this, you know that, don't you?' She looked at Nat.

When he nodded, she realised he'd shown her purposely.

In the kitchen, she rejoined Sara. The Ellises' kitchen was extremely inviting, even considering the circumstances. The units were Shaker style, a large red AGA cooker in the middle of a row of cream doors. There were numerous magnets covering the fridge and the smell of coffee in the air.

Lucy Redfern was sitting at the kitchen table with Sara. Grace thought she might get up to leave when she saw her but she didn't. She sensed the women wanted to talk.

She looked at each one in turn before pulling out a chair herself. 'Ladies, I have something to show you.'

TWENTY-TWO

As neither of them spoke, Grace placed the envelope of cash on the table.

'Where did you get that?' Sara gasped, reaching across to it.

Grace stopped her from touching it. 'It was in Nat's bedroom.'

'But—'

'He invited me in to show me photos of Erin. But I think he needed to tell someone about it.'

'He could have given it to me.'

'He can see you're upset and he was probably trying to protect you. He's done the right thing, though. Do you know where it's come from? Does Erin have a part-time job?'

'No.' Sara shook her head.

'Do you know if she was saving for anything in particular?'

'If she was, she wouldn't have hidden it in Nat's room.' Sara glanced at Lucy.

Grace watched Lucy reach for Sara's hand and give a little nod of encouragement.

'Lucy and I have been worried about the girls for some time

now,' Sara began. 'They've become,' she paused with a grimace, 'a little unruly over the past few months.'

Grace took out her notepad. 'Any particular incident occur, or is this just in general?'

'I'd noticed that when Erin would come home at night, sometimes she was drunk; other times she'd be upset and argumentative.'

'Did either of them look as if they were doing drugs?'

'I don't think so,' Lucy joined in. 'But I couldn't be sure. Sara?'

Sara shook her head. 'We didn't know about that money, though. They could be runners for someone, couldn't they?'

'It's possible. I noticed a scarf in Erin's wardrobe. It's quite an expensive designer brand. Did you buy it for her?'

'No, she said she got it from a charity shop in town.'

'Ah.'

'They've been coming home with real attitudes too. It's been hard to watch as they used to be such sweet little girls. The past year, they've been glued to each other's sides. I'd often catch them whispering and they'd never let you in on anything they were saying. I know this could be construed as normal teen behaviour but even so, it was out of character. And Erin was coming in late.'

'And where was Molly on these occasions?'

'She was always at home,' Lucy said.

'Do you think Erin might have had a boyfriend that she wasn't telling you about, Sara?' Grace pressed.

Sara hung her head for a moment. 'I feel so ashamed not knowing what my daughter was doing, but it's hard when they become so unresponsive. Erin would be her usual self one moment and jump up into a rage the next.'

'They stopped out for a night last month too,' Lucy added. 'They told us they were at each other's houses. They're always doing something like this so it didn't cross our minds to say no. But one of the neighbours saw them out and when we asked them about it, they said they'd stayed overnight at a party.'

'Did they say where?'

Both women shook their heads.

'We should have done more,' Sara replied.

'This isn't your fault.' Grace moved her hands from the table for fear of reaching over and getting too emotional. 'I'm not sure there are many of us who didn't fib to our parents for a night out to a party when we were teenagers.'

'I suppose.' Sara didn't seem convinced.

'Is there anything else you can think of?'

Sara glanced at Lucy, who shook her head.

'Thank you, ladies, for your honesty and for your time.' Grace nodded. 'I know how difficult this is for both of you. Well, we'll keep you up to date with our enquiries.'

Sara nodded, tears welling in her eyes. 'Thank you for earlier too.' She pointed to the ceiling. 'You were gentle with Nat, even though you were seeking information.'

'I'd like to try and figure out what state of mind Erin was in, as well as find out what happened to her, Mrs Ellis.'

'I know, but you treated him like an adult. I guess this may become the thing that defines him now. He'll always be known as the brother of a murdered girl.'

Grace nodded her understanding. 'Is there anything else you'd like me to see of Erin's?'

'No.' Sara gnawed her bottom lip. 'She was a good girl, you know. It won't be anyone she knows.'

'Why do you say that?' Grace couldn't understand the assertion.

'I just know. It was a random attack, which means that man who Molly saw could do it again.'

'We'll be working that angle too. In the meantime, if there's anything you feel that might be helpful, please don't hesitate to call us.'

'Thanks. My ex-husband is still out in the garden. I don't think he can face things yet.'

'I can see what this is doing to your family and I am truly sorry. But the more you can let us know, the better while we continue with the investigation.' Grace turned to Lucy. 'I'll need to speak to Molly about this too. Shall I come across with you now?'

TWENTY-THREE

Sampson Street was still full of police and search teams. The pathway remained cordoned off as a crime scene, but the street had been reopened a little more to the public.

Even so, Grace knew that there would be neighbours watching them all to see what they were up to, where they were going; knew it would no doubt be all over social media as to which houses they visited.

Walking across to the Redfern home gave Grace some valuable time to talk to Lucy alone.

'What were the girls like at school?' she asked. 'Were they popular, competitive, part of a gang at all?'

'Nothing like that, as far as we were aware,' Lucy replied, moving to one side to let three officers past. 'Neither of them skipped school, they both had good attendance and like I said earlier, they were popular.'

'Even over the course of the past few months?'

'Well, now you come to mention it, it has been very much the two of them for a while. Usually there would be girls and boys calling for Molly all the time. I wasn't worried by it though.

Those two only needed each other. They were so close, very much like me and Sara at that age.'

'Who would you say was the stronger one?'

'I don't follow.' Lucy's brow furrowed.

'Did Erin tend to look after Molly, or vice versa? Or were they both equals?'

'Oh, I see. I guess it was Molly then. Erin was the shy one, Molly the loudest.' Lucy paused at the door as she searched her keys from her pocket. 'You don't think Erin was killed because she didn't fight back?'

Grace shrugged, choosing to stay quiet to see if Lucy would say anything else.

But Lucy just shook her head. 'Molly's going to be distraught without her.'

Inside the house, Grace followed Lucy through to the kitchen. In the daylight, the family home was warm and inviting, colours of autumn flowing through from the hallway.

Molly was sitting on a small settee, staring into space. She looked up, a worried expression appearing when she saw Grace.

'Hi Molly, how are you feeling today?'

'Tired. I haven't slept much.'

'I hope you'll be okay to answer a few more questions, in light of new information we've received.'

'Okay.' Molly glanced at her mum for reassurance.

Lucy went over and sat next to Molly. Grace took out her notebook, smiling at the young girl, hoping to alleviate her nerves.

'Molly, do you know if Erin had a boyfriend?' she asked.

Molly shook her head. 'We were both single. We weren't interested in boys.'

'I thought everyone was interested in boys.' Grace smiled. 'I know I was when I was your age.'

'Most of the ones I know are immature.'

'I've been chatting to your mum, and Erin's mum too. They tell me they've been a bit worried about the two of you lately.'

Molly said nothing.

'Your mum mentioned that, recently, you and Erin said you were staying at each other's houses but instead you stayed out all night.'

Molly looked uncomfortable. 'We said we were sorry.'

'I know, and these things happen. Can you tell me whose party it was?'

'Just one of the girls from school.'

'Did her parents know about it?'

'Not at the time. They were on holiday, but the neighbours told them. She got into a lot of trouble for it. And we didn't even trash the house. There was no damage at all.'

Grace tried not to smile at Molly's outrage. She remembered back to her seventeenth birthday when her friend Gemma's parents had gone away for the weekend. They hadn't had a party, but had sung karaoke and eaten pizza and chocolate until she'd felt sick. But when Gemma's mum came home, they had been accused of it anyway and no matter how many times they denied it, they weren't believed, to the point that Gemma wished she'd had the party she was being accused of.

'Can I take the name and address of your friend?'

'I don't want to get anyone into strife.'

'That won't happen. I promise I'll be discreet.'

Molly shook her head.

Grace stared at her pointedly. Molly needed to understand the gravity of the situation.

'Molly, your information is vital to this investigation, do you understand?'

'It was only a stupid party.'

'Nevertheless.'

'I can't remember who it was. It was a friend of a friend.'

Grace decided to change tack for now. 'So you don't know anyone who Erin was friendly with?'

'I keep telling you. There was no one special.'

Lucy put her arm around Molly and squeezed her shoulder in encouragement. 'Help us out, Mol. We're trying to find out as much about Erin as possible. We thought you'd know if she had a boyfriend. You told each other everything, didn't you?'

'Most things.'

'So you didn't see her with anyone?' Grace asked again.

'No.'

'Are you sure?' Lucy probed. 'You're not covering for someone? It wasn't a boy's house that you stayed over at for the party?'

Molly shook her head.

'Okay. Do you know what Erin might have been saving money for? We found quite a lot hidden in an envelope, and it would be useful for us to know how she got it.'

Molly looked at Grace sharply. 'I don't know anything about that.'

Grace frowned. The girl had almost snapped her head off. 'You sure about that? I thought you were best friends, sharing everything with each other?'

'I'm positive. It has nothing to do with me.'

Grace paused for a moment. She was about to speak again but changed her mind. There was no indication that Molly would know about the money, so she didn't have reason to doubt her. But something was off.

And she wanted to have a think about why Molly might be lying.

As her mum showed the detective out, Molly held in her tears. She couldn't believe she had lied about Erin like that. But there was no one there to dispute what she had said.

The party she was being asked about was at Angela's house. They'd both gone, and they'd had a great time. Molly had been with Chad and Erin had been talking to Max until the rest of the men had arrived.

But she couldn't say any of that without getting into trouble. So it had been best to say nothing, until she absolutely had to.

And the money! Erin had been looking after both their earnings. Molly knew she'd keep dipping into it if she kept it at her house, so Erin had offered to hide it all. Molly trusted her with it. They were saving for a holiday but now it was never going to happen.

And all the things they'd done to get it had been for nothing.

Outside Grace saw Frankie coming out of the nosy neighbour's house. She beckoned him over.

'Got anything?' she asked.

'Useful intel about the girls,' he replied. 'Not sure it helps with the case, but it builds up a picture of how they were. He said they were good girls, never in any trouble. Mostly he saw them together, always happy, smiling and laughing.'

'Did he say anything about their parents?'

'Only that they'd done a lot together until Mr Ellis left. They'd been a close bunch. Genuine people you could rely on. He said they'd looked after him when his wife had gone into hospital. The girls would bring food their mums had cooked, the women would run errands for him and the men would take him to the hospital as he doesn't have a car.' Frankie sighed. 'It's not much to go on but it tells us the girls were great friends, so maybe the argument was a one-off or they bicker all the time like some married couples.'

'I think you got more than you realised from him,' Grace begged to differ. 'You can tell a lot about a street and its occupants with that intel. It seems a nice place to live. Sure, I reckon everywhere has its odd or noisy neighbour, but in general, it appears okay. It also tells us about their parents, how the girls were brought up. Nice work, Frankie.'

Frankie smiled at her praise. 'I'm going to do some more house-to-house, if that's okay with you?'

'Yes, I'll leave you here while I head back to the station with Perry. I'll be back soon.'

TWENTY-FOUR

Grace thought about Molly Redfern as she walked towards the main road to locate Perry. She was definitely lying about something. It could have been a case of both girls staying over at a boy's house, maybe kipping on the floor with a group of friends. She'd certainly done that herself on more than one occasion. Or perhaps Molly might not have wanted to tell the truth in front of her mum, for fear of getting in more trouble? She'd ask her later when she figured out if it was important or not.

Having gone around the long way rather than walk through the crime scene, she spotted the pool car in Steele's Gym's car park. A huge sigh escaped her, disappointment clear that she'd missed the chance to be derisive. She liked nothing better than throwing sarcasm Leon Steele's way.

She had almost crossed the road when she heard someone shout her name. A car door opened in front of her and a woman climbed out of the seat.

Grace groaned. It was Kathleen Steele, the matriarch of the family. Kathleen had had three children with Grace's father, two of them while he was still with Grace's mum – Leon was two months older than Grace; Eddie two years. Her mother had stood by George Steele through fifteen cruel years, and all that time he'd been messing around with other women. After Grace and her mum had left, he'd married Kathleen.

Grace could never understand why Kathleen had stayed with her violent father. She wondered if she too had nightmares that woke her up crying. Did she still finger scars that brought back hurt, along with bad memories of how they were acquired? Was she afraid of the dark, having to put a light on whenever she went to the bathroom in the middle of the night because of an overactive imagination?

'Could I have a word please, Grace?' Kathleen interrupted her thoughts.

'I'm afraid not. I'm at work right now.' Grace took out her phone and pretended to be busy.

'It will only take a moment.'

Her tone was persistent. It piqued Grace's curiosity.

Kathleen moved closer, to drown out the sound of the passing traffic. She was a smart woman, knocking on sixty. Every time Grace had seen her she'd been well-presented, keeping herself immaculate and looking remarkable for her age. Grace often wondered if it was a front; armour to say to the world that everything was good in her life.

'I know you helped me a while ago with Megan and that . . . that lout she was seeing.'

The lout was Seth Forrester. Kathleen had asked Grace to have a word with her half-niece because she was dating him. She wanted her to choose someone better. Grace had obliged because she hadn't liked what she'd heard about Forrester even before she helped to get him sent down last year. She'd felt responsible for putting Megan's mother in prison and it was her way of rectifying it.

Grace was glad she'd taken the time to meet Megan now; pleased that she'd listened to her, although, to be fair, Megan probably would have made her own mind up eventually. Forrester wasn't a likeable soul. Even a charmer can become too unpleasant to keep their friends and lovers on side.

'I need you to find out if—'

Oh, here we go, Grace thought.

'Why is it that you Steeles always want me to do something for you?' she questioned. 'If I wasn't a police officer, you'd have nothing to do with me.'

'I think that's the opposite of what would happen.' Kathleen raised her eyebrows. 'If you weren't a police officer, I would love to have you as part of the family.'

'We have my father in common. That and nothing else.'

'But we could have been so much closer, seeing as you're flesh and blood.'

Grace checked her watch. 'What do you want me to do, Kathleen? Lose my job because I'm finding out information so that you can sort things out behind closed doors?'

'No, I just want to know if Megan was seen at the takeaway.'

'Why?'

'Because.' Kathleen paused as a car came into the car park and drove past them.

Grace waited for her to elaborate.

'I don't want her involved with it, okay?' Kathleen placed her hand on Grace's forearm. 'But you should look into it. There's more going on there than meets the eye.'

Grace wasn't surprised to hear the allegation. She wanted Kathleen to know they were already one step ahead of her, but she didn't want to alert the family to the things they were looking into at the moment and she assumed Kathleen was fishing for that information.

'I'm not going to help you again,' Grace told her.

'Not even for Megan?'

'Nice try, but no.'

'I don't understand you at times.'

There was so much venom in Kathleen's voice now she knew she wasn't going to get her own way. Grace wouldn't have been surprised if the woman poked her in the shoulder as she spoke.

Grace squared up to Kathleen as she said, 'I'm not helping you. And quite frankly, if you're letting Megan anywhere near that takeaway when you think something is going on there, then you're not fit to be her guardian. She needs someone she can rely on to look after her.'

'She has a family to do that.'

Grace held back her response knowing she'd say something she'd come to regret, and she wasn't going to give Kathleen the satisfaction of having a go at her. She turned to leave but Kathleen stopped her, grabbing her arm.

'You need to look into that takeaway, but this' – Kathleen pointed behind her at the gym – 'is none of your business. So keep your nose out of our affairs if you won't help.'

Grace watched Kathleen march away. 'It will always be my business until the place is closed down,' she muttered.

TWENTY-FIVE

As Kathleen scuttled into the gym, Perry was coming out. He held up his phone as he drew level with Grace.

'Possible murder weapon found in Sampson Street,' he said. 'A knife with a four-inch blade. Something you'd have for camping rather than shanking, which could mean the attack was carried out by an amateur on the spur of the moment if it is connected.'

'Or it could mean that's what our assailant wants us to think.'

He nodded. 'Let's leave the car here and walk across. Did you find out anything?'

Grace updated him about the money Erin had been hiding, and her chat with the two mums.

'Interesting. What're your thoughts?'

'I spoke to Molly, who said she wasn't aware that Erin had a boyfriend, which I find hard to believe, and she said she had no idea about the money, although she was more horrified than curious when I mentioned it. Both mums said they didn't think the girls had been taking any kind of drugs, but Sara and Lucy were definitely worried about their daughters.'

'Interesting.' They jogged across the road as a gap in the traffic opened up.

'How did you get on at the gym?' she asked as they reached the other side.

'I saw Eddie and Leon. Neither of them were giving much away. Leon said he was at the Potteries Takeaway on business as he owns the building.'

'Yeah, right. I don't think I'll ever trust a word either of them say.'

'That's not what I gathered from my chat with Eddie.'

Grace turned to him, eyes wide.

'He made out like you were some sort of informant.'

'That's ridiculous! I would never get that close. It isn't something I would even *declare* and do.'

'So what did he mean then?'

Grace pinched the bridge of her nose. 'He's told me a few things, given me a couple of pointers, but I've done nothing for him.' She hoped her reddening skin wouldn't betray her. 'Sometimes he's given me some great intel but I always figure it's for his own end. Take Seth Forrester, for example. He told me what he was up to, to ensure that Seth was put away, which was in the Steeles' interests. Eddie does it for himself, and not to help me.'

'You sure about that? It didn't seem that way.'

'You know Eddie. He's trying to wind you up. And he loves seeing Leon angry too. It's his thing. Eddie's all in it for himself and Leon doesn't care if he never sees me again, quite frankly. I don't think he'd even bother to spit on me, never mind offer up information.'

'As long as that's all there is to it.' Perry nodded.

Grace looked straight ahead then. She hated lying to Perry but she hadn't done anything wrong. So why was she feeling so guilty?

That family would be the death of her. She couldn't wait to finally get the opportunity to put one or both of the brothers behind bars. See how they liked being on the other side – because they would slip up one day.

As Grace and Perry drew closer to Sampson Street, she noticed the strong police presence. Uniformed officers were suited up in forensic gear going over every inch of the pathway and its surroundings. The city council had arrived to give them access to the grids and bins nearby.

Walking round again, they ignored the cries from the journalists who were starting to cram the far end of the cul-de-sac. TV crews had set up since they'd first got there that morning; the local radio stations too.

Grace spotted Simon and gave him a faint smile. He winked at her as they passed through. She threw a thumb over her shoulder.

'It's like feeding time at the zoo,' she told Perry.

'They can sense something.'

'Don't give them too much credit. They can see what's happening, more like.'

'I'm going to get the cordon moved back a little but it's hard when there are houses at the head of the road.'

'People will understand,' Grace pacified. 'At least they can get into their homes.'

They both stopped to grab a mug of tea being offered by a resident and mouthed their thanks.

'I'm off to have a quick chat with Simon,' she told Perry.

'Love's young dream.' He rolled his eyes comically.

Grace grinned before heading towards the press. She lifted up the crime scene tape and went over to Simon.

'Preferential treatment again, Cole,' a man she vaguely recognised bantered. He was in his mid-thirties at a push, with receding blonde hair, spiked at the front in a way that Grace thought looked ridiculous rather than hip. He was the only one in the pack of eight reporters wearing shorts, with thick-soled boots and a red raincoat that would suit a five-year-old. He certainly stood out in the crowd for the wrong reasons.

'He's got a kind face,' Grace threw back at him, her voice laced with sarcasm. As chuckles broke out all around them, they moved away from the group.

Simon stared lovingly at the mug until she handed it over with a sigh.

'I'm freezing standing there,' he mocked. 'You should take pity on me.'

'I did.' She took the mug from him. 'I gave you a slurp of my tea.'

'You're so generous.'

Glancing around to see the press looking back in the direction of Sampson Street, she leaned forward and pressed herself close to him for a moment. She kissed him.

'Your lips are cold,' she teased. 'I can't warm you up right now, but I can certainly do better this evening,' she murmured, stepping away from him reluctantly.

'I'll hold that thought.' He cocked his head to one side. 'So you don't have anything to share with me?'

'Don't push it, Cole.' She stared at him, then smiled. 'We're still building up background. It's going slowly.' She nodded over to the crowd. 'Remind me who the knob with the gob is.'

'You have such a way with words.' Simon roared with laughter. 'It's Will Lawrence, *Staffordshire News*. He's only recently started working there, but you're right. He is a knob.'

'Well, I'm very happy to keep him out in the cold.' Grace offered Simon her mug again but he shook his head. 'Right, I'll be off to see what's happening.'

'Text me if you find anything juicy.'

She wanted to chastise him, say that this was no laughing

matter. But instead she smiled. Their jobs were depressing at the best of times. It was only a way of letting off steam.

'There's something going on outside,' Sara said as Rob entered the kitchen. 'I want to go out but I don't want to know either.' She stopped, aware by his face that something was wrong.

When he gave her Erin's diary, she was surprised.

'What's that?' she asked, spotting tears in his eyes.

'I don't want you to look through it all.' He turned to a particular page. 'Just read a bit from there so I don't have to say the words aloud.'

Reading the page, Sara was sickened.

Immediate thoughts of letting her child down rushed through her mind. How had this happened?

She looked at Rob, with tears in her eyes. 'Why didn't you give it to the detective earlier?'

'I . . . I couldn't.'

Suddenly they were crying in each other's arms.

'What did we do wrong?' she asked him. 'We weren't terrible parents. Erin wanted for nothing.'

'Maybe the divorce hit her harder than we thought.'

'But Molly was involved too. I wonder if it was her that made Erin go to the parties.'

'You can't blame Molly for this.'

'But you know that Erin worshipped the ground she walked on. We used to call her a little sheep as she followed her everywhere.'

Sara pulled away but Rob resisted.

'Just keep on holding me,' he whispered, hugging her to him tightly.

Sara did as she was told, even though it felt awkward.

'I know we have to hand it to the police, but I want to read it all first. I don't want them to take it away yet.'

'Please don't, Sara. You'll only upset yourself.'

She looked up at him, rested a hand on his face. 'Just let me have it for today. We can give it to them this evening.'

He sighed and nodded. 'Okay.'

She went upstairs and lay on her bed. She opened the diary and began to read the excerpts. Rob was right: it was torturous to read, but she wanted to understand her daughter, find out why she would do those things. She wondered why Erin felt she couldn't speak to her, tell her what was happening.

Tears poured down Sara's face. The more entries she read, the more her blood boiled. Eventually, she had to stop.

This was Molly's fault. She was always the confident one of the girls. The pushy one, the mouthy one, even. Erin wouldn't have wanted to go to those parties.

Molly would have dragged her into this, she was certain.

And there was only one way to find out.

TWENTY-SIX

Downstairs, Sara pulled on a jacket and a hat, and slipped out of the front door. Even though there was a cold wind blowing, there were people there; lots of press in the distance. Remembering what the detective had told her about shielding herself from them, she kept her head down and was at Lucy's in no time.

She banged on the back door.

'I need to see Molly.' She pushed past Lucy as she opened it.

'She's asleep.' Lucy followed quickly after her. 'It's taken her ages to settle.'

'What's going on?' Phil came in behind them.

Sara stood at the bottom of the stairs, about to rush up but Lucy put a hand over hers on the banister rail.

'Can it wait until later?' she asked. 'I know this is hard for you, but Molly is grieving too. She's exhausted.'

'No. I want to know what's been going on.'

'I don't understand.'

'I knew they'd been falling out lately, but I had no idea why any of this was happening.' She pointed up the stairs. 'This is Molly's fault.'

'What is?' Lucy frowned.

'Molly knows more than she's letting on about who . . . whoever killed my daughter.'

'Slow down, I don't understand. How do you know that?'

When it came to it, Sara couldn't bring herself to tell Lucy everything but she had to say something.

'They were going to these . . . parties.' Sara closed her eyes momentarily as images flooded her mind. 'They were servicing men.'

She watched the colour drain from Lucy's face. 'You mean like prostitutes?'

Sara nodded. 'Rob found a diary of Erin's in the summer house. It says she and Molly have been going to these parties once a month. That's where all that money must have come from.'

Phil ran a hand through his hair. 'Fuck, this changes everything, doesn't it?'

'It takes the police on a different route, and it could even have been one of those men. All I'm bothered about is finding out who killed Erin.' Sara looked at them both in turn. 'Why did someone do that to her? She's no more than a child.'

'Did the diary go into detail?'

'Is that all you're interested in?'

'No, I—'

'It will be Molly who got her into this. My Erin was the quiet one.'

'Erin wasn't as sweet and innocent as you think,' Lucy said, going on the defensive. 'Once Rob left, she went off the rails. I tried to hide a lot from you but now you're blaming Molly, I might have to tell you a few home truths.'

'If anyone had an influence over Erin, it was your daughter.' Sara moved towards Lucy as she continued. 'She would do anything for her. Which is why I need to speak to her. Erin

125

wrote that she was scared about upsetting her, and that Molly said she would tell me if she didn't do as she was told. *Do what*, that's what I want to know.'

Lucy went pale. 'You're lying.'

'How could you think that?' Sara gasped. 'Molly knows more about what happened last night in the walkway, and I'm going to get to the bottom of it.'

'What do you mean?'

'She clearly knows more than she's letting on and I can't understand why she won't tell the truth. She's too worried about protecting herself while my daughter is lying dead in a mortuary.'

'Come on, guys.' Phil held up his hands to try and pacify the situation.

Lucy's eyes rested on Sara's. 'Let me speak to Molly and see if I can find out anything.' She moved forward.

Sara stepped away before racing out of the door. 'Leave me alone.'

'Sara,' Lucy cried behind her.

Once outside, Sara ran across the road, not caring who saw her. She hurriedly let herself into her house, slammed the front door, and dropped to the floor behind it.

'What's wrong?' Rob appeared from the kitchen looking concerned. 'Have the police told you something?'

'There's nothing new,' she sobbed.

'I'll make a cup of tea.'

'I don't want a cup of fucking tea! It's not the answer to anything.'

'I don't know what else to do. I'm struggling as well.'

She heard the door slam as he went back to the kitchen. From the corner of her eye, she spotted Nat sitting on the top stair. She raced up to him as he burst into tears.

She pulled him into her arms and ran a hand over his head. 'I'm sorry. We're all upset, Nat. It's hard to know what to say or do at the moment. Is there anything you want to ask me about?'

'No, I just want my sister back.'

As she held her little boy close to her and they cried together, Sara couldn't tell who sobbed the loudest.

TWENTY-SEVEN

Nine months ago

Erin stood still for a few seconds until the man in the chair clocked her watching Molly and the other man on the bed.

'Want to play?' He pressed his hand to his crotch. 'I'm waiting for him to finish but you'll do just the same.'

Molly looked over at Erin. She mouthed the word 'go', a serious look in her eyes.

It broke her heart to close the door and leave her best friend in there. On the landing, all alone, Erin dropped to the floor. The alcohol she'd been plied with was beginning to wear off. What was happening? She was confused about what this party had turned into, but she knew she had to get out of there in case anyone dragged her into a room. She could wait for Molly outside, but she was leaving.

Taking the stairs two at a time she ran straight into a man. 'Hey, what's going on?' he asked.

'Nothing. I . . . I . .'

'What are you so scared of?'

His eyes looked so sincere that she burst into tears.

'Was it you who was locked in the bathroom earlier?'

She nodded. 'He . . . he . . .'

'Did someone hurt you?' He wanted to know. 'Someone here?'

She nodded again, sobbing hard now. She couldn't get the image of Molly out of her mind, knew she needed to help her friend.

'Come on.' He took her hand. 'You'll be safe with me.'

'My friend.' She stopped, looking back over her shoulder up the staircase.

'Where is she?'

'Up there, with two men.'

'Wait here. If anyone says anything to you, say you're with Chad.'

He took the stairs two at a time. Within a couple of minutes, he was back and had Molly with him. She was dressed, looking a little spaced out, but she was okay.

Chad took them home, dropping them off at the end of the road.

'These parties,' he turned to face them both. 'They're fine if you want things to happen. You can earn decent money, but you have to want to be there. There's no point in getting scared about it. There will always be someone who wants more than they've paid for but if you tell me, I'll handle it.'

Erin looked out of the window. She wasn't exactly sure why yet, but despite him helping her and Molly, she didn't trust him. He was at the party so he was in this to make money out of them, surely. He would exploit them and then when they were drunk get them to do things that they wouldn't remember.

'Hey,' he said to her.

She looked at him.

'No one's going to hurt you. If you don't want to come again, you don't have to.'

'I do,' Molly said.

Erin's eyes widened. Surely she didn't think it was a good idea?

'Think about it and let me know.'

Molly scrambled out of the car and Erin followed. When he'd driven away, she let rip.

'What were you doing in that room?' she cried. 'I saw you with two men.'

'They paid me to have sex with them.' Molly was nonchalant. 'I made fifty pounds in less than half an hour.'

'But it's wrong.'

'It's good money for a bit of fun. They were nice to me.'

'Well, I had some sweaty old man push me into the bathroom. He locked the door and tried to make me give him a blow job.'

Molly's face crumbled with laughter. 'You've done it before.'

'Only the once, and I didn't like it much. I was lucky Chad saw him and stopped him. And then I came to find you.'

'I was okay, nothing bad happened,' Molly tried to reassure her. 'You'll get used to it soon.'

'Used to it?' Erin shook her head. 'I'm not going to any more parties.'

'But you promised you would!'

'That was before he—'

'Think of the holiday – just the two of us. Once we have enough money for that, we can stop going to the parties.'

'That will be ages yet though.'

'Well, you could look at it another way. It's good experience for the future. We'll know what to do to please our men.'

Erin threw her a funny look. 'Who told you that?'

'Chad did.' Molly linked her arm through Erin's and they began to walk. 'Come to the next party and see. Once I've made a few friends, I'll be fine to go alone. But for now, I need you.'

Erin shook her head.

'Please! You know I'd do the same for you.'

'No, you wouldn't. You only ever do what you want.'

'But you'll come?' Molly put out her bottom lip like a child about to cry.

Erin was torn. Had she overreacted? Molly didn't seem to have any problem with it, so why should she? And fifty quid in half an hour! Their holiday fund would be massive by the time they finished school for summer if they saved it all.

Or was Molly trying to get her own way as usual? Erin wished she wasn't so naïve at times like this, but she didn't want to annoy Molly and let an argument break out.

'Okay,' she nodded. 'I'll give it a go one more time.'

Molly smiled and gave Erin a hug. 'I can always rely on you.'

Yes, Erin knew she was a pushover. She'd just have to drink more next time so she enjoyed herself.

TWENTY-EIGHT

Traffic was backing up on the main road, the evening rush-hour in full swing as Grace got out of the car alongside Perry and Frankie. They were going in to Potteries Takeaway. As well as putting out appeals on social media, Perry had rung ahead to see if Jeff Harvey could get word to any of the teens spotted there the night before, to see if they would be willing to talk to the police.

She wondered if any of them would speak out. Some were so anti-police they would assume they were being set up and wouldn't be helpful, so she was pleasantly surprised to see at least a dozen people through the shop window.

They went inside, conversations coming to a halt as everyone's eyes fell on them. Perry flashed his warrant card, Grace and Frankie following suit.

'Just a friendly chat, guys,' he said. 'We'd like to speak to anyone who knew Erin Ellis.'

'You haven't got her murderer yet then?' a small boy with an alarming display of acne shouted up.

'Shut up, Harry. They wouldn't be here if they had.' The girl next to him rolled her eyes and then looked at Perry. 'We all knew her.'

'Did any of you see Erin and Molly here last night?'

Three girls' hands shot up in the air. Two boys followed, a little slower.

'Are either of you Ethan or Christian?' Grace questioned.

'I'm Ethan,' a dark-haired teenager said. 'Chris isn't here yet, but he will be soon.'

Aware they were standing in the middle of the room, Grace piped up. 'I'm starving, Perry. Chips all round?' She looked at the group who either nodded or shrugged a shoulder.

'Can you do us a job lot of chips, Jeff, please?' Perry shouted to the man who had just come through from the back. 'To eat in.'

'Sure will.'

Grace sat down next to the two girls while Perry and Frankie went to speak to the boys at another table. None of them got their notepads out. They'd agreed before they came in that they would just grab information. They may get something or nothing but they needed to win the teens' trust first – and what better way to do that than with free food.

'Here you go.' Jeff brought over the food and placed everything in the middle of the table. 'Tuck in.'

Grace smiled in appreciation. 'Did Erin hang around with you?' she asked as she grabbed a chip.

'With most of us, really,' a girl with two plaits told her. 'Or, she used to, at least.'

Grace had learned her name was Lacey. Her friend beside her was Suzi. Lacey's hair was long, grey with a lilac tint. Suzi had short dark hair, and the most enticing blue eyes. Both of them were made up as if they were going clubbing. Each had their phones in their hands as they helped themselves to chips.

'Did you ever see Erin with a boyfriend?' Grace went on.

A look passed between them. She waited for one of them to fill the silence.

'She was always lording it up in here as if she was something special,' Lacey said. 'Actually, Molly did too.'

'That's not what I asked.'

'Erin was seeing Max,' Suzi enlightened her.

Grace frowned. 'Max who?'

'I don't know his surname. He used to pick her up in his car.'

'From here?' Grace's ears had pricked up.

Lacey nodded. 'Erin and Molly, well, they were into these parties. Me and Suzi didn't want anything to do with them, did we?'

Suzi shook her head. 'There had been rumours.'

Grace saw Frankie coming towards her and shook her head. He went to talk to someone else. She didn't want the girls to stop talking now and seeing a man may have spooked them. There was something about this conversation that she didn't like.

'Oh?' she asked.

'About what went on at the parties.' Suzi leaned forward so their conversation wouldn't be overheard. 'There was a lot of sex at them.' She snorted, clearly embarrassed.

Grace tried not to show her emotion. 'Who told you that?'

'I can't remember. Jeff might know. He chats to a lot of us if we're upset, or have something on our minds.'

Grace stored away that information for later. 'Did either of you ever go?' she continued.

They both shook their heads.

'Max asked us if we wanted to once, but Erin warned us off. You have to make your mind up if it's worth selling yourself.' Suzi pointed at herself and Lacey. 'We would *never* do anything like that.'

'Do you know anyone else in here apart from Erin and Molly who did?'

She shook her head, looked away. Grace realised Suzi was worried she might have said too much.

'Do they come in here too?' she continued.

'Who?'

'The people who arrange the parties.'

Lacey shrugged. 'We're not in here all the time. Only when the weather is bad.'

'What about the boys? Are they ever invited to the parties?'

'No.' They spoke in unison.

'Molly told us about a woman called Angela,' Lacey said. 'She was after more girls, asking Erin and Molly if they had any friends who'd like to come along too. But Erin went mad when Molly told us. She was so angry with her. They had a huge row and no one mentioned it again. I'm glad we didn't go now. Is that what happened to Erin? Did she upset someone so they killed her?'

'Why do you say that?'

'Like I said, she has quite a temper on her at times. We all used to be friends . . .'

Grace paused whilst she thought for a moment. 'This Angela who invited you to the parties. Can you tell me anything about her? Where she lives? The car she drives?'

'Everything okay over there, girls?' Jeff shouted over.

Grace noticed the two of them jump back as if burnt.

'Could we get some cans of coke, please?' Grace asked, raising a hand to get his attention.

'It's okay.' Lacey stood up quickly. 'We were just leaving, weren't we, Suzi?'

Suzi stood up too.

'If you have information, then it's very important you tell us.' Grace handed them each a contact card and looked at them pointedly. 'This is a murder enquiry and if the police find out you've been withholding anything that might be useful in catching Erin's killer, then you'll land yourselves in a lot of trouble.'

TWENTY-NINE

From behind the counter, Jeff watched the police in action. He'd been in the back room when they'd arrived but he'd come out to stand behind the counter, choosing to stay where he could see what was happening. He didn't like them there, messing and interfering, but he couldn't do much about it. His job now was to make sure no one here said anything to the officers that they shouldn't.

'You okay there, Jeff?'

He looked in front of him to see the woman detective.

'Yes,' he nodded. 'It's just such a tragic thing to happen. I can't stop thinking about Erin. Those girls were such close friends. It's going to be hard on everyone who knows them as well as their families. And poor Molly – I bet she's distraught.'

'Everyone is upset.' Grace nodded. 'As you say, at that age friends are like family, and Erin's going to be missed by a lot of people. Did you know the girls well?'

'Not really. Like most of the teens, I had a laugh and a joke with them. Often they'd tell me their troubles; looked to me as a father figure, I guess.'

'Had you noticed any changes in either girl lately?'

Jeff moved aside as a load of chipped potatoes were brought through in a bucket. They were emptied into a fryer by a young man with a red Mohican and an arm full of tattoos. The sizzle of steam made conversation difficult for a few seconds.

'I don't recall any,' Jeff replied, once the sound had died down. 'They were kids. They seemed really close. I'm going to miss them. I doubt Molly will come in now.'

'Perhaps not.'

Jeff decided to dig for information. 'Do you get this kind of thing often?'

Grace shook her head. 'Nine times out of ten, the victims know the killer. There aren't many who attack strangers – and when they do, they mostly act on impulse with huge bursts of anger that result in an accidental death that we deal with as manslaughter. It's devastating for everyone involved either way.'

Jeff moved out of the way as more chipped potatoes were thrown into the fryer. 'I'll keep my eyes and ears open and let you know if I hear anything.'

'Thanks.' Grace turned to go but stopped. 'One more thing. The name Max kept coming up. Do you know who that might be?'

'I have a customer named Max, although I don't know his surname,' Jeff offered. 'Lots of the girls like him. He's a good-looking bastard.'

Grace smiled. She seemed unintimidated by him.

'Did he have a soft spot for Erin?'

'Not that I know of. He's a charmer, a smooth talker, friendly with everyone. But he's mid-twenties. I doubt he'd be interested in the girls. He's a bit old for teenagers.'

'So you think mention of him is more to do with a teenage crush?'

'It's possible. You'll have to ask him, I suppose.'

'Do you know where I can find him? Where he works, or lives?'

'Sorry, no.'

'Not to worry. I'm sure we'll find him on the security footage you gave to my colleague this morning.'

'There was nothing untoward going on, as far as I could see.'

Grace nodded and went over to join the other officers.

It seemed as if they were getting ready to leave, but Jeff was no happier than he'd been before the conversation had begun. He hated how the police let you think they were finished with you, only then to throw in one more question. He'd seen it enough on TV – it meant they suspected him of something. He hadn't got a clue who had killed the girl. It wasn't on his radar.

Yet, even without the murder, if they found out half of what was going on, he was looking at some serious jail time. He had to get everyone out of there. But he didn't know how to do it without drawing attention to himself. And that woman detective kept staring at him.

Did she sense he was involved in something?

Maybe he should warn Max that they were on to him. He ran a hand back and forth over his chin.

Maybe not. No one had loyalties any more. It was every man for himself.

After a few minutes, the three officers left and made their way to the car. When Grace thought back to the free food they'd used to entice the teenagers to talk to them, she shook her head in disgust.

'I can't believe we bought them food after what I've just heard.' She enlightened Frankie and Perry on her conversation with the two girls. 'I feel so ashamed. In one way, we're no better than the people who preyed on them.'

'Come off it, Grace.' Perry shook his head as he put his keys into the door. 'We were doing it for the right reasons – to help find Erin Ellis's killer. We weren't currying favours.'

'I know, but it feels,' she shuddered as she looked over the roof at him, 'icky.'

'Icky?' Perry laughed. 'That's something my little Alfie would come out with.'

'Archie too,' Frankie joined in.

Grace smiled to ease her tension. 'It doesn't make me feel good about myself.'

'We never put those teens under pressure.'

They got into the car.

'Don't beat yourself up about it,' Perry insisted. 'There's absolutely no comparison.'

But Grace wasn't convinced. 'What do you make of the owner, Jeff? He seems a bit . . . greasy to me.'

'You really do have a way with words today, Grace.' Frankie laughed.

'That's what Simon said earlier when I called one of the reporters a knob.'

'Well, it's one way of putting it.' Perry smirked.

'Jeff kept looking over at me when I was talking to the girls,' Grace said. 'I'm not sure if he was listening in or being a lech.'

'He told me he acts like a kind of father figure,' Frankie said.

'He said that to me too. More like he garners trust when he's really after information.'

Perry frowned but Grace didn't enlighten him. Thoughts of her conversation with Kathleen Steele sprang to mind. Maybe there was more to things underneath the facade of the takeaway.

'I'm going to do some digging on him when I get back,' she said. 'Let's see what his past has to say about him.'

THIRTY

It was pouring with rain as they raced into the police station. Thick black clouds hung not only over the investigation, but they seemed to hover just above their building in Bethesda Street too. The day was already disappearing and they had so much to do.

A few minutes later, Grace was sipping a much-welcomed coffee. She shared a bank of desks with Frankie, Perry, and Sam, who were all there too. There was action everywhere she looked, people in the larger team gathering evidence and intel as they worked.

This was always the most frustrating time for her, when everything hadn't yet fallen into place. It was speculation, crossing out, ruling in: too soon for the jigsaw to be complete yet. The search team were nowhere near finished and, as well as going house-to-house, uniformed officers were still scouring the area close by.

Grace could see Allie in her office on the phone, a frown on her face as she sat forward, leaning on her elbow and looking at the monitor.

Once she'd finished the call, Allie came out to them. 'Just a heads-up, there will be a press conference with the parents tomorrow morning. But we've also had results back from the post-mortem. As we knew, Erin died of a stab wound to the chest. The blade sliced through a vital artery, causing her to bleed out. There was nothing anyone could have done for her.'

'Do we have any more information about the weapon that was used?' Grace enquired.

'It doesn't look like a match to the one that was recovered near to the scene but we'll know more tomorrow. Either way, it was something that could be concealed from view quite easily.' Allie blew out her breath. 'But there's more. Our victim was four months pregnant.'

'Holy crap.' Perry whistled. 'So that could be a motive?'

'We should speak to Molly again. Erin was clearly sleeping with someone on a regular basis and those girls were as thick as thieves so the chances of her knowing are high,' Grace said. 'I also questioned Jeff Harvey about someone called Max too, as one of the girls we chatted to in the takeaway mentioned him. He said he was a regular customer, but he only knew him as such and didn't know his surname. I wonder if that was why he was cagey. Perhaps he knows him more than he's making out to me? And if Harvey knew about the pregnancy, this could mean he's been withholding information from us. Could this Max be the father, do you think?'

'It's too early to tell. Are we thinking that the takeaway joint is a pick-up place for young girls to groom?'

'As much as it pains me to say it,' Grace sighed, 'I think so. Although I've been digging for intel on Harvey and he's coming back clean so far. Sam, is there anything you can see on the footage that we've not covered? Max with Erin perhaps? Or from the cameras on the road?'

'I haven't spotted anything yet,' Sam said. 'We've ruled out Thomas Haddington as he is indeed in Spain with his mum, but that tattoo is still a clue. The guy who went through the walkway fifteen minutes before the girls was forty-two-year-old Malcolm Finney. He'd come off the bus after finishing work and went straight home. His family can confirm he was there. He was in the shower at the estimated time of attack. He doesn't fit the description of our suspect, with no tattoo on his neck, and he's a lot taller than Molly Redfern said. Which leaves us with one more male lead. No luck with him yet, but we're pushing all the media we have.'

'It could be someone who doesn't use social media channels, I guess.'

'Ah.' Grace put up a hand. 'Here's someone now who might be able to shed some light on the sleazier side of things.'

The woman coming towards them was tall, and wore snazzy white trainers with a sharp grey trouser suit. The smart casual attire on her feet had nothing to do with fashion. Camilla Preston walked with a slight limp, a permanent injury from a car accident several years ago. She'd thought at the time that she would have to retire from the police but finding a position in a team that were less active did the trick. She was still a valued asset though, having helped with lots of court cases and convictions.

'Hi.' Grace smiled. 'Come to share your knowledge and wisdom with us?'

Camilla worked in SET, the sexual exploitation team. Grace had first met her when she had interviewed Regan Peters with Allie. Two years ago, as part of Operation Wedgwood, Regan had come forward to say that she had been raped and assaulted by a group of men at a house party. She'd been willing to testify but there hadn't been enough evidence for them to convict, nor catch, who was behind it all. Since then, Regan had been helping out with a women's group set up for victims of sexual assaults.

Grace had kept in touch with Regan, checking in with her

every few months to see how she was doing. It saddened her that she may have to visit her now to find out information for this case.

'It's going to be hard to crack if the girls won't come forward,' Camilla said, tucking her blonde bob behind her ears as she joined them. 'There's only so much information I've been able to seek from the ones I've spoken to over the past few years. They're frightened of repercussions. Lots of them are vulnerable, young and timid. Some are dependent on drugs. It sickens me how men can treat women like meat. So I'm happy to help you catch the bastards. What can I help with first?'

THIRTY-ONE

It was eight thirty that evening when Grace and Allie pulled up outside the Ellises' home.

'Can you take the lead on this update, Grace?' Allie turned to her. 'I'd like to keep you as the main contact so I think it would be better coming from you.'

'Yes, ma'am.' Grace nodded, a mixture of pride and dread running through her simultaneously.

'It's boss, or Allie, but not ma'am.' Allie shook her head. 'Ma'am feels way too old for me.'

Grace smiled. 'Okay, Allie it is.'

A large police presence was still in operation in Sampson Street and, despite the wet weather, members of the general public stood watching; umbrellas up, some with phone cameras held aloft.

There was a sombre mood when they stepped into the house – as if the family were already expecting the worst. It wasn't a nice feeling to be walking into their home, the place where Erin should have been, to deliver such devastating news.

'The post-mortem has identified something we weren't

expecting,' Grace began, thinking it best to get it over and done with once they were seated in the living room. 'Did either of you know that Erin was pregnant?'

Sara shook her head. 'That's impossible. She's . . . she was only sixteen.'

'How far gone was she?' Rob asked, his face ashen as he moved to sit next to his ex-wife.

'Approximately sixteen weeks.'

'Four months pregnant?' Sara gasped. 'Why hadn't she told me?'

Grace knew it was a question that no one could answer.

As Sara fell into Rob's arms and began to cry, Grace looked away momentarily to give them time to take in the news. In the doorway, Nat stood holding on to the frame, unsure whether to come into the room or not.

'Would you go and play upstairs for a moment please, son?' Rob asked him gently.

Sara wiped at her cheeks as Nat disappeared. 'I can't understand why she hadn't told me. I would have been shocked but these things happen. I would rather have known than find out like this.'

'When I get my hands on the bastard that did this . . .' Rob stopped short, a sob caught in his throat. 'People have obviously been taking advantage of her.'

'When you mentioned Erin changing during the past few months, do you think it could have been because of this?' Allie asked.

Sara sniffed. 'I suppose you could put that down to pregnancy hormones.'

'Why didn't you tell me she was acting differently?' Rob asked Sara.

'What would you have done about it? You'd blame me, say her change in attitude was because I was giving her too much

146

leeway. If anything, she was missing a father figure. You weren't there for her.'

Grace watched Rob recoil from Sara's words. She wanted to intervene but it wasn't her place. Instead she tried to steer the conversation back on course.

'Mrs Ellis, could you explain a bit more about Erin's moods?' she encouraged.

'There had been the usual "I'm sixteen and I can do what I like" argument, which I had countered with "not under my roof" but never for one moment did I think she was pregnant. Four months gone meant that she either didn't realise, which I doubt very much, or she wanted to be far enough along for no one to stop her having it.

'Erin's moods had started to upset me and Nat. Erin had become volatile and disruptive, to the point that I'd grounded her on one or two occasions. And as I mentioned, she'd come in drunk several times too; one time she said she'd been celebrating a friend's birthday. I didn't think it would be *that* kind of party.'

'What do you mean by not that kind of party?' Allie asked before Grace had a chance to.

Sara stood up and left the room.

Grace thought she'd gone to be alone for a moment and was about to start talking to Rob when she came back. She had a notebook in her hand, which she handed to Grace.

'It's a diary. Rob found it in the summer house. It was hidden away.'

Grace took it from her, glancing surreptitiously at Allie. 'Have you read it?' she asked.

'Yes, but not all of the entries,' Rob replied. 'I found it earlier today. We knew it was important to give it to you, but it's all a bit raw and we wanted time to digest the content.'

'To be honest, we didn't want to give it to you at all,' Sara admitted. 'Rob said it would help you, and I agree, but it's hurtful. We know other people will see it and think the worst of Erin.'

'Let me take it with me and I'll treat it with the respect it deserves,' Grace said. 'Rest assured.'

'These . . . parties.' Sara's voice broke with emotion. 'It seems like she was being paid, like a prostitute, to service men. Could that be true?'

Grace shivered inwardly as she flicked through the pages, skim reading a few lines, trying to catch up quickly. Could this be the motive they were after, a man attacking Erin because she was pregnant with his child? The case had just turned a very sinister corner if so.

It might even be connected to the sex parties they unearthed as part of Operation Wedgwood. During the Jade Steele case two years ago, it had come to light that young girls were being groomed for sex parties but at the time the evidence wasn't strong enough to link any suspects.

'We'll look into everything as quickly as we can, Sara,' she said. 'Thank you for this. I know it will be hard for you to take everything in at the moment, but this diary could be a huge help.'

'So what happens now?' Rob asked. 'Do we just wait for him to do it again?'

'We're working on the assumption that there will only be one victim, Mr Ellis,' Allie replied. 'And we are concentrating all of our resources on this case.'

'It's one of those evil bastards from those parties, isn't it?' Sara broke down. 'Someone found out and killed her.'

'You have to find him.' Rob shook his head in resignation. 'Please.'

'We're all doing our best,' Allie jumped in to reassure them.

Grace could understand their frustration but this was the

first they'd heard about the diary; the first solid piece of evidence about parties.

Rob showed them out.

'Sara Ellis was right,' Grace said once they were out of his hearing range. 'If what she's saying in that diary is true, it could give any of those men a motive for murder.'

'Exactly,' agreed Allie. 'I think we need to speak to Molly Redfern again while we're here, don't you?'

THIRTY-TWO

Grace and Allie were shown into the Redferns' living room by Lucy. Molly was sitting in her usual spot on the settee, Phil on the armchair in front of the window. They'd decided not to mention the pregnancy, leaving that to the Ellises' discretion.

'Molly, we have to talk to you again,' Allie said. 'We may need to take you down to the station, but for now, I'm happy to conduct a first statement here.'

'What do you mean?' Lucy questioned. 'What's happened?'

'We found a diary that belonged to Erin.' Allie looked at Molly. 'Do you know anyone named Angela?'

Still keeping her eyes down, Molly shook her head.

'You're sure about that, Molly?' Grace pressed.

This time Molly looked up. 'I don't know anyone called Angela.'

'Some of your friends from Potteries Takeaway know her.'

'Molly?' Phil asked, when she remained quiet.

'I don't know, Dad.' Molly wouldn't look at him.

'We also know about Max,' Allie said. 'So I think you need to start talking. Can you tell me about these parties you've been going to? Is that where you were when you stayed out overnight?'

Lucy gave an involuntary sob.

'I'm not proud of what we did, but it wasn't all Erin's fault,' Molly said, her voice low. 'They didn't make us do anything we didn't want to. We felt as if they loved us. They looked after us, made sure we weren't abused.'

'They exploited you!' Lucy cried. 'You're too young to see that.'

'They didn't. Max looked out for me and Erin. Chad did too.'

'Chad?' Grace questioned.

'He looked after me like Max looked after Erin.'

'You mean he was your pimp?' Lucy shook her head and closed her eyes momentarily.

'No! What do you take me for, Mum?'

'He made you have sex with other men and you got paid.'

'Lucy, please,' Allie interrupted.

Phil moved across to sit with his wife, throwing a comforting arm around her shoulders.

'He never took money from us,' Molly continued. 'He watched over us.'

'While you slept with other men!'

'Come on, love,' Phil said. 'Why don't we go and make tea in the kitchen; let the police do their jobs.'

'I can see that you're upset and—' Allie started.

'That's a bit of an understatement.' Lucy wiped tears from her eyes. 'She has no idea how dangerous it was.'

'No one ever hurt me,' Molly said.

'You expect us to believe that?'

Molly hung her head down. 'But don't you see, that was because of Max and Chad. They made sure there was nothing heavy.'

Lucy began to cry, and then apologised. 'There is so much to take in.'

'We're also a bit baffled,' Allie took the lead from Grace.

151

'We've seen camera footage of you and Molly going into the walkway, but there doesn't seem to be anyone going in behind you, so it could mean that someone was waiting for you. Are you sure of the direction the man came from as he carried out the attack on Erin?'

Molly shook her head. 'It all happened so fast.'

'But you're our only witness. If you know who this is and you're afraid to say, I want you to understand that we will protect you at all times.'

Tears began to spill down Molly's face.

'What is it?' Lucy covered her daughter's hand with her own.

Molly looked at Grace. 'I wasn't with her when it happened.'

There was silence for a moment.

'We were arguing,' Molly continued. 'It was Erin who bruised my face. She hit me and I walked away from her. But then I heard her scream. I went back for her and that's when I saw her, on the path.'

'Molly, this is a completely different story to the one you told us last night.' Grace wanted to feel sympathy for the girl but equally knew that this misinformation had held them back.

'I know, but I felt so ashamed.' Molly shook her head. 'I shouldn't have left her.'

'Right, going back to the beginning, then. Do you even know if it was a male or a female that attacked Erin?'

'No. I'm so sorry.' Molly began to cry. 'I didn't want anyone to know that I'd let her down, especially Sara. She would be so disappointed in me.'

'So let me get this clear,' Grace made a note of what had been said so far. 'You didn't see what happened to Erin and now you're saying that it might not even have *been* a man with a distinctive tattoo on his neck?'

'I can't remember!'

'Can't you see she's confused because she's upset?' Lucy cried.

'Mrs Redfern,' Allie snapped. 'Molly has led us on a merry dance and we've been searching for a suspect who we now don't have a description for. It's an offence to waste police time. I'm sure you're aware of the term "perverting the course of justice".'

Molly lowered her eyes. 'It was my fault.'

'No, it wasn't,' Lucy soothed.

'If we have to speak to you again, Molly, it will be at the police station,' Allie added. 'This is a serious matter and you've lied to us. Do you understand?'

Molly nodded, tears trickling down her cheeks as she looked at the floor.

Back in the car, Grace turned to Allie. 'I can't get the hang of the girl at the moment.' She fastened her seatbelt. 'I'm not sure if Molly is upset because she's lied, or because she's been found out. Either way, I don't believe her for a minute. Do you?'

'Not a word. She's covering for someone. Let her stew for the night.' Allie started the engine. 'And then I think we need to bring her in tomorrow for more questioning.'

THIRTY-THREE

Once the police had gone, Sara sat on the settee in silence. Rob was in the kitchen with Nat. It was such a surreal time. None of them knew what to do. They couldn't even arrange a funeral until the police had finished their enquiries. She'd been told it could be months if they were still waiting for evidence.

Sara squeezed her eyes shut to rid herself of the image of Erin lying in the mortuary. Her pregnant sixteen-year-old daughter. Wait until news got out about that. She was going to be the talk of the neighbourhood: a murdered girl up to goodness knows what.

People would say Erin got what she deserved, getting herself into trouble like that. They wouldn't be bothered about the circumstances, or whether or not it was a stranger who attacked her.

Why hadn't her daughter been able to confide in her about the pregnancy? She would have been angry, disappointed too, but she would have stuck by Erin and whatever decision she had made.

She still couldn't go into Erin's bedroom; couldn't bring herself to step over the threshold after she'd shown Grace around earlier. Yet suddenly she really wanted to lie on the bed, curl up with Erin's pink teddy bear, the one she'd had since she was a baby.

How could she not have known what had been going on with her own daughter? How could she not have realised Erin was carrying a child?

Memories of Erin as a baby had been flooding her mind since she'd found out the news. She recalled seeing her for the first time after a frantic labour lasting twenty-two hours. Both mother and daughter had been exhausted afterwards; it had been touch and go whether she was to have a C-section but in the end Erin had been born naturally.

She remembered that first meeting, when Erin was put into her arms, wrapped in a blanket, eyes closed as she snuffled. The feeling of love rushing through her was intense and she would have done anything to keep her safe. That was her job after all. Mum.

Through the years as she grew up, Erin and Molly had become inseparable, even replacing time spent with her mum for time spent with her friend. It was heart-warming to see as she and Lucy were also such good friends. They'd spent so much time together. Either her house was quiet and they were both at Lucy's, or her home was a riot because they were in Erin's bedroom.

She thought back to when she was pregnant with Nat. Back then, she and Rob had been so happy. But when Rob had lost his job and things had become hard, they'd drifted apart. Speaking resulted in arguments as both apportioned blame to the other.

She wondered now if they were responsible for Erin misbehaving. Would she have been okay in a stable environment, with two loving parents instead of two people who couldn't stand the sight of each other?

Once Nat had come along, she'd thought her family was

complete. When Rob left, they'd survived together, becoming a little unit of three. But now, losing Erin meant it would be just the two of them. Poor Nat. It was going to be so different.

Sara would have to speak to Lucy and Molly soon, see if she could find out who the father of the child was. The detective was right, Molly would probably know.

She watched until the police left Lucy and Phil's and then she raced down the stairs. Before Rob could stop her, she was marching across to Lucy's house.

Two knocks on the back door and Lucy answered.

'I haven't come to argue,' Sara said. 'Can I speak to Molly?'

They went through to the kitchen where Molly was sitting at the kitchen island.

'I just need to know if Molly knew that Erin was pregnant.'

'Oh, Sara.' Lucy's hand shot to her mouth.

'Yes, she told me,' Molly replied.

'When?' Sara asked.

'I . . . I can't remember.'

'You must do. Please! Was it a week ago, a month? Even longer?'

'A few weeks at the most.'

Sara looked at Lucy. 'Did you know?'

'Of course not!' Lucy shook her head fervently. 'I would have told you if I had the slightest inkling.'

Sara stood in silence, not knowing what else to say, afraid of what someone might tell her. She sat down across from Molly.

'I don't know what to think. I thought I knew her but it seems that I didn't. How could she be pregnant?'

Lucy flinched at the word. Molly squirmed in her seat.

Sara reached across and placed her hand on Molly's. 'Do you know who the father is? You won't be in any trouble if you tell us. Is it one of those *men*?'

156

'Why is everyone questioning me all the time? I don't know, okay!' Molly pulled her hand free from under Sara's and ran out of the room.

'Molly!' Lucy stood up to follow her but Phil came to the doorway and stopped her.

'What's wrong?'

'Erin was pregnant,' Sara told him. 'I was asking . . . I wanted to see if Molly knew.'

Silence fell on the room.

'We barely knew them, did we?' Lucy's voice was quiet.

'Why don't I take you home, Sara?' Phil said.

'I can't be there. I'm lost without her. I don't know what to do.'

'Go and be with your son,' he urged. 'Nat will need your support.'

Sara realised he was right. She needed to look after Nat. He would be grieving too.

'Come on, I'll walk you across.'

She stepped outside with Phil. 'I'll be fine by myself, you know,' she said, the hint of a smile.

'I want to do it anyway.'

She had known Phil since she was eighteen, when he had first walked into Lucy's life. He was Lucy's second long-term boyfriend and she'd married him three years later. At the time, Sara hadn't met Rob, but once she had, the four of them had been out together on numerous occasions. He'd ended up being Rob's best man; Lucy her maid of honour. She would trust him with her life.

At the end of her drive, he gave her a hug. 'What am I going to do without her?' She broke down in his arms.

He kissed the top of her head as he held her close. 'I'm sorry. I'm so sorry.'

They stood together for a while before breaking apart. Sara wiped at her eyes. 'I keep doing that. Bursting into tears.'

'It's understandable.' Phil thrust his hands into his pockets. 'I hope you and Lucy come out of this okay. I'd hate it to ruin your friendship.'

'I'm not sure there will be one left.'

'She's hurting. She has Molly and you to think about. Her loyalties are split – and she's lost Erin too.' He put a hand to his mouth momentarily. 'Sorry, that should have all stayed in my head. You've lost Erin, that's the main thing.'

'I know what you were trying to say.' She hugged him again before turning to go inside. 'I'll get through this one way or another.'

As she went back inside the house, the oppressive atmosphere crushed her. She closed her eyes, pinching the bridge of her nose to stop tears from forming again. But images of Erin with predatory men sprang to her mind so she opened them again quickly, taking a deep breath before she burst into angry sobs.

She couldn't switch off.

And she couldn't help thinking that Molly still knew more than she was letting on. Was Lucy covering for her? Because she had no right to do that. Not in these circumstances.

She needed to get the information out of Molly soon. Lucy should be trying to find out too.

There was no loyalty in their friendship right now. Someone had killed her daughter.

THIRTY-FOUR

As soon as Sara had gone, Lucy went upstairs to Molly.

'You lied to everyone,' she cried.

'I'm sorry.'

'Sorry doesn't cut it this time, Mol. You could get into a lot of trouble. You weren't helping at all.' She sat down on the bed beside her. 'Is there anything you want to tell me? Something you couldn't say in front of the detectives or Sara?'

'What about?'

'Who the father is.'

'I don't know.'

'I find that hard to believe.' Lucy tried not to show her disgust that it could be any of the men at the parties. 'You were always together. How could you not have seen her with someone?'

'We weren't *always* together. When we went to the chippie . . .' Molly stopped.

'Go on,' Lucy told her.

'We used to hang around with some of the boys.' Molly looked down at the floor.

'And?'

But Molly had clammed up again.

The front door opened. Lucy sighed and then went downstairs. Seeing Phil in the kitchen, she flew into his arms and broke down.

'Not our Mol,' she sobbed. 'Did Sara show you the diary?'

'The police have it. She gave it to them.'

'Surely it should be private?'

'It could contain vital clues to who attacked her.'

'But it also contains things about Molly. They had no right to do that without asking us.'

'I'd want the police to look into it if the shoe were on the other foot. You would too, if you think about it.'

'Yes, but everyone is going to know what they've been up to.' She paused. 'Oh, what am I thinking about that for? Surely I should be more disgusted in what they've been up to. Concerned about what they were dragged into. Did the diary go into a lot of detail?'

'I didn't ask.'

Lucy pulled away and sat down with a thump. 'Why would Molly do something like that?'

'Teenagers are vulnerable. They can be lured in by . . . by bastards who use them for their own means.' Tears welled in his eyes. 'I'm finding this hard to take in too. She's our child.'

'A *child* – that's exactly it. She isn't even old enough to vote. I'm going to talk to her again.'

'Be gentle, don't go in feet first.'

'I won't.'

But as soon as she saw Molly, she couldn't help but burst out angrily. 'Molly, I need to ask you about these parties. What was so attractive that you had to go and . . . and have sex with men?'

Molly's face paled. 'It's all lies.'

'*You're* lying! Tell me the truth. I'm your mother.'

'It has nothing to do with anyone else,' Molly snapped. 'And why am I getting the blame for everything?'

'I can't very well chat to Erin about it now, can I?'

The words were out of her mouth before she'd had time to think about them. She watched Molly's face screw up. 'Oh, Molly, I'm sorry. I shouldn't have said that. But sometimes you make me so angry, and I'm trying to understand you and I can't.'

Molly bowed her head, unable to look her mum in the eye. 'It was just a bit of fun.'

'So it was true?'

Molly didn't reply.

'They were exploiting you! They groomed you, took you to parties and then made you have sex with men you didn't know.'

'They didn't make us.'

Lucy put up her hand. 'I don't want to know all the details. I just want to know why.'

'We enjoyed it, is that what you want to hear?'

'Of course not!' Lucy flinched. 'Who's *they*, Molly? Who took you to the parties?'

'I can't remember.'

'You'll have to answer questions when the police find out, anyway.'

'There's only me and Erin who know what went on and she's dead, so I'm keeping it to myself.' A sob escaped her.

'You won't be able to, don't you understand? Once they find out who killed Erin, if it's anything to do with these parties, you'll have to testify.'

Molly bit at her lip. 'Then I'll lie.'

'You'll go to prison!'

'And then everyone will know what bad parents I have.'

Lucy recoiled. 'That was uncalled for. We've given you everything we could. You have wanted for nothing, and you repay us like this?'

'I can't tell you anything. I can't tell anyone,' Molly cried. 'I've lost my best friend and I don't want to talk about it.'

161

Lucy stayed where she was for a full minute but Molly turned her back on her. She could hear her sniffing, knew she was crying. Why wouldn't she trust her? Why wouldn't she let her comfort her?

Finally, she left the room. She'd have to try again when Molly was calmer, because she needed to know what had been going on.

Phil was still in the kitchen, the kettle warming as he reached for mugs out of the cupboard.

'How is she?' he asked.

'Being defiant and adamant she didn't do anything. Saying she'll deny everything.'

'Do you want me to try?'

She shook her head. 'I doubt she'll tell us any more yet.'

He took her hand and gave it a squeeze. 'We'll get through this,' he said. 'She's out of it now.'

'Is she?' Lucy drew in her breath. 'You don't think she'll be next, do you? If someone killed Erin, they could come after Molly.'

'Let's not think any further than day to day at the moment. The police will catch who is responsible. I know they will.'

As Phil took her in his arms again, Lucy wished she shared his optimism. He was always the positive one of the family. She recalled how much he had taken control when her parents had died within two months of each other. Lucy had been inconsolable and Phil had organised everything, shouldered the burden.

Right now, she was so glad to have him. Because if she was with Molly alone, she wouldn't be able to control her temper.

And right now, her daughter needed love and affection, rather than a dressing down.

THIRTY-FIVE

Seven months ago

Erin wasn't sure when they stopped giving her and Molly money and changed it to alcohol and drugs. They were taken to more parties and got to know a few of the other girls. Some of the men became friends. Before they realised what was happening, it was too late to stop. But she didn't think it was wrong to get affection from these men. It was nice to spend time with most of them.

She had felt better at the next party she and Molly went to and started to enjoy herself more. It wasn't so bad sticking up for herself if anyone got too pushy, so she went to the next one as well. It was only a few hours once a month.

She was still seeing Max, but not as much as at first. He'd brought several other girls to the parties. When she'd questioned him about it, he said it was only fair as she slept with other men. She wouldn't have, she'd told him, if he was her boyfriend. But he'd smiled at her and said it was too complicated.

Erin was a little drunk when a man took her by the hand and urged her to stand up. Molly nudged her.

'Go on, you'll be fine with him.' Molly's speech sounded slurred as someone took her hand too. 'He's really nice.'

Erin stood up. The man was smiling at her as they left the room and found a bedroom upstairs. He was good-looking with tidy grey hair, clean shaven and he smelt clean too. Musky aftershave invaded her senses.

He pushed her down onto the bed and jumped on it beside her, laughing as they ended up rolling together. He kissed her then, the drink she'd consumed making her feel light-headed. She let him remove her dress and then lay still as he took off his clothes, thinking about the red jacket she might treat herself to that weekend.

As she let her mind wander, he pushed into her. For a while she moved with him, wanting to seem as grown up as Molly. She had told her what she'd been doing. Maybe she should practise some things on him.

But then his demeanour changed and he pushed into her harder.

'Be careful,' she mumbled, her voice sounding alien.

But he kept on. His hands moved to her throat as he thrust into her. She struggled to breathe, managing to call out before he squeezed tighter.

'Stop!' She roared at the top of her voice.

The door burst open and Chad came bowling into the room. He pulled the man off her, the force sending him reeling across the room and into the wall. Chad laid into him, punching him several times in the face before a last kick in the back.

'Get dressed and get the fuck out of here,' he told him afterwards. 'You won't be invited again.'

Erin scrambled to the top of the bed, putting her hands around her knees as she tried to cover her nakedness. The man grabbed his clothes and shoes and left the room.

Chad picked up her dress and gave it to her. He sat on the end of the bed looking the other way while she put it on.

'Are you okay?' He turned back to her afterwards. 'He didn't hurt you too much?'

She dried her eyes and nodded at him.

'I'm fine,' she whispered. 'Thanks.'

'You have to be more careful. Some of them will always want to hurt you. There are certain things you don't do. If you're not comfortable with someone, then don't go in a room with them.'

'He was nice . . . until we were alone. Then he changed.'

'So you tell us about them. We want you to feel safe while you're here.' He leaned across and brushed a finger lightly down her cheek. 'You're precious, don't you forget that.'

She smiled, the fear dissipating at last.

'Come on, have a drink with me while you wait for Molly. Then I'll take you both home.'

Once Dave had finished with her, Molly waited for him to leave and then sat in silence for a while. Her head was spinning but there was something about sex with an older man. She had only been with one boy before the parties. Denton Martin had been her first attempt at it. They'd been going out for two months before anything serious happened, and once it had, she'd wondered what all the fuss was about. But now she knew.

Some of the men treated her as if she was their own. They were patient, considerate, teaching her things so that she could pleasure them. A couple of them even made time to pleasure her too. Like Dave, he was kind to her. She liked him, knew she was special to him. He only ever asked for her.

She searched out her clothes and dressed as quickly as she could, all the time her eyes trying to focus. How much drink had she had? She knew one of the men had brought a bottle of wine with him but it had only been half full. Had he had any of it or had he given it all to her? She couldn't remember.

Finally, she went downstairs and into the kitchen. Chad and Erin were sitting at the marble breakfast bar. They were laughing, heads together. Molly glared at them as best she could. What was Erin doing with him?

'Ah, the wanderer returns.' Chad smiled at her. 'Had a good time?'

'Not really.' Molly reached for a glass and ran the cold water tap. It was then she noticed Erin's face. 'What's up with you?'

'She got a bit spooked, that's all,' Chad said. 'One of the guys was a little rough.'

Molly snorted. 'They're all like that, if you ask me.'

'If you ever have a problem, you only have to say.' Chad's tone was one of reasoning and she grasped hold of it. Maybe he did like her best.

'Sometimes it's too late by then,' she admitted.

'Then tell me afterwards. I don't want any unwelcome guests at our parties.'

He reached into his wallet and gave them both a few notes. 'I like you two. Why don't you buy yourselves something nice?' He clocked the time. 'Come on, let's get you home.'

'Where's Max?' Erin asked.

'He had a little business to take care of. Asked me to see you got a lift.'

When Chad pulled in at the bottom of Sampson Street, Erin got out but Molly stayed in the car. 'I just want a word with Chad,' she told her. 'I'll see you tomorrow.'

'Okay, night.'

As soon as Erin had disappeared from view, Molly turned to Chad. 'I thought I was your favourite girl. That's what you told me the other night.'

Chad reached over to her, wiping his thumb across her chin.

'You are, but we have to be careful.' He put his thumb to her lips and prised them open gently. 'That's why I look out for Erin too. She's your friend.'

'She won't be if I catch her fooling around with you.'

'Hey, don't be like that.' He stared at her. 'She's not as street savvy as you are. She's a bit shy with the men. Whereas you, you're all woman, or so I'm told.'

'You could always find out.' Molly turned to him and pressed out her chest.

She had wanted to feel his lips on hers for so long. When he leaned across and kissed her, she was swept away with infatuation. His kiss was the most passionate she had ever experienced. It was as if he wanted her and no one else.

She reached for his zip, pulled it down and slipped her hand inside. She would do anything to please him.

THIRTY-SIX

Sara stood in the kitchen, her back resting against the worktop as she sipped at a hot mug of tea. Rob was taking a shower. He'd been keeping Nat occupied for most of the evening until it was time for him to go to bed. They'd been playing a football game on his computer. Every now and then she'd heard a roar as one or the other scored a goal. It was good of Rob to try and entertain Nat. She was glad he was here, despite it feeling unnatural.

A few minutes later, he came into the kitchen. His hair was wet and for a moment, a whole load of nostalgia crept up on her. She remembered the first time they'd slept together, their wedding night, and how for years after they would take cheeky opportunities when the kids were grown up and out of the way for an odd hour here and there.

But then she recalled the arguments, the betrayal when he'd had an affair. The anger, the hurt, the guilt.

'What happened across the road?' he asked, as he filled the kettle with water. 'I would have come across with you. Nat would have been okay for half an hour.'

'I wanted to see Lucy by myself.' She moved along the worktop as he reached for a mug.

'And how was she?'

'Oh, I don't know. I just feel she's trying to shield Molly against the hurt of losing Erin to the detriment of helping us find her killer.'

'Oh?'

'I'm sure Molly is hiding something from us, and the police. Lucy and I have barely had a cross word for years. Why else would we argue like we have?'

'Don't you trust her to tell you the truth?'

'I do.' Sara paused. 'But I wonder how much I would cover for Erin in the same circumstances.'

'It's rational, I guess. I'd want to protect Erin too.'

'I know Molly was more involved than Erin. I just can't prove it.'

'There might be nothing to prove.'

'How could Lucy not want to know? It would tear me apart – it *has* torn me apart. I've a good mind to show her the diary, put her and Phil through the same pain as we've experienced. Maybe then she would get Molly to talk.'

'But that's not like you, and you know it. You wouldn't want to hurt either of them.'

She sighed. He was right. Despite her current frustration, she harboured no real ill-feeling towards Lucy.

'Don't you think Lucy is being naive if she thinks Molly will tell her everything? I can remember lots of times when we lied to our parents about staying out, meeting boys.'

'That's trivial. Part of growing up.'

'We thought the girls were out doing just that, though. This is much worse.'

'Molly and Erin were good friends,' Rob added. 'There's

nothing Molly would hide, surely, to purposely hinder the police with their investigation.'

'You're probably right.' She moved through to the living room with him, and sat down on the settee.

She closed her eyes, hoping when she reopened them that this would all have been a dream. How had her life been shattered into so many pieces in the matter of a day? She wasn't sure she was strong enough to cope with what was going to happen during the next few either. Because the worst was still to come when they found Erin's killer.

At least they would get some justice then though, if not any peace.

Molly curled up into a foetal position on top of her bed. This had all started because Erin had kept a stupid diary. Why hadn't she told her? Whatever was in it would damn her too.

She could tell by Sara's reaction earlier that afternoon that Erin must have gone into detail about what they'd been doing at the parties. She was in for it if Sara showed her mum and dad. Everything was going to come out.

She sat up suddenly. She had ample reason to contact him now, meet up with him. She had to warn him. She picked up her mobile and called him. There was no answer so she sent a message.

I have to see you. There's something you need to know.

A reply came in a few minutes later.

Tell me over the phone.

No, I have to see you.

It's not safe.

She didn't reply.

I can meet you in twenty minutes if you can get out.

Where

Our usual place.

Okay.

Molly crept down the stairs. Her mum and dad were in the living room and she slipped out of the back door before they noticed. She ran down the side path onto the drive and into the street. It was dark, not many people around at that time of night, but she pulled up her hood just in case. The walkway was still closed but the police presence had tapered off. She'd been told it was to get things back to normal for the residents of the street, but that didn't mean they had given up on finding Erin's killer.

At the bottom of the street, she turned left and hot-footed it back to the main road. She wanted to get to the Bennett Estate. Once there, she headed for Mount Street, where he would be waiting for her.

She saw his car and ran to it. As soon as she had climbed into the passenger seat, her tears came.

He drew her into his arms, comforting her while she sobbed.

'They know about the parties.' She pulled back from him. 'Erin kept a secret diary and her dad found it. Even I didn't know about it.'

He groaned aloud.

'My mum went mad at me when she realised what had been going on. I tried to say it was made up but I bet my mum and Erin's mum will work it all out.'

She stayed in his arms for a while, all the time he played with her hair. She was safe with him. He would make things right. No one would find everything out. Not her mum, not Sara, not the police. This was her secret and she wasn't sharing it with anyone.

'Do they know everything?' he broke into the silence.

'They know she was pregnant.'

'What? Fuck.' He put his head back on the headrest in resignation. 'This had better not get any worse.' He turned to her again. 'We'll have to stop contact for a while.'

'Why?' Molly frowned.

'Because we might get found out and you don't want that, do you?'

'I don't care.'

'Your parents would stop you seeing me.'

'They can try. I won't let them.'

'It's not that simple, don't you understand?'

'But I love you.' Molly watched as he stiffened at her words. 'You love me, don't you?'

The look he gave her could have turned her to stone.

'I don't love you, Molly. I never have and I never will.'

'But you said—'

'I say a lot of things that I don't mean.'

Molly gasped in between sobs. 'How can you say that after what happened to Erin? I have no one now.'

'You had no one before. Erin wasn't a good friend to you.'

'What do you mean?'

He stared at her without speaking and then he started the engine.

'Get out of the car.'

172

'No!' She began to wail. 'I'm not leaving you.'

'I said get out of the car!' He reached over, pressing down on her as he opened the door. 'Get out and don't call me again. Do you hear?'

'But I did it for you. You can't dump me! Not after everything that's happened.'

He pushed her towards the door. She took one last look at him and then scrambled out. The second she had closed the door, he screeched away from the kerb.

She cried, broken again. Was everyone she loved going to leave her? She couldn't live with the pain, the guilt of not being there for Erin.

THIRTY-SEVEN

Lucy dipped her fingertips into the bath water to see if it was hot enough. She turned off the taps, removed her dressing gown and stepped in. Immersing herself in the heat, she let out a sigh. Usually she loved lounging in the bath for half an hour with a good book but today she was using the routine to escape. The house had an atmosphere hanging over it and she had to get away from it for a while. From Erin and the tragedy.

Lucy had been friends with Sara since they'd been four years old. At nursery school, they had bonded over a game in the sand pit and had been inseparable ever since. They'd grown up living three streets away from each other, only a few minutes' walk from Sampson Street and, like Erin and Molly, had been in and out of each other's houses all the time.

Sara loved coming to see Lucy's parents and she'd stay over most weekends from Friday after school. They went everywhere together, until boys and dating came along – though they often did that together too. A weak smile formed on her lips as she thought back to the two of them going out with the Morgan twins and not really being sure which one was which. She was sure the boys played them, often swapping purposely to tease them. But they had soon been history when Phil had come onto the scene.

Lucy had been besotted with Phil from the moment she saw him. He lived in the south of the city in Meir, so they didn't know each other from school. They met one evening at the roller rink – long replaced by several nightclubs – and Phil had been showing off, skating in and out around her and Sara as they held hands around the rink. Suddenly, he'd stopped and turned quickly, aiming to skate backward towards them. It had ended badly, with Lucy's legs being knocked out from under her, and she'd crashed to the floor. Phil had literally fallen for her, landing heavily on her foot.

She'd hobbled off the rink with him helping her, his arm around her waist. They'd sat the rest of the night out as Sara skated around, putting up her thumbs when she thought Phil wasn't watching.

They'd gone on four dates that week and after that, became a permanent item. When he'd asked her to marry him three years later, she had been ecstatic.

Sara had gone on to meet Rob two years later and the four of them had become firm friends until they split up after Rob had an affair. Lucy recalled that it had been hard on Phil. He'd lost his friend, his confidant, and a part of her knew he hadn't forgiven Rob for leaving him too.

She and Sara hadn't planned to have children at the same time, but really, their timing couldn't have been better. Enjoying, and moaning, through their pregnancies together had been fun. It was like having her own personal ally all the time. Sara was there for her when she'd been afraid because Molly hadn't moved for a while, insisting they go to the hospital, and there afterwards when she'd been told she was worrying too much but still couldn't stop. And when Molly had been born, after a long and laborious labour, Sara, still pregnant with Erin, had been the one who had helped her to get Molly to feed.

Two weeks later, Erin had come along and they had spent that first summer in a daze of baby memories and bliss. It had helped them both immensely to know what the other was going through. And when her parents had died, shortly after Molly was five, Sara had helped her through that, too.

And now, was all that going to change? Lucy really hoped their friendship would strengthen rather than split. She wasn't sure how she would cope without Sara in her life. Sara had always been there for her, and vice versa. And yet, here she was now, at a complete loss as to what to do. All she wanted was to know what had happened, the contents of that diary. And Sara didn't want to share them.

It made her want to see it more. Was she protecting her against things Erin had said about Molly, or what they had been doing together at those parties?

It had hurt her so much when Sara had said that Erin's death was down to Molly. Of course she knew her daughter was no saint, but neither was Erin and it was wrong to lay the blame at her feet. Molly loved Erin as much as Lucy did. She had lost her best friend. Things were never going to be the same for her.

Perhaps they could get Molly some counselling. She might need to talk to someone about her ordeal.

Groomed. How could that have happened? They had brought her up better than that, surely?

She closed her eyes, held her nose and sank her head beneath the water, relishing the silence in her ears as she lay submerged. She wanted to stay here, shield herself from what was to come. She had to find out what was in that diary. It wasn't fair that Sara and Rob had seen it and yet she and Phil still didn't know the details of what had been going on. Because she hadn't seen the diary entries, she was imagining all sorts of things. Images of Molly with those men kept flashing through her head. And what happened if it was leaked to the press?

A loud knock on the bathroom door brought her out of the water, gasping for air.

'Lucy, Molly isn't in her room. She's left the house and she's not answering her mobile.'

'I'm coming.' She sat up so quickly that the water in the bath sloshed everywhere. 'Try her phone again while I get dressed.'

THIRTY-EIGHT

Leon was at home when his phone rang. When he saw who the caller was, he went to take the call in his office. Trudy had been sitting across from him and he didn't want her to hear the conversation.

'Where the fuck have you been?' he asked, sitting down at his desk. 'I've been trying to contact you all day.'

'I've been keeping a low profile. The police are on to the parties. Erin kept a diary. Her parents found it and handed it in.'

'For fuck's sake. Do you know what was said?'

'Molly said she never saw it; didn't know anything about it.'

Leon sighed dramatically. 'Is there any way you can find out?'

'You mean inside contacts? I doubt anyone will trust me, but I can try.'

'Do that and come back to me. I need to know how much clearing up I have to do.'

'Wait – did you know she was pregnant?'

'Yeah. Jeff told me. Molly has been spouting her mouth off. Does everyone know?'

'I'm not sure. I can try and find out.'

'No, leave it for now. The less people know, the better.' Leon disconnected the call and went back into the living room.

'What was all that about?' Trudy wanted to know.

'Just a bit of business. Nothing to worry about.'

'It is if you're up to no good.'

'Like I said . . .'

'What's going on, Leon? Being secretive will only piss me off, as well you know.'

'Just leave it, will you?'

'If it's anything to do with Ranger Street . . .'

Leon's eyes met hers as he turned his head sharply. 'Everything is fine there.'

'That's not what I've heard.'

'Then you should get better sources.'

'I'm warning you, Leon. If you're bringing—'

'Give it a rest, woman,' he roared. 'I'm tired of all your insinuations. Nothing is going on!'

He stormed out of the room and into the kitchen. He paced the floor then stood with his hands on the worktop, staring out of the window. That phone call had got his back up. Business was going to be affected by this. There was no way he could concentrate on getting any new orders in, and the runners had been scarce since the trouble with Caleb Campbell, and Seth Forrester going to prison last year.

Things were going from bad to worse. Something had to be done.

Molly hadn't wanted to go straight back home so she walked around for about half an hour. It was raining so there weren't many people about. But she didn't mind if anyone saw her crying. She was in a living hell that she didn't know how to get out of.

Chad's manner had shocked her. She thought he cared for her. Was it all words to get her to do things for him?

She loved him, but he didn't love her . . . yet. She could change that. Everyone was upset about Erin, maybe things were getting on top of him too. It was all raw. He would come around.

Convincing herself of this made her feel a little better so she finally went home. She walked into the kitchen and jumped as a shout came out.

'Molly! Where have you been?' Lucy cried.

'I went for a walk.' Molly wiped at her tears, glad her parents would assume she was upset about Erin.

'But it's pouring down! You're soaked.'

'I needed a bit of fresh air.'

'I've been calling you on your mobile.'

Molly had switched it off after speaking to Chad. She got it out and looked at the screen. 'I must have knocked it onto silent,' she lied.

Lucy stared at her before embracing her. 'Your dad and I are so worried about you, Mol. We don't want you going to see anyone involved in those parties.'

'I wasn't. It's so claustrophobic in here with everything going on. I wanted to see something apart from these walls.'

'It's not safe out there at this time of night,' Phil chastised.

'This is Stoke, Dad, not Manchester.'

'But there is a killer on the loose and for all we know . . .' Lucy paused.

Molly burst into tears again.

'Oh, Molly, it will be okay, duck. The police will catch whoever did this soon. But in the meantime, I'd rather you stay in.'

Her mum was right. What else could Molly do if Chad didn't want to see her? She couldn't go out with friends, she couldn't go to Potteries Takeaway, and she couldn't sneak out to the party tomorrow night to see if she could make Chad change his mind about seeing her again. It was too risky.

How had so much changed over the course of two days? Erin was dead, and everything had fallen to pieces.

THIRTY-NINE

It was half past nine by the time they got back to the station with the diary. Grace was looking through its contents, shocked by some of the things she was reading. It seemed as though Erin had been mixed up with the parties for nearly a year. No wonder the girls' behaviour had been up and down if they were being plied with alcohol, and possibly drugs, as well as given money for sex with strangers on a regular basis.

It turned her stomach to think of what they had to do to earn their keep, so to speak. She knew they would likely have been asked to do many degrading and disgusting things, most of which they would never have agreed to if they hadn't been under the influence. A lot of things they wouldn't remember either, if they were given the date rape drug Rohypnol. It was a common method used by groomers, and something she had seen several times in previous cases.

She was making notes at her desk and looked up when her name was called. It was Shaun Ericson from the tech team.

'Got some things from the victim's phone.' He wheeled over a chair, his huge body spilling over its sides. Shaun was a giant of a man.

'I've found several interesting photographs. Both Erin and Molly are predominant through the photo album – lots of selfies, the usual stuff – but there's also a youngish male with Erin, and from what I can gather, he seems like a boyfriend.'

Grace shouted Perry over and Sam and Frankie also came to stand behind her as Shaun flicked through a number of images: one of Erin sitting on the man's knee all smiles, one of them arm in arm – someone else evidently doing the snapping – another of them in a car, a selfie this time.

'Max Croydon,' several people said at once, and a rumbling went around the room.

'Croydon is known to us,' Perry explained to Grace. 'He's been involved in trafficking young girls and exploiting females.'

'Interesting, because there are also lots of images of a party with older men and lots of young women on here,' Shaun said.

'Any indecent ones?' Grace asked.

'No, although I'm not sure that isn't going on behind closed doors.' Shaun brought up more images and Grace's shoulders sagged as he scrolled through. She could see Erin and Molly among the girls, but didn't recognise any of the men other than Max.

'I wonder who's organising this.' Perry said.

'Maybe someone who Molly is protecting?' Grace suggested.

Frankie pointed to a photo of Erin by the side of a car. 'I recognise that street. It's off Sandon Road, Meir Heath. There aren't many properties on it, if I remember rightly. Yeah, it's Sandon Crescent.'

'Well spotted, Frankie,' Grace said.

'That might explain my next point.' Shaun clicked the mouse a few more times. 'I found these images we're looking at in the deleted file. Based on the time stamp, whoever was there at the time of the murder erased them, thinking they'd done it permanently.'

'So that could be our suspect, not wanting us to see them?' Perry asked. 'Maybe he's worried we'll find out about the house—'

'Molly changed her story to say she didn't see it happen, by the way,' Grace interjected.

'Maybe she did, but now she's scared the killer will find out she's talking to us.'

'Well, we need to talk to her again.' Allie had joined them. 'I think we have a line of enquiry to examine her phone now too. Let's see what's on there and pretty sharpish. Grace, can you do that?'

'Sure can.'

Allie nodded. 'Let's bring Croydon in for questioning tomorrow and go from there. It's interesting, if he is a suspect, that he didn't take the phone and dispose of it. Why take the time erasing only some of the images – leaving ones of himself – and then fling it into the hedges rather than swipe it and run?'

'To make it look like it could have been Molly? Envious that Erin had a boyfriend? Maybe Erin was spending too much time with Max, and Molly was jealous?'

'That's possible. We need to find more evidence that puts him near the scene at the time of Erin's murder.' Allie looked at Sam. 'We also need to check what car he drives and if it comes up on camera anywhere nearby in the period before or after.'

Sam nodded. 'I'm on it.'

'We also need to see if we can find out the identity of anyone else in these photos. Thanks for the information, Shaun.' Allie brought the chat to an end. 'Let us have a list of the text messages as soon as possible. We need to get Croydon's phone number and see if we can link it to Erin's phone asap. I'm sure he's going to be on there, even if the messages have all been deleted.'

Shaun nodded. Allie went back into her office, Grace following behind. After all the trouble Nick Carter had got her into, Grace very much wanted to keep the trust that she'd built since with her colleagues.

Nick was their former detective inspector, before Allie, and he'd made things uncomfortable for Grace as soon as she'd been posted to Stoke because he'd wanted her to keep it to herself that she was related to the Steele family. She'd got into a couple of scrapes with him until the news had been broken by the *Stoke News*. That was when colleagues had turned on her and she'd had to work hard ever since to gain their trust again.

She needed to be open with her DI.

'Allie, Max Croydon is a known associate of the Steele family,' she said.

Allie nodded. 'Don't worry about it. I know Nick pushed you hard to find out information from them but I won't be doing anything like that. Just come to me if things start to overlap.'

'But I—'

Allie stopped her. 'We'll play it by ear until then. I don't want to remove you from this case unless absolutely necessary.'

Grace nodded her appreciation. She had been worried about just that since she'd heard Croydon's name, but if her connection to the Steeles meant coming off the case, she would. She wouldn't get involved if it put the team in jeopardy again.

And at least she had let Allie know.

FORTY

It was around ten thirty when Grace finished for the evening. She got home to an empty house, having rung Simon to find he was still at the office. He'd said he'd be home within the hour so while he was out, she took the chance to get on the treadmill.

Sometimes it seemed as if a week had passed rather than a day since she'd left the house in the morning. So much had happened and been crammed into the time available.

It was easy to forget things as she ran, her mind clearing of everything but the effort to breathe sensibly.

Before she'd left for the night, they had started to dig more into Max Croydon's background. He'd been in prison for two short spells for thieving but he'd been off the radar for a good eighteen months now. This annoyed Grace even more, as she knew it meant he was likely up to no good and purposely keeping a low profile. At least if it did come out that he was involved, they now knew where to find him.

Once her run was over and she was in the shower, memories from her childhood rushed back at her. Being shut in the room behind the garage, not knowing when she would be let out. Not even knowing what she had done. Being scared of her father whenever he returned to the house. Not wanting to be alone with him. Seeing what her mum went through day after day, month after month, year after year, until she could take no more.

Tears poured down her face and in the end she gave in to them, letting out all of her anguish. The day would have been hard enough without all the talk of the sex parties. To think that they'd started up again after the team had successfully shut them down two years ago. It was beyond her comprehension.

Or had they even stopped? Had they still been going on and only brought to their attention because of Erin Ellis's murder?

She heard the front door open as she was padding through to the bedroom wrapped in a bath sheet.

'Honey, I'm home!' Simon shouted up to her.

'I'm upstairs!'

She heard him take the steps two at a time and immediately he was in the doorway. He raised an arm and placed a hand on the frame. 'Now, there's a sight for sore eyes,' he grinned. Then immediately, spotting the look on her face, he backtracked. 'What's wrong?'

Grace sighed. 'It's just been a long and tiring day.'

He took her into his arms and gave her a hug. 'I'm in desperate need of a shower. How about I do that, and then I'll fetch you a glass of wine?'

'That would be perfect.'

He disappeared out of the room and Grace climbed into bed, getting out her laptop. She flicked through the news pages but nothing else was coming forward. Simon was back with her within ten minutes.

'Did you get to speak to Teagan?' she asked as he climbed into bed beside her.

'Yes, she's got a grade A for her artwork. She's really pleased.'

'That's good.'

'I told her we'd take her shopping soon. Well, I said you would and I'd wait in Wetherspoons for you.'

She rolled towards him and laughed. 'You know I don't mind going shopping with her, as long as this case is sorted by then.'

'Do you think it will be?'

'It's hard to tell.'

'Oh, before I forget. Luke called, asking if I want to play golf on Saturday. And then afterwards, he's invited us to dinner. Are you okay with that?'

'Yes, sure. I like Caroline. We have a laugh.'

'Mostly at our expense,' he teased.

'Of course.' They lay quietly for a moment.

'Have you wondered if Molly Redfern could be a suspect?' Simon asked.

'Oh my god, no! And I can't believe that I didn't,' Grace said in mock surprise, then slapped him playfully on his chest. 'Of course I have. She could have used the knife and then run for help saying it was someone else.'

'What do you think about that?'

'I think Erin and Molly were close. They were teenagers, both sixteen. Hormones aplenty. And there was the pregnancy to contend with. But to stab your best friend you've known since birth?' She shook her head. 'I have to keep an open mind. And that is why I'm a copper and you're a senior editor.'

She snuggled into him and they turned the lights off to go to sleep. But an hour later, Grace's mind still wouldn't rest so she got up and went downstairs to get a drink.

Hot chocolate made, she sat at the table and clicked on Google Street Maps, bringing up the street that Frankie had recognised. There were only a few houses there, all regal-looking, individually designed homes. She'd get him to pay a visit in the morning, see if anyone could remember any parties.

She shuddered at the thought of those men with the girls.

And every time she did think about them it brought her back to the Steeles. She wondered if it would be worth popping in to see Eddie first thing, see if he could identify any of the men in the images. If she could get him alone, without Leon to muddy things, maybe he might tell her some names.

She shouldn't, but it was worth a shot. And Allie had said she was doing okay . . .

Grace sent Eddie a message, asking to see him early the next day, before she could change her mind.

FORTY-ONE

Three months ago

'I miss seeing you.'

'I know, babe. But I've been really busy.'

Erin was in Max's bed. She'd been with him for the past hour. At the party last Friday, she'd been moaning at him that she didn't see as much of him as she'd like to, so tonight he'd brought her to his flat. She'd never been there before. It was on Ford Green Road above Skinjase, a tattoo studio.

Even though it was small, it was exceedingly tidy. The living room shared the space with a tiny galley kitchen of cream units. Two navy blue settees were set in an L-shape, a coffee table in the corner, to accommodate a small dining table and chairs. The walls were decorated in a blue and cream striped wallpaper, and poppy red cushions added a dash of bright to the space.

Erin fell in love with it instantly, picturing herself cooking meals for her and Max, then putting her feet up next to him on the settee as they watched TV together. She imagined them having friends round at the table, and long hot showers together every morning.

But the first thing Max showed her was the bedroom. He pushed her onto the bed, not even bothering to remove her clothes, just moving aside the necessary items.

Afterwards, they went to sit in the living room.

'Is the tattoo place downstairs busy?' she asked for want of something to say.

'Yeah, Jase is an amazing artist.'

'Did you have any of your tattoos done by him?'

'He added a few to my sleeve.' He pointed to an image of a tiger on his forearm. 'He did this one too.'

'Does it hurt?' She ran a finger over it. 'I'd be too scared.'

'They sting for the first minute or so and then it's okay. Some places hurt more than others too.'

'If I had a tattoo, I'd have a butterfly. It's a symbol of hope, you know. Flying away from your past and emerging as something else.'

'Why would you want to do that?' He shook his head. 'No. Your body is pure. No tats, no piercings. Just beauty to enjoy as it is.'

'Why don't you enjoy it a little more?' She reached for his hand and placed it on her breast.

'Not got enough time, I'm afraid.' He checked his watch. 'I have to be at work in half an hour.'

'But we've only just got here.' She pouted.

'I told you it wouldn't be long.'

'It's not fair. I never get to see you now.'

'I've squeezed you in tonight when I don't really have time,' he protested.

'I bet you make time for Annabel.' She folded her arms like an insolent child. 'I've seen her all over you.'

'Don't be like that.' Max pulled her into his arms. 'Being jealous doesn't suit you.'

'I'm not jealous!'

191

He laughed. She found herself joining in.

'The next time we meet you should take me to Ranger Street,' she said. But she felt his body freeze.

'Where did you hear about that?'

'I overheard Melana talking about it. That it's a place for the special girls only. I'm special, aren't I?'

'Course you are.'

'Then take me to Ranger Street.'

Max shook his head. 'You're too precious to go there.'

'I could go with you?'

'I don't have a key.'

'You could get one?'

'No.'

'But—'

'Be quiet, woman.' He silenced her with a kiss, pushed her down onto the settee and moved until he was on top of her. 'Isn't my gaff enough for you?' he teased.

She grinned, realising as she melted into his embrace that she was special to him. But she made it a goal to get to Ranger Street and see what it was like. She wasn't going to be fobbed off by Max. She *was* special, never mind Annabel or that other girl Rachel thinking he was theirs.

And if Max wouldn't take her, maybe she could go there with someone else. It didn't have to be him, not now someone else was giving her attention . . .

FRIDAY

FORTY-TWO

Grace had messaged Eddie mainly because she wanted to see him on his own first thing, before anyone was around. She pushed open the door at Steele's Gym, hoping it would be quiet.

She was right. There were only two men pumping iron in the far corner, spotting one another. Neither gave her a second look as she marched across the room.

'What can I do for you, officer?' Eddie smiled.

No matter what, he still liked to tease her. But, as usual, she didn't rise to the bait.

She produced an envelope from her bag and removed the stills Shaun had given her from Erin's phone. 'Can you identify any of these men?'

Eddie took the images and spread them out on his desk as he examined each one. His face darkened the more he saw. By the time he had seen all three, Grace could see veins in his temple twitching.

Eddie pointed to a man.

'Max Croydon,' Grace said. 'We know that one.'

'He works for me on the doors at Flynn's Nightclub. He's also a member of the gym.'

'Anything you can tell me about him?'

'You probably know more than me.' Eddie sat back in his chair, stretched his legs out and steepled his hand. 'Let's just say, you're barking up the right tree.'

Grace sighed dramatically and sat down. 'If you have information, then I'm going to have to bring you in for questioning.'

'I don't know anything,' he said.

'But you clearly do.' She raised her eyebrows.

They stared at each other across the desk.

'Look, if Leon is involved in this,' she tapped a finger on one of the stills, 'then we need to put a stop to it. And him. Do you understand?'

'Oh, I do. And believe me, I had no idea it had started up again. I'm as sickened by it as you are.'

'Then help me to nail him.'

'I can't.'

'Why, because of your loyalty to family?' Grace taunted. 'You say yourself often enough that I'm family. I'd like to play that card right now.'

Eddie laughed. 'You don't get to pick and choose.'

'Fine, have it your way. I'll maybe come back with a warrant to fish through Leon's belongings. And then we'll do a thorough search of the place. I'm sure we'll find a lot more than we're looking for.'

'Empty threats, Grace. You can't do any of that without evidence, and I can't give that to you. That's what I meant.'

She gnawed at her bottom lip for a moment. Then she leaned forward and collected the photos. 'If you don't want to help, I'll do it my way.'

She didn't speak again until she was at the door. 'He's exploiting young women for his own personal gains. He makes money from those parties. He's a criminal.'

'He's still family.'

Grace laughed. 'You don't get to pick and choose.'

She left him to it, annoyed she had done nothing but rattle him. And herself. She was so sure he was going to help her. The hints he'd given her before, the tip-off about Forrester on her last case. It had been for his own purposes but he had still forewarned her. Why wouldn't he help her now?

She knew, really. It was because he'd never forgive her for being on the other side.

Eddie waited a few minutes after Grace had gone. It was a good job it was too early to speak to Leon, as he was so angry.

That stupid fucking idiot. Why was he doing this again? It was obviously lucrative but after their upbringing, he thought Leon would have more compassion. They had both watched their father lay into their mother on several occasions. It seemed Leon would always be his father's son.

But Eddie wouldn't. He'd warned Leon after the first time and he had stopped. Now he'd started it up again, even though he knew the police would be on to him.

Should Eddie tell him that they were getting close?

No, he'd bailed Leon out enough over the years. If the law came down on him, then it was his own fault.

As long as it didn't take him down too.

FORTY-THREE

Phil hadn't had much sleep the night before, so when he received the text message from Sara in the early hours, he got up, put on his coat, pulled on a hat, and wrapped a scarf round his neck so he wasn't too recognisable. He had to slip across to see Rob.

Sara answered the door and gave him a hug. 'How are you feeling?'

'Like a train wreck.' She pointed to the kitchen. 'Rob is through there. I think he'll appreciate someone to talk to.'

He followed her through to the kitchen, where he could see Rob in the conservatory. He knocked on the door before going in.

'Hey, bud.' Phil raised a faint smile.

'Hey.'

Rob didn't look up. Phil could see he was close to tears so he sat down across from him and waited for him to say something.

'I don't think either of us knew her when she died,' Rob spoke eventually, his voice breaking. 'I hadn't realised the divorce had hit her so hard. Sara wasn't telling me half the stuff that had been going on.'

'I guess she was trying to show she could cope without you.'

'But pregnant at sixteen?' Rob shook his head. 'We didn't bring her up to do that.'

'Teenagers make mistakes. We all do, no matter what age, really.'

'Erin had everything. You know my parents didn't have much, and neither did Sara's, so we always vowed we'd give our kids the best we could. Nice home, good holidays, clothes, the latest gadgets – whatever they wanted.' He sneered. 'A fat lot of good that did.'

'You'll just have to remember her as she was the last time you saw her.'

'You're blaming me because I moved out?' Rob folded his arms. 'That she went off the rails because I wasn't here for her?'

'Of course not!'

'I saw her in summer. She and Nat came to stay with me for a week.' He smiled then. 'I live half an hour from the beach now. We spent a lot of time there. The weather was hot and sunny. We were lucky.'

'And how was she then? Did she seem any different to you? I know I never noticed *that* much change in Molly.' Phil struggled to keep his emotion in check.

'She seemed like any normal sixteen-year-old. I wasn't sure she'd be happy spending a week without your Mol, but the longer she was with us – that's me and my partner, Lyn – the happier she became. In some ways, she was like my little girl again. I just thought it was because she was enjoying herself.'

'Were there any indications she had a boyfriend?'

'She didn't say. But she was on her phone a lot, texting and scrolling mainly. She could have been in contact with someone.' Rob paused for thought. 'She was drinking a bit too much, come to think of it. She wanted wine with everything and I told her no. She said Sara let her and I knew that would be a lie. It was the only thing we had words about during her visit. I let her have the odd glass, but nothing else.'

When Rob was silent for a while, Phil decided to leave him in peace.

'I'm here if you need to talk,' he said. 'I know there are some things you might not want to discuss with a bunch of women. You'll be staying here a while?'

'For as long as I can before I have to go back to work.'

'I guess it's not appropriate for us to go out for a pint, but I'd love to have a drink with you before you go. Sounds soft, I know, but I've missed you.'

'Missed you too, fella.' Rob nodded his thanks. 'Let's do that soon.'

They stood up and, after shaking hands, Phil let himself out from the side door, not wanting to go back into the house to see Sara. Tears welled in his eyes and he pushed the balls of his hands against them to stop them falling.

Before he reached the drive, he stopped to catch his breath. He couldn't begin to imagine how it would feel as a father to think your child died because you left their mother. Rob would blame himself, and he would blame Sara. But the world was a tough place. No one could wrap a child up in cotton wool, keep them close all the time. One day you had to let them go and pray they returned safely.

But look what had happened to Molly and Erin. If he could get his hands on the bastards who had violated their daughters, he wouldn't be responsible for his actions. Every time he closed his eyes, images raced through his mind. It was hard to think of anything else.

He hoped Molly would be able to move on after this. They could get her some counselling. She'd already had so much to deal with even before Erin's murder because of those men. The man who stabbed Erin had to be one of them. This wasn't a mugging gone too far – although knife crime and gang mentality seemed to be becoming the norm. Only a few weeks back, he remembered a report on the front page of the *Stoke News*. There had been two teenagers stabbed on their way home from a nightclub. They'd both survived but the reasons for the attack had been pathetic to him. One of the victims had looked at the perpetrator in the wrong way, 'disrespecting' him. It seemed the attack was more of a show for his mates, like an initiation. Do as we do, and you can stay with us. If you don't, we'll turn on you so fast that you won't know what's hit you.

He wiped at his eyes, then continued home. At the bottom of the street, he noticed one of the female detectives who had visited Molly yesterday walking up the street. He liked this one; she was softly spoken, made everyone feel as if she was there for them, and not just doing her job.

He paused as she came closer, not expecting her to stop at his house.

'We need to speak to Molly.' Grace showed her warrant card again. 'I'm afraid that this time, it will need to be at the station.'

Desperate to see Nat happy, Sara had given him some money to call at the local shop and buy a comic and some sweets as he wasn't going to school. She didn't expect him to come home in such a state at eight thirty in the morning. A nasty bruise was forming on his cheek, and his eye was swelling above the brow line. His clothes were dirty too, patches of mud on his knees.

'Nat!' Sara cried. 'What happened to you?'

He burst into tears.

'Did someone hit you?'

'Not before I hit them.'

Sara opened her arms and he ran into them. He was ten years old, what was going on?

'They called Erin mean names,' he sobbed into her shoulder.

'Who did?'

'Some of the boys from my school. One of them said she was a slag and she deserved to die, so I hit him.'

'Oh, Nat.'

'He said everyone knew what she was like except me. What do they mean, Mum?'

She held him tighter to her. 'It's just name calling. You know your sister better than anyone. They will never know her like that. So that's what you need to remember.'

Sara closed her eyes as she held on to Nat. He was going to be broken when he found out what had been going on with Erin and Molly and all these revolting parties. Because the boys from his school were right: Erin had been putting it about and none of her family had known about it.

As a mother, she had missed the signs. She'd thought Erin was being moody, pushing her luck like she had with her own parents at that age, about staying out late, about being a woman and not a child.

The truth was going to break them all eventually.

Rob came in when he heard the commotion.

'What's happened?' He put a hand under Nat's chin and lifted it to take a better look at his face.

'Someone was calling Erin names and he hit out at them,' Sara explained.

'You should see the other boy,' Nat said with a frown, although a little smile crept in.

'It's wrong to fight, Nat, under any other circumstances. But this time? I'm glad you did.' Rob gave him a hug. 'Whoever it was deserved it. They had no right to say things like that.'

'We can have a word with your teachers once you go back to school,' Sara added.

'I'm not going back to school, ever.'

'Nice try, kiddo, but that won't wash with me.' She tried to smile as she wiped furiously at her tears. 'Why don't you get cleaned up and I make you something nice for breakfast? Did you get the oatcakes?'

As Nat went upstairs, she looked at Rob. 'Everyone will be thinking those things about her if the contents of Erin's diary have to be made public.'

'She was a vulnerable young girl who was groomed. So was Molly. None of this is their fault. They were lured in by . . . by . . .' He hung his head down and cried, then left the room before she could comfort him.

Sara didn't know what to do. So used to being mum, chief hugger and there to cheer everyone up, her family as she knew it was broken and she had a feeling there was so much worse to come. Once they found the men who were behind these parties, more details would emerge.

She hugged herself, feeling as though she had no one to talk to or comfort her. She was as alone as Erin was, lying on a slab while the police searched for her killer.

A sob escaped her. She was never going to get over this.

Ever.

FORTY-FOUR

Grace was sitting in the soft interview room with Lucy and Molly Redfern. It was set out as a living room – a three-piece suite, coffee table, dining table and a few paintings hanging on the walls – as its sole intention was to put people at ease.

Grace tried to use this room as often as she could. She found she could get more from the general public if they didn't feel threatened. There was often enough pressure for some just to walk into the police station, even when they had committed no crime.

She took out her notebook, flipped it to the next blank page and wrote out the date.

'Molly, as you know, we found a diary of Erin's. Well, we've been reading through it and now have some questions for you.' She paused for a moment. 'We've also found some images on Erin's phone. They were deleted at the approximate time of her death. Are you covering for someone?'

Molly wouldn't look Grace in the eye, preferring to inspect the carpet.

Grace took an enlarged image from her file and handed it

204

to Molly. 'Can you tell me the names of anyone in this photo with you and Erin?'

Molly didn't look at it but shook her head. 'I can't remember.'

'But that's you there, on someone's knee.' Grace pointed to the photo. 'Who is he?'

'I don't know. We used to drink so much that sometimes I wouldn't even remember getting home from the party the next day, never mind what went on while we were there.'

'Did you and Erin ever fall out about the parties, or the men who went to them?'

'No, we were really good friends.'

'But you were seen on the security footage at Potteries Takeaway having words about something. On the night Erin was killed, do you remember?'

'She'd borrowed my shoes and I wanted them back.'

'Okay. And when you and Erin stayed out overnight – can you now tell me the address this party was at?'

Molly shook her head. 'No.'

'That doesn't cut it, I'm afraid.' Grace pointed to the photo again. 'And if you're not going to give us an address then I need more details from you as to what you know about the man she is with here. Max.'

Molly recoiled. 'I am so dead right now.'

'Why would you say that? Is it because he will be angry with you to know you're talking to us?'

'No, it's because he'll know *you're* on to him and he won't like it.'

'How would he find out?'

Molly shrugged.

'You need to start telling us the truth, Molly, no matter how scared you are. No more lies. Do you understand?'

Molly stayed quiet for a moment and then nodded slightly.

'So you *do* know more than you're letting on!' Lucy barked.

'Lucy, please let me ask the questions,' Grace spoke softly.

Lucy waved the comment away with her hand but she said nothing else. Grace turned back to Molly.

'You mentioned to your mum that Erin had a boyfriend. Was it this man in the photo?'

'Yes.'

'Were you aware of how old he is?'

'When you say old . . . ?' Lucy queried.

'He's twenty-five.'

'But she was barely sixteen.' Lucy looked at Molly for answers but she was still, her eyes down. 'Do you know anything about this?'

Molly looked up then, defeated. 'Erin had been seeing him for a few months.'

'Molly?' Grace pressed for more when she went silent again.

'Erin and Max had been getting closer and closer. I wasn't sure what to think of it, but he seemed okay.'

'What were you doing when Erin was seeing Max?' Lucy asked. 'Because you've still been going out every night as if you were seeing her.'

'I hung around with the gang in the chippie.'

'Potteries Takeaway?' Grace checked.

Molly nodded. 'There's always someone there I can talk to.'

'How often were they seeing each other?'

'Two or three times a week. Sometimes she'd be with him all evening. Sometimes he'd see her for an hour and drop her back to the chippie.'

'So you weren't pleased about that, I guess?' Grace could understand how Molly's nose would feel pushed out of joint.

'She was happy with Max,' Molly insisted.

'*How* happy?' Grace pushed.

Molly blushed before speaking again. 'Erin was in love with him.'

'She told you that?' Lucy shook her head. 'She was barely more than a child.'

'Old enough for some things though, right Molly?' Grace pressed.

'But isn't it obvious now?' Lucy nodded knowingly. 'You should be talking to him, not Molly. Perhaps he didn't want her to have the baby and . . . and killed her deliberately. You need to speak to him!'

'Mum, stop it!' Molly stood up quickly. 'Erin is dead and we can't bring her back. So it doesn't really matter if she was pregnant or not.'

'Of course it does!' Lucy reached for Molly's hand. 'He could be a suspect. It could have been him.'

'You're sure now that you didn't see the killer's face?' Grace pressed again. 'I know you changed your story but I'm also aware that you may have been frightened into doing so.'

'I didn't see who it was.' A lone tear fell down Molly's cheek, followed closely by another. 'I wish I had, but I didn't. She died because of me. All because of a stupid argument. It was my fault.'

Molly sat down again. Lucy gave her a hug as she cried.

Grace sat back in her chair to give them a little space. It was hard on them both but she had to find out the facts. Molly had known that Erin was pregnant, that she was going out with Max, but she hadn't told them. She couldn't help wondering why. She wouldn't be afraid of her friend's boyfriend, surely? She would probably have known him well.

'We need to examine your phone, Molly.' Grace held out a hand. 'Can you give it to me?'

'But I can't do without it,' Molly cried.

'I'll get it back to you as soon as I can,' Grace continued. 'But we're going to look at it for evidence.'

'What are you saying?' Lucy barked.

'It's routine, Mrs Redfern. We do this with every person who was one of the last people to see a victim alive.'

Molly handed over the phone, a worried look on her face.

'There's nothing to be afraid of, Molly. We just need to rule you out of things.'

FORTY-FIVE

One month ago

Erin woke up that morning and felt an ache between her legs. She looked under the covers, pulled up her nightie to see a fist-shaped bruise on her thigh. She couldn't recall how it had happened. She must have been wasted. But she had a much bigger thing on her mind right then.

She met Molly outside her house. They were heading in to Hanley to window shop.

As soon as they were out of Sampson Street, on the path that would take them through to the main road, Erin turned to her friend.

'I think I might be pregnant,' she blurted out.

Molly stopped. 'No way.'

'My period is late. It's been seven weeks since my last one. I feel funny too. I can't explain.' Tears brimmed her eyes.

'You need to take a test.'

'How am I going to do that without anyone finding out? Dr Bishop would probably tell my mum.'

'He can't. Doctor–patient confidentiality.'

'But he's known us since we were kids. I can't go to him.'

They started walking again.

'You can get a test from lots of places now,' Molly said. 'No one will see us if we just nip in to Superdrug.'

'I'm not sure I want to know anyway.'

'You have to. Then you can decide what to do next.'

'I can't have a baby at my age.' Erin shook her head vehemently. 'There's so much more to life than living around here.'

Molly raised her eyebrows. 'Face facts, we're going to amount to nothing, even if we get a good set of exams.'

'I'll be able to do even less with a baby in tow.' She burst into tears. 'What am I going to do?'

Molly was in a foul mood by the time they got to Hanley. If Erin was pregnant, it could ruin everything. If they didn't go to the parties, she wouldn't see Chad and she couldn't bear that. Even though he knew she slept around, he wanted to be with her. He looked out for her. He took care of her, made sure that she came to no harm.

And fancy being stupid enough to have let it happen, if it turned out to be true. She had always used protection; always pushed it on Erin too.

As the bus stopped to allow passengers to get off, she wondered if she was actually jealous that Erin might be pregnant. No, that couldn't be it. Although if it was true, it would mean she could have more control over things at the parties.

But maybe they wouldn't want them to visit now, because who wants to have sex with a pregnant girl? Although some of the dirty bastards invited might be turned on by that.

They bought a test and went up to the second floor of the shopping centre to the ladies'. As Erin went into a cubicle, Molly waited impatiently for the minute that could change both their lives forever.

A woman came in to use the toilets. Molly moved to sit on the bench below the mirrors, her feet dangling to and fro.

'It's time,' she shouted once the woman had gone. 'It's been over a minute.'

Erin came out of the cubicle. She looked at Molly with tears in her eyes. 'What happens if I am pregnant?'

'I wouldn't have the baby if it were me.'

'You'd have an abortion?'

Molly nodded. 'You're too young. Just think of all the things you wouldn't be able to do.'

'But it isn't right to kill a baby.'

'It won't be a baby yet.'

'I know, but—'

'I think you'd better check first. You could be wrong.'

Erin paused, and then nodded. She held up the stick so they could both see. The word PREGNANT was spelled out in blue letters.

'Holy shit.' Erin gasped, her hand flying to her mouth. 'I think I'm going to be sick.'

She rushed into the cubicle and had only just managed to shut the door before she threw up.

She came out a minute later, wiping her mouth and looking pale. Molly genuinely felt sorry for her.

'My mum's going to be so angry.' Erin's bottom lip began to quiver.

'You don't have to tell her anything if you decide not to keep it.'

She burst into tears. 'I can't kill it, though.'

Molly pulled Erin into her embrace, letting her cry.

'What am I going to do, Mols?' she sobbed.

'Why don't you do nothing for a few days? Let it sink in and then decide.'

'I have to tell my mum.'

'You need to have a good think about what to do without anyone interfering.'

'But she's my mum. She'll know what to do.'

'Yeah, but if you tell her about the baby then you'll have to tell her about everything else.'

Erin balked. 'I can't do that.'

'So don't you see? Having an abortion might be the best thing all round. You can keep everything to yourself then. Imagine if it gets out what we've been up to.'

'We haven't been doing anything wrong,' Erin protested.

'Taking uppers, getting drunk? Of course we have. And besides, you could have harmed the baby by now. Have you thought of that?'

Erin began to cry.

'It will work out, you'll see,' Molly comforted.

'But you're going to hate me too.'

'I will never hate you.'

'Oh god, I don't even know who the father is.'

'Well, you know some of the men you've been with. You'll have to count them up.'

'And then do what?'

'I don't really know.'

'There's something I have to tell you first.' Erin looked up at her. 'I-I've been sleeping with Lion Man.'

'No way!' Molly recoiled. 'I don't believe you.'

When Erin didn't speak, Molly demanded to know what had been going on.

'Tell me,' she said. 'You need to tell me everything.'

FORTY-SIX

Max Croydon had been picked up that morning and Perry was about to start the interview, Grace by his side.

Grace could see that Max didn't look nervous. There were folded arms but no tapping of the feet, no jiggling of the knees. No looking around tentatively. She wondered if he'd be the same after he'd been questioned. Some of the men she dealt with on a regular basis thought they were above the law, always sharp to prove her wrong as a woman.

She could also see how, like Jeff Harvey had indicated, lots of women would be enchanted by Max's appearance. With strong Roman features and intense brown eyes, he had the look of a model. But good looks and charm didn't interest Grace, unless they were packaged with a good personality and a warm affection towards other people. She wasn't one to make her mind up about anyone on first impressions though.

'You're not under arrest at this time,' Perry informed Max, 'but we'd be grateful for your assistance in our enquiry.'

Grace listened as Perry went through the routine, saying that the interview would be recorded, that Max could leave at any time. Max hadn't wanted a solicitor present but could request one if things changed.

'How well did you know Erin Ellis?' Perry started.

'We dated a few times over the past few months.'

'You were an item?'

'I wouldn't say that. I saw her maybe once or twice a week, when I was at a loss for something to do.'

Grace stared at him. What an arrogant prick.

'Where did you go when you met up?' she asked.

'Mostly to my place.'

'Which is?'

'Ford Green Road. I rent a flat.'

'Were you in a sexual relationship with Erin?' Perry said next.

'We had sex a lot, nothing wrong with that.'

'Her age didn't put you off?'

'She was over the legal requirement, if that's what you're getting at.'

'She seems a bit young for you.'

'What's a guy to do when a girl throws herself at his feet? She was a bit of a goer, if you know what I mean.'

The room dropped into silence as they waited for him to fill it. Grace knew guys like Max; she saw them all the time. They wanted to shout out about their exploits, tell the world how much of a babe magnet they were. How women worshipped them. He'd talk more, she was certain.

She was right.

'She was a sweet kid, wanting to be shown the ropes by an older man. I taught her a trick or two she wouldn't have learned from someone her own age. She always liked it, wanted more. There were no complaints. But for me, it was all about having something to do.'

'So you had no feelings for her?' Perry questioned.

'None whatsoever. Like I said, she was sweet. Not like her slapper of a mate.'

Grace leaned forward. Was he saying he was sleeping with them both? Maybe that was why Molly and Erin had been arguing before her death.

'Did you have a sexual relationship with Molly too?' she asked next.

'Not me. I have standards.' Max sat back in his chair. 'Erin was okay but Molly was a bitch. She'd snipe at me all the time. I reckon she was jealous because Erin was getting some from me. You know what sixteen-year-old girls are like.'

'Not sure I do, actually.' Perry shook his head. 'Care to enlighten me?'

'They're all jealousy and hormones. They can become quite clingy at times too.'

'Is that what happened with Erin?'

'Now you're putting words into my mouth.'

Grace saw Perry looking through his notes, purposely taking the time to pause before he played their last card.

'Were you aware that Erin was pregnant?'

Max lowered his eyes for a second. 'Molly told me. It's not mine, though.'

'But Erin thought you were an item.'

Max sniggered. 'We might have fooled around a little every now and then but we weren't any more than bed buddies.'

'At sixteen, she would have been besotted with you, though?'

'Maybe so, but she was infatuated by a lot of men.' Max stared at Perry before sitting forward again. 'Look, Erin was a sleep around. She might have looked as if butter wouldn't melt in her mouth but believe me, she was the total opposite. I wasn't the only man she was sleeping with. She was a wild thing on the quiet.'

'Regardless of that, the baby she was carrying could have been yours.'

Max paused to think, working out what to say next, Grace assumed. No matter what, he had to be careful.

'No, we always used protection.'

'What would you have said if she'd told you she was carrying your child?'

'Exactly what I've just said to you, and that she'd have to prove it was mine when it was born. I don't know her well enough to be saddled with a child either way, but I'd need to know for certain before committing to anything.'

'So, you're saying she was okay to sleep with but for nothing else?' Grace tried to keep the anger from her voice.

'She was sixteen. Not exactly waiting to get married.'

'But old enough to get pregnant.'

Max shrugged. 'Not my problem.'

'Two nights before she was murdered, you were seen talking to her in Potteries Takeaway,' Perry said. 'What was that about?'

'Things in general, TV and stuff.'

'She wasn't telling you she was pregnant and you weren't reacting in a way she wouldn't be happy with?'

'If you saw us together on camera, then you'll see that she was fine when we parted.'

Grace knew he had them there. Sam had shown them footage of the night in question and she'd watched Erin rejoin Molly afterwards. The two girls had sat chatting for a while after Max had gone. She realised the argument between Molly and Erin on the same night had now became far more important.

Perry got out the images they'd found on Erin's phone, laid them on the desk facing Max and pointed to them.

'That's you, sitting on the settee with Erin on your knee. Care to tell me where and when this was taken?'

Max took a long look at each image. Grace could see he was

using the time to get his thoughts in order again before he said anything.

'I think it was a party a few months back. I went through a rough patch and I was drinking heavily.' Max shook his head. 'No, I can't actually remember where I was.'

'Do you recognise any of the people who were with you?'

'Only Erin and Molly.'

'Can you remember whose party it was?'

He pressed his lips together and raised his eyes to the ceiling. 'Sorry, like I say I was drinking heavily.'

Perry collected the images, put them away in his notebook and turned to Grace. 'Any more questions?'

'Nothing for now.'

'Okay, Max. You're free to go.'

While Perry led him out of the building, Grace went back to her desk. She updated Frankie with their findings, ending with a huge sigh.

'Not what we'd planned,' she admitted, running a hand through her hair. 'He's a sleazy git, though. Made my stomach turn how he spoke about our victim as if she was just a plaything.'

'Sadly, she was,' Frankie acknowledged.

'We need to find something to rule him out completely now or else gather evidence to arrest him and look into him further. Can you help Sam with more CCTV trawling? Perhaps his car was in the vicinity of Potteries Takeaway after the girls left on Wednesday evening. See if you can locate it anywhere else nearby if not.'

'Will do.'

Perry came in then. He sat down with a huge sigh too. 'I thought we were getting somewhere.'

Grace was scrolling through her phone to check out what was being said on social media about their case but she stopped. 'He's into more than he's letting on.'

Perry nodded in agreement. 'Has anything come back from Shaun yet re text messages?'

Grace held up a sheaf of paper, with a roll of her eyes. 'I was thinking I might grab a drink and make a start on it.'

'Pass half of them to me. It may make for interesting reading.'

Outside the station, as soon as he was out of view, Max got out his phone. As he waited for the call to connect, he walked past the city library and down the side of the museum, away from the noise of the traffic.

'Things are getting muddied,' he said when the call was finally answered.

'Don't worry, we'll smooth things over if necessary.'

'But—'

'There's no evidence linked to you. You'll be fine.'

'But they have images of the parties.'

A slight pause. 'Anyone on there they would know?'

'Not really.'

'Well then, there's no need to worry. Everything is covered.'

'So when do I get paid?'

'Come and get it tomorrow – around midday.'

Max disconnected the call, knowing he'd been untruthful. There were several people in that photo that he needed to contact straight away. They all needed to get their stories straight.

But then again, keeping quiet might mean the light wouldn't be shone on him.

Maybe he'd better say nothing about that either.

FORTY-SEVEN

It took Grace twenty minutes to get to Tunstall from the station for her next call. She parked on the road in front of a large green, houses and maisonettes bordering three sides of it.

The area was owned predominantly by the city council and was a good locale to live in. Here, people took pride in their homes and gardens, and neighbours looked out for one another. It had been the perfect place to rehouse one of the vulnerable women she'd encountered as part of Operation Wedgwood two years ago.

Grace knocked on the door of the first block of maisonettes. When it was answered, she didn't need to hold up her warrant card.

'Grace!'

'Hi, Regan. Can I come in and talk to you for a moment?'

'Yes.' She beckoned her in. 'It's good to see you.'

Regan Peters was in her early twenties, but she looked much older. She was a former drug addict and had visible signs of it left. Her skin was pale, hair long and thin; hands as wrinkled as an old woman's. Her mental health had also suffered because of what she had been through.

Grace followed her into the tiny kitchen. It had the standard units she saw so often during her day-to-day work. White cupboards, black marble-effect worktops. Often that was all she would see, but sometimes people would add their own personal touches.

Regan's kitchen had bright yellow accessories, giving it an instant burst of summer. Grace spotted photos of her and a man on the fridge door, held on by yellow magnets in all shapes and sizes.

'Is this a social call or a work one?' Regan asked, holding up a mug.

'A bit of both.' Grace shook her head. 'I don't want a drink, thanks.' They moved into the living room.

'You've decorated,' she exclaimed, eyeing the floral wallpaper and new carpets. 'It looks lovely, so bright and inviting.'

'I have a boyfriend, Steve.' Regan grinned. 'It's early days yet, but he helped me with it.'

'Ooh, get you,' Grace grinned back. 'You look happy. It's nice to see.'

'I hope you're not going to burst my bubble.'

'I hope I'm not either. But I need your help in identifying some people in a photo.'

'They're not at it again?'

'It's looking possible.'

Regan sighed, shaking her head.

They sat down and Grace took out her phone where she had stored the images from Erin's mobile. She swiped through to the ones that she wanted and showed them to Regan.

Regan took her time going through them and then pointed to one. 'He's Max Croydon,' she said. 'He introduced me to Clara, got me into the parties.'

In 2018 Clara Emery had been involved in finding young girls to attend the sex parties. During Operation Wedgwood there had been no solid evidence to link her, so she'd been charged with perverting the course of justice. She'd lied during her interview and was given a suspended sentence because of it. As far as Grace was aware, she'd stayed out of trouble since.

'Do you know any of the others?' she asked.

Regan held the phone closer to her eyes, enlarging the image with her thumb and index finger. She pointed to another man. 'I know him, and the one sitting next to Max. I don't know all of their names, but they used to come to the parties.'

Grace sighed inwardly. 'I'm so sorry to dredge up raw memories for you.'

Regan shrugged. 'They're not painful any more. It's like it was in a different life. Now I've met Steve, I'm a lot happier. And not taking drugs keeps me from wanting money to buy them. I'm out of that horrible time in my life, and I'm going to continue trying not to relapse.'

'That's so good to hear.'

Regan smiled and then it dropped almost as quickly. 'This is to do with that dead girl, isn't it?'

'We're looking into some things at the moment.'

'Can you tell me what's been going on?'

Grace shook her head. 'We're following up on several leads, though. Does the name Chad mean anything to you?'

Regan paused, but then shook her head. 'I don't think so.'

'We think he was one of the ringleaders.'

'And he isn't in these images?'

'We don't know what he looks like.'

'There were a few men who didn't get involved in the parties – more they kept an eye on things. There was one who used to go with some of the girls, though. Away from the parties.'

Grace frowned. 'What does he look like?'

'Like they all did, men in suits.'

Grace felt Regan clam up then.

'So you don't know who Chad would be?'

Regan shook her head. 'Sorry, no.'

Grace stared at her for a moment but if she knew more, Regan wasn't telling her. She stood up. 'I'll see myself out.' She gave her a quick hug. 'Thanks for your help and I hope things go well with Steve.'

Regan grinned. 'He knows about my past, that's a good start. And before you say anything, he's not a former addict or anything. He's just, well, a nice guy.'

Grace left the flat, feeling glad she had seen Regan happy for a change. But she wasn't convinced she was telling her everything. It seemed as if she knew something but was afraid to speak.

'Hey, Grace!'

She turned to see Regan running towards her. 'I've just remembered someone's name. The man on the settee with the blonde on his knee – the fat one. His name is Trevor.'

FORTY-EIGHT

Grace and Allie were waiting for DCI Brindley to show before they went in to face the reporters. It was always a worrying time for the team at a press conference when members of the deceased's family were taking part. No one wanted to put undue pressure on them.

Erin's parents had been brought to the station. They were in the side room at the moment, waiting to go in to the main room and Grace, Allie and Perry went through to see them.

'Now remember, you don't have to say anything if you don't want to,' Allie said. 'It's always better coming from either of you, but please believe you are under no pressure. I can take over if you prefer.'

Sara shook her head. 'I want to do it. I need to do it.'

Grace could tell she'd been crying. Her eyes were puffy and red, the tissue in her hands wet and scrunched up.

Rob looked at Allie. 'What questions will they ask?'

'It will be about the case. They'll try to wheedle things out of us, hoping that we give them information that we can't release yet. That's why we have specialist training to deal with this sort of thing.' She stood up as she could see Jenny arriving.

'Do you both understand what's about to happen?' Jenny said after she'd been introduced to everyone. 'I know it's hard for you to go through, but it won't take long to do and we find these kind of press conferences extremely useful as they can often jog people's memories, producing new leads.'

There were a few minutes' small talk and then a man came into the room. Grace recognised him as the station's press officer. He nodded at Jenny. 'If everyone's ready, please follow me.'

Mr and Mrs Ellis walked into the room, Jenny in front of them and Allie at the rear. Grace moved with Perry to stand at the back of the room as cameras began to flash.

Once they were all seated, Jenny updated everyone about Operation Doulton.

'Mrs Ellis would like to say a few words now,' she finished, 'and then there will be time for questions afterwards.'

The room dropped into silence but the minute Sara began to speak there was a blinding light from cameras, clicks from phones.

'My daughter was murdered on Wednesday evening after someone mugged her,' Sara said, then cleared her throat. 'Erin was sixteen years old and was changing from a lovely girl to a beautiful woman. She was warm, kind and considerate. She had lots of friends and a loving family. Whoever killed her took all that away from her.

'If you know anything about what happened, or if you saw something out of the ordinary happening around the time of the murder, please contact the police. The killer is still out there and I'd hate for any more parents to go through what we're going through right now. Erin will be missed by us all. We need your help to bring her killer to justice.' Sara looked directly into the camera then. 'Help us find who murdered our Erin. I beg of you. If you have information, please come forward.'

Her voice finally broke and she sat back in her chair, spent, exhausted and broken.

'We'll take questions now,' Jenny said.

'Is it true that Erin had been going to some kind of sex parties?' A voice came from the back.

Grace searched out the speaker and tried not to roll her eyes. It was Will Lawrence, the thoughtless idiot with the dodgy shorts.

'We have no further comments on that at the moment,' Jenny said. 'Next question please?'

'But there is speculation about this. Can you deny it if you can't confirm it?'

Grace had to admire his persistence. She knew that was the same question but asked in a different way.

'Like I've just said we have no further comments on that at the moment. Next, please.' Jenny pointed to a woman.

'So that's a yes, then.' Will Lawrence raised his eyebrows in an inquisitive manner.

Grace could only glare at him when all she wanted was to call him out for being a dick.

'What's your name again?' Jenny asked.

'Will Lawrence, *Staffordshire News*.'

'Well, Mr Lawrence, I suggest you find your manners for the next time we meet or else you won't be coming to many press conferences in the future.'

A few sniggers went around the room as Will turned the colour of a tomato. Grace tried hard not to smirk as she and Perry shared a surreptitious glance. She loved it when an idiot had a good put down by a strong woman. And he was a jerk, Simon had told her quite a few times. She spotted him now, glaring at Will once things started to calm down again.

Jenny continued to answer questions from the crowd. In a matter of minutes, it was all over and they left the room.

As she watched Sara and Rob Ellis comforting each other, Grace hoped there would be good news for them soon. A press conference was always heartbreaking to watch but seeing the parents in the flesh brought it home even more.

In his office at the gym, Leon switched off the TV and sat deep in thought. He had no sympathy for the parents of the dead girl. They should have kept their daughter safe, checking where she was going of an evening. Surely they must have known she was up to something given the amount of times she would have come home drunk. And how could Erin hide a pregnancy from them for so long? He'd certainly noticed her growing over the past few weeks.

Those girls, Erin and Molly, were collateral damage to him, just like he'd been to his father. Yes, he blamed the parents. If they'd kept an eye on Erin, this wouldn't have happened. Still, it had worked out in his favour. Seeing the press conference had convinced him he needed to cancel that night's party. He'd left it until the last minute in case he could get away with it, but it was too risky this month, especially on top of the ongoing investigation.

He picked up the phone to ring Max; he could give him the job of letting everyone know, and also to find and relay new dates for when things had died down.

Leon wouldn't be stopping altogether. The parties were far too lucrative. Maybe he'd be better changing their locations again though. He sighed dramatically. There was always something to do.

As Eddie came into the office, he finished his call abruptly and put his head down. He didn't want to speak about the matter with him.

FORTY-NINE

Molly's eyes were red raw with all the crying she'd done since seeing Chad. It was easy for her to pretend it was down to Erin but she knew it was only a matter of time before her parents or the police wanted to know the truth. Everyone was going to find out some time and she wasn't sure she could cope with it.

She'd been taking her chances and using the landline when she could to ring Chad but there had been no response from him, so he was obviously ignoring the number. The last time she'd tried, his mobile had been switched off. She tried one last time. If he didn't want to see her, then she would do something to get his attention.

This time he picked up.

'I told you not to contact me on this number,' he bellowed down the line when he found out it was her.

'But I wanted to talk to you and—'

'Not over the—'

'When then? I have to see you.'

'I told you yesterday. We have to stay away from each other.'

'I have to see you!' She almost shouted.

There was a pause on the line.

'Don't call this number again, do you hear me?'

'But, Chad.'

'No.'

Before she could say anything else, the line went dead.

Molly ran upstairs and threw herself on her bed. She couldn't cope with Chad ignoring her but she would show him. She picked up one of the boxes of paracetamols she'd collected from downstairs. Then she pressed eight tablets out of their blister packaging and laid them on her bedside cabinet. She'd read online that you had to take enough to make sure you didn't come around again.

Molly didn't want to end up having her stomach pumped and then have to explain why she had done it. She wouldn't be known for the rest of her life as the girl who tried to commit suicide. She was going to do this properly.

Molly didn't want to live another day without her best friend. Erin had been too young to die and everything had been Molly's fault. She picked up four tablets and held them in her hand. She knew if she shoved them all down at once they might work faster, but decided she would take one at a time for now.

With tears pouring down her face, she popped one on her tongue, drank a sip of water and swallowed. All the time she thought about Erin and how she had let her down. Finding out she was pregnant had been a bitter blow. Then when she'd realised Erin wanted to keep the baby, Molly felt as if *she* was being side-lined, that Erin was getting the attention that Molly deserved.

But then she thought about what had happened to Erin and she swallowed another tablet.

Molly used to look after Erin but it had all changed when they'd started going to the parties. Erin had hated them at first but she'd soon begun to enjoy the attention as much as Molly, and then she'd become more popular. It was a complete role reversal. Molly had always been the leader but lately she'd had to take a back seat.

When they'd been in junior school, Molly had stuck up for Erin to no end if the other kids bullied her. Erin had been a prime target for it as she wouldn't stand up for herself. But then again she hadn't had to because Molly was there to protect her.

She remembered hitting out at Ronan Finlay when he'd pulled Erin around the playground by her pigtails. She'd pushed him to the floor, straddled him and slapped him around the face. She'd only stopped when she saw he was crying. Luckily no teachers had caught her.

She swallowed another tablet, retching as this one went down, so she took more water.

This time she thought back to their first school disco when they had fancied Danny Thurston and Richard Johnson. They were all twelve, with experimental roaming hands and tongues, illicit kisses behind the wall of the school hall. She remembered laughing with Erin when she'd told her that Danny kissed like a hoover. Erin had said that Richard shoved his tongue down her throat so much that she almost gagged and couldn't breathe.

Two more tablets went down with a struggle.

She thought back to their last birthday party. Being born two weeks apart had meant a double celebration every year. They'd had a huge party in her back garden. The weather had been glorious and her dad had been in charge of a barbecue that most of the street had ended up at. There had been about thirty of their friends, presents galore.

Back then they hadn't really acquired a taste for alcohol. Neither of them had been interested in it until they'd started to hang around at Potteries Takeaway. But once they had, it had seemed brave and bold to them to drink so much, parade around in front of their friends as if they owned the place. How wrong they were.

She pushed out more tablets into the palm of her hand.

Stuff it, there was no point in waiting any longer. She shoved them all in her mouth, trying to swallow them down with the water quickly.

But the taste made her retch and as quick as she swallowed one, it came back up again. In less than ten seconds, every tablet she had taken was on her bedroom carpet.

Defeated, she curled up on the bed and sobbed, closing her eyes against the world. She couldn't start again. It was useless. What was she going to do now?

Exhausted, she fell asleep. The next thing she knew her mum was shaking her awake forcefully.

'Molly,' she cried. 'Molly, wake up! What have you done?'

'It's okay, Mum. I vomited the tablets up again,' she explained. 'I couldn't do it. I couldn't do it.'

'Oh, Molly, love.' Her mum held her close. 'It will be okay, you'll see. Everything will be okay.'

Molly cried hard at those words. There were so many questions to answer now. The police would want to know more as they dug into her and Erin's background. And she was the one who could put all the pieces together.

She wondered how much she should tell them. Just enough, or everything?

No, she couldn't tell anyone. How she had let her best friend down. How she had lost the one person she truly cared for. How she didn't want to go on without her; couldn't ever think of living her life without Erin by her side. How things wouldn't get better with the passing of time. Everything was going to get much worse.

FIFTY

Grace had only been back at her desk for half an hour, eating a sandwich as quickly as she could, when Perry said her name.

'There's someone to see us. David West – says he's seen the press conference and has information about Erin Ellis. Want to speak to him with me?'

Grace nodded and reached for her lanyard. She hung it around her neck, took another quick bite of her sandwich, and followed Perry downstairs.

'Interesting that he's come forward, don't you think?' she said.

Perry raised his eyebrows. 'We shall see.'

The man had been put into interview room three and was sitting at the table. He wore a tailored grey suit, white shirt and a pale lilac tie. His black patent shoes were square-toed. He seemed to be mid to late thirties, clean shaven with short greying hair.

His eyes skirted from Grace to Perry and back again as they sat down across from him.

Grace exchanged a quick look with Perry. Mr West was one of the men in the images they'd retrieved from Erin's phone. It changed everything. They needed to book him into custody and interview him under caution.

Once this had been done, they started again.

'I believe you have some information for us after the press conference this morning?' Perry said, his notepad at the ready.

'I do, but it's sensitive.' West sat forward and clasped his hands together. 'What I tell you might get me in trouble if it's leaked that you found out from me.'

When they said nothing, he ran his hands through his hair and looked at the floor for a moment.

'Mr West?' Perry questioned. 'May I call you David?'

'It's Dave. I was with the victim at a party a few months ago.'

'A birthday party?'

'A house party.' He stopped for a moment.

Grace wondered if he was thinking what best to tell them, to give himself maximum credibility and minimum fallout.

'Where was the party?' Perry wanted to know.

'At a friend's house.'

'His name?'

'Trevor Merchant.'

Grace sighed inwardly, recalling that Trevor was the name mentioned by Regan earlier that day.

'Where did you meet him?' Perry went on.

'I was out with a group of friends one night. He invited me to a get together in a week's time. Said there would be lots of women there. I've been on my own for a while and so I fancied some company. If you catch my drift.'

'You mean escorts?'

'Not quite.' He coughed while he gained his composure, his cheeks reddening by the second.

'What?' Grace snapped, urging him to speak. 'What was going on?'

'There were lots of young girls. They were there for . . . fun.'

'How old were they?'

'All over the age of consent!'

'You knew this for certain?' Grace scoffed.

'Well, I—'

'So these girls were there for you to have sex with?' Perry rested a hand on Grace's arm. 'Is that what you're telling us?'

Dave nodded, not looking them in the eye.

'Why are you coming forward with this information now?'

'I thought it was wrong, what they were doing.'

'And if one of the girls hadn't been murdered, would you have come to see us then?'

Dave shook his head. 'I'm not proud of what I did. And I never went to another party. I was shocked, if I'm honest. I was expecting a little lap dancing at the most.'

'Where was the party held?'

'At a house over in Lightwood, by the park.'

Grace sat forward. 'The address?'

'Seven Park Avenue. It was one of those big old houses. It was a beautiful thing. Full of fancy stuff.'

Grace glanced at Perry, who was looking at her surreptitiously. It was a different address from the one in the photographs which Frankie had recognised.

'Approximately how many men would you say were there?' Perry continued.

'Ten.'

'And females?'

'About the same.'

'All young?'

He nodded. 'It was their thing, all right.'

'Yours too.'

'I told you, I was invited by Trevor. I had no idea what to expect.'

Perry paused. 'Did you see Erin Ellis there?'

'Yes.'

'Did you have sex with her, or any of the other girls while you were there?'

'No. It was like a cattle market, men being paired off with whoever they took a fancy to. When I saw what had happened to that girl on the news, I thought you needed to know. That house might not be connected but she was into some bad stuff.'

Grace tutted. 'Did you watch her being exploited?'

'No!'

'So you don't know if she gave her full consent?' she went on.

'You're not pinning anything like this on me,' he cried. 'From what I saw, she was willing and able. I left quite early.'

'Yet you—'

'What is this? I come to you with information and you're trying to turn me into some kind of predator? She seemed okay with it.'

'How could you tell?'

'Because she had her hands all over the men.'

'Somehow I doubt that very much,' Grace couldn't help but answer.

Perry took out the images from the file he'd brought in with him and laid them out on the desk.

'Care to tell me when and where this was?' he questioned.

Dave leaned forward and looked at the image.

Grace watched his features change, taking great delight in the fact Dave knew he was in too deep.

'She wasn't an innocent woman,' he said in his own defence.

'She was an innocent *child*,' Perry said. 'Exploited by a group of men who should have known better.'

Dave was about to protest but seemed to know he was beat. 'I'm beginning to wish I hadn't come in to see you now.'

'We're so glad you did.' Grace's smile was a sarcastic one. 'In the meantime, we need to take a full statement from you.'

'Come again.'

'Visiting a brothel. Paying for sex. Need I go on?'

'But I didn't come here to get arrested. I came here as a witness!'

'For which we are extremely grateful. We have a duty of care to everyone who is vulnerable in the hands of men like you. We'll be asking you questions of our own soon. I assume you'll want a solicitor present.'

The man held his head in his hands. 'I don't believe this.'

'Tell us the names of these people.' She pointed to two of the men.

'I don't know.'

Grace stared at him.

'I swear! I don't know. I only went for the one night so I wasn't introduced to many of them.'

Grace had no sympathy for him. He'd come forward thinking he was doing the right thing, but had landed himself in a mess. Ultimately, it would depend on the CPS if charges would be brought, and if so, what for. It would also depend on how he cooperated with them now they needed different information. If he came up with a no comment quip, then he deserved what he got.

'You must know one of them,' she pushed. 'Is the man whose party it was in there?'

Dave ran a hand through his hair, pausing as if the words were stuck in his throat.

He nodded slowly.

'Which one?'

Dave touched the photo with his index finger. 'That's Trevor Merchant.'

Grace stayed poker-faced. It was the same man that Regan had pointed out to her.

The interview over, Grace followed Perry out of the room.

They left a uniformed officer to show West out. As they went back upstairs, Perry held the door open for Grace and she walked through.

'What was all that about?' he asked. 'I wasn't aware we were playing good cop, bad cop. You could have warned me.'

'Sorry,' she apologised as they took the stairs. 'But after seeing Regan Peters this morning, and all this talk about those parties, it's got under my skin a little more than I'd thought.'

'You can't save everyone, Grace.'

'Maybe not, but we're nowhere near catching Erin's killer and if it is one of the men involved then I want him off the streets asap. It's frustrating to know we haven't got a suspect yet.'

'It's early days. We'll nab someone soon.' He grinned at her. 'Just keep your temper under control, hmm?'

'Yes, sir.' She thumped him on the arm. 'When have I ever let you down?'

But as he went before her chuckling, Grace stepped away and dashed outside to get some fresh air. She could feel tears forming and she didn't want them to fall. She leaned on the wall of the building, letting the noise of the traffic and the city fill her brain.

She *had* overreacted with David West. She shouldn't make it personal, but how could she not? The Ellis family needed answers, but this felt like history might be repeating itself. She hoped this wasn't another time she wouldn't be able to make a difference.

No, that was not going to happen.

Not on her watch.

FIFTY-ONE

One month ago

Erin sneaked out of the back door and into the garden as quietly as she could. Her mum and Nat were watching the TV and she was due to meet *him* soon, but she needed to get some things off her chest and she couldn't speak to Molly about it.

In the summer house, Erin took out her diary that she'd hidden. She began to write:

> *I wish I could talk to my mum. I'm sure she would understand but I can't bear to see the disappointment in her eyes. The shock of what I've done. That her daughter is a disgusting slag. That she got herself knocked up at sixteen. That she doesn't know who the father is as it could be one of many.*
>
> *How will she feel when I tell her? Because I can't get rid of my baby. I just can't. I know Molly thinks I'm too young to have a child, but that's probably because she is selfish and wouldn't want anything to take away the limelight. Molly has changed so much in the past few months that I don't even know her any more. So why should I listen to her?*

I'm glad I stopped drinking as soon as I was sure. From now, I won't take any uppers to get me through the night either. And I'm not going to any more parties. Stuff what Molly says. Stuff what Max says. Stuff what Chad says. This is my life. They can't tell me what to do.

If I could just confide in Mum, I'm sure everything would be okay. I love my mum and I know she is miserable since Dad left but she's doing fine really. I wish I was closer to her. I wish I could tell her. But I can't. Well, not until it's too late for anyone to do anything about it.

Because I'm not having an abortion. Lots of girls my age have babies and go on to do things with their lives. I've been checking up on the internet. A lot of young mothers have their children early and then have careers. If I want to do that, I will.

But for now, it's just me and the little bump. I have enough love for two.

Erin ripped the page from her diary. She shredded it into tiny pieces and put it in the bin outside before slipping back into the kitchen.

One thing was certain, she wasn't going to tell him yet. He'd know what to do when the time came, but for now it was her secret.

Molly lay on her bed, her right leg over her left and her foot jangling back and forth furiously. She was waiting for a reply to the text message she had sent to Erin. They were supposed to be going to the party and were being picked up in an hour. Erin had been throwing up all afternoon due to that bloody baby.

She still couldn't believe she hadn't got rid of it, like Molly had suggested. An abortion would have put an end to it all. She would have terminated the pregnancy if it was her. But, oh no, Erin was being all high and mighty about it, saying it was morally wrong to kill a child. Well, it was morally wrong what they'd been doing every month at the parties but she hadn't been so high and mighty about that!

She picked up her phone again, knowing that no new messages had come in as she would have heard them. She groaned loudly: she wouldn't be happy if Erin let her down.

She waited five more minutes before calling.

'Are you coming or not?' she snapped as Erin answered.

'I don't think I can. I can't stop vomiting.'

'Take something for it. We'll only be out for a few hours.'

'My legs are wobbly and I smell of sick.'

'Take a shower!'

'I can't.'

'You have to!'

There was silence down the line.

'Erin? Erin!'

'I can't make it.'

'I'll come across to you then.'

'No!'

'Why not?'

'It smells in my room. It won't be nice. I'll be fine tomorrow. I'm sorry.'

'Sometimes you really get on my nerves, you and this baby. You're a selfish cow!' Molly disconnected the phone and threw it down on the bed.

She didn't want to go to the party on her own. Despite being the confident one, she didn't feel safe going alone. Erin was always there to come and get her if she was out of it, or if she was pushed into something she didn't like.

239

And Erin stopped her making too much of a fool of herself by watching out for her. Now she'd have to stay in. It wasn't fair.

Erin sat on her bed, feeling terrible that she was lying to Molly. But she was going out on her own to meet Lion Man and she couldn't tell her about that. She'd be mad that she wasn't coming along, but also she'd be annoyed by who she was going to see.

Erin had been invited to Ranger Street. She hadn't told Molly as she would be furious to know she was going without her. It was somewhere they both wanted to go, because some of the other girls said it paid serious money.

But she was going with Lion Man, alone. He wanted to spend some time with her, and no one else.

And not even Molly was going to spoil that for her.

FIFTY-TWO

After being cooped up for most of the morning, Grace was glad to get out of the station again. With Frankie driving, she made her way to Lightwood, in the south of the city. Seven Park Avenue was a large property, set back from the main road, with a high wall and wrought iron gates.

Frankie parked outside and they made their way up the drive.

Grace glanced around. The house was Georgian, renovated to take into consideration all of its finest points. It was two storeys high, a real specimen, with ivy growing over a third of it. Leaded windows peeped out like eyes.

'It's quite secluded considering it's on a main road,' Frankie said.

Grace nodded. 'I reckon you could fit at least fifteen vehicles on the frontage, and even if there were noisy parties here, would anyone hear too much? I checked before I came out and no one has reported any anti-social behaviour.'

There were three cars parked in front of a garage. Grace rang the bell and waited for it to be answered. A man in his mid-

241

fifties came to the door. He was dressed smart-casually, wearing a checked shirt, cardigan and moleskin trousers.

Grace didn't recognise him from the images they had. They showed their warrant cards and introduced themselves.

'We're looking for Trevor and Angela Merchant,' she said.

The man shook his head. 'You have the wrong address. I'm Peter Townley. I've lived here with my wife and daughter for the past twenty-seven years.'

'Are they at home too?'

'Yes.'

'May we speak to them?'

'Of course.'

They were shown through a hallway and into a large sitting room. The floor had been stripped back to its original parquet, panels on the wall had been painted cream and the areas above them were covered in wallpaper with a delicate pattern. Three chesterfields surrounded a coffee table, and a TV cabinet sat by the side of the fireplace. At the back of the room was a grand piano, sitting in front of a set of French doors.

Grace saw Frankie raise his eyebrows slightly in recognition as he saw the two women who were sitting on the settee.

'These are detectives, Rita,' Mr Townley said. 'They're after people named Merchant.'

Rita shook her head. 'I don't know anyone of that name around the vicinity.' She glanced at the young woman sitting beside her. 'Do you, Rachel?'

'No.' Rachel dipped her eyes to the floor.

'What's this about?' Rita asked them.

'We'd like to talk to them about an on-going case, and we were given this address.' Grace looked at them all in turn. 'It's obvious that the Merchants don't live here. But Rachel – you look as though you might know something about them.'

242

All eyes fell on the younger woman as she seemed to sink into the cushions.

'Do you go away often, Mr and Mrs Townley?' Grace asked.

'Yes, we have a villa in the south of France,' Peter responded. 'We go for weeks at a time.'

'And you've been there this summer?'

'For the most part, yes.' Peter frowned. 'Rachel stays to look after the house. Now, would someone mind telling me what's been going on?'

'I think your daughter might be able to explain, but we'll need to speak to her at the station first.'

'I don't think so.' Peter shook his head.

Grace took out one of the printed photos they'd retrieved from Erin's phone and showed it to them. It had been taken in the room they were standing in.

'This is you, isn't it, Rachel?' She held out the photo so they could all see.

Peter frowned and looked at his daughter. 'Who are these people? And why are they all in our house?' He gave it to his wife, who covered her mouth with her hand for a moment.

'What are you doing on that man's knee, Rachel?' Grace asked.

'I'm not talking without legal representation,' Rachel said quietly.

'Do you have someone in mind or would you like us to appoint a duty solicitor for you?'

Rachel looked up at her parents for help. 'Dad, I can explain. I—'

'I'm not sure what's going on,' Peter said, 'but I'll call the family lawyer. He'll get to the bottom of this.' He bent over to point a finger in Rachel's face. 'And then you can tell us what the hell has been going on while we've been in France.'

Grace took Rachel's arm as they led her outside to their car.

'Dad,' Rachel said. 'Dad!'

Grace opened the rear door to the car. 'Mind your head,' she said, before closing the door.

At Bethesda Police Station, the lawyer who represented the Townley family was unavailable to be there in person as he was in Singapore. Rachel took advice from him over the phone instead and as there wouldn't be a duty solicitor free for some hours, she decided to go ahead with the interview alone for now.

'Okay, Rachel,' Grace said as she sat across from her in the interview room. 'You're here under caution but not under arrest, and you can stop and ask for legal representation at any time if you feel you require it. I do hope you'll cooperate with us, though – I think it will be much better for you in the long run – but any time you feel like you want to stop, you only have to say.'

Rachel nodded, fidgeting in her seat.

'Can you tell me the names of anyone in this photo?'

Rachel pointed out the people that they knew already, and herself, but no one else.

'Why were they all at your house on the evening of August 17?'

'I had a party.'

'Any special occasion?'

'My parents were out of town and I had a few friends round.'

'Do you have these parties often?'

She shook her head. 'It was a one-off.'

'So if we ask the neighbours either side of you, they would back you up?'

'Of course. Nothing happened and our neighbours keep themselves to themselves anyway. We don't live on a social housing estate, you know.'

Grace ignored her pompous attitude.

'Can you tell me why you had so many parties?'

'I told you, there was only the one.'

'The girls seem a little young for you to be friends with.'

'There isn't a law against that, is there?'

'Not at all. How old are you?'

'Nineteen.'

'Were any of the men at the party your partner?'

Rachel scoffed. 'Have you seen them? Most of them are old enough to be my father.'

'Do you know why a lot of the men in that image are known to us already?'

'I can't see the relevance of that question.'

'Rachel, you're not being smart. These men may be involved in grooming teenage women and taking them to parties purely to have sex with older men. These men then pay the girls.' She tapped the image. 'I'd call that procuring a prostitute and you've allowed it at a property which you were in complete control of at the time it happened.'

'But—'

'Now either you start telling the truth or we can arrest you and you can go into a cell and bide your time until we want to talk to you again. I'm sure you'd rather be at home than here, though . . .'

'Hardly! You've made certain I won't be welcome there,' Rachel almost spat the words out.

'Your parents give the impression they're a nice couple,' Grace replied. 'I'm sure they'll be disappointed in you but I'm also certain they won't disown you. They seem to think a lot of you. Although perhaps that does depend on whether or not you were being paid to have sex with the men, too.'

'I never did anything like that,' Rachel protested. She ran a hand through her hair and sat forward. 'I was paid to provide a place for the party, all right?'

'By who?'

'Someone called Chad.'

'Chad . . .'

'I don't know his surname. I met him at a party a few months ago.'

'Is he in the photo?' Grace pointed to it.

Rachel shook her head. 'No, but he was there. He stays in the background. He doesn't join in, just keeps an eye on things.'

'Meaning?'

'He makes sure the girls are well looked after. And they are. No one harms them and they have fun with the men.'

'So you don't condone their behaviour?'

Rachel shook her head. 'Why shouldn't women do what they want to in this day and age?'

'I agree, if it's legal and they know what they're getting themselves into. But these are *girls* we're talking about.'

'They're all streetwise.'

Grace held her tongue. Rachel Townley seemed no more than a spoiled brat who was using her father's property to make money from illegal parties.

'How much did they pay you?'

Rachel gnawed at her bottom lip. 'Five hundred pounds. It's not a lot of money, really. You should see the mess they make and I have to pay a cleaner out of that.'

Oh poor you, Grace wanted to say but refrained. She handed Rachel a piece of paper and a pen. 'I need you to write down every person who came to the parties.'

'Do you think they would give their real names?'

'Give me what you know then.'

Rachel looked from Grace to Perry and back. 'I think I'd like to wait until I have a lawyer present now.'

Walking upstairs with Perry, they went over the conversation.

'I can't believe anyone like Rachel Townley would be interested in the likes of Max Croydon.'

'Really?' Grace laughed. 'You obviously don't see the attraction of the bad boy.'

'Of course I see it, but I can't understand it.'

'It also shows that it isn't just working class girls who get taken in by creeps. Rachel comes from a wealthy family and hasn't wanted for anything in her life. I wonder how she got sucked into all of this. It doesn't seem the kind of scene her upbringing would get her into.'

'Either way, she has some explaining to do to her parents. I wouldn't like to be in her position right now.'

FIFTY-THREE

Max had been surprised to get a call from Rachel, even more so when she said she needed a lift home from Bethesda Police Station. After speaking to David West, he began to make more sense of things. The police were closing in.

In Bethesda Street, he waited on level two of the multi-storey car park for her to emerge.

Once in the car, she slammed the door behind her. She turned to glare at him as she pulled on the seatbelt to fasten it.

'That was the worst experience of my life,' she exclaimed. 'And it's something I don't want to repeat ever again.'

'What the hell were you in there for?' Max asked.

'The police turned up at my house.' She clicked the belt in place. 'Two detectives. Someone had told them that Trevor and Angela Merchant lived there. They came in with photos of the party in the house.' She prodded him in the chest. 'Photos with you and the dead girl sitting on your lap.'

Max ran a hand over his head trying to think of the implications. 'What the hell does that mean?'

'It means that I am in deep shit with my parents. They were home too and want to know about the party.'

'Stuff the party. How did they know about the Merchants? Did you tell them?'

'Of course not!'

'What did you say to the police?'

'I said that the party was a one-off and I'd held it for a friend. That's what I'm going to tell my parents too. I'm going to lie through my teeth. They're already livid with me. If they find out what I'm involved in—'

'How will they do that?'

Rachel gasped. 'You don't think the police are closing in on everything?'

'No, they're clutching at straws.'

He was lying to keep her from panicking. The police knew way too much information for him to be comfortable but he wanted to keep Rachel sweet.

'What else did they ask you?' he went on. 'Do they know about any of the other houses?'

'No. They never mentioned anything but my address.'

'Well that's a relief.' He smirked.

'For you maybe, but not for me.' She put a finger to her cheek to wipe away a stray tear.

'Hey, don't get upset. I'll give you a lift home and you can sort it all out,' he offered, an idea forming in his head.

'I can't go back. Not until they've calmed down.'

'But you've never been in trouble before.'

'Exactly. Which is why I will be a huge disappointment to my father.'

He leaned close to her and gave her a long kiss. 'I love that I'm your sugar daddy.'

Rachel snorted at the suggestion. 'Sugar daddies give their women presents.'

'I give you good loving, don't I?'

'Me and plenty others.' She pouted.

'You're my special girl, though.' He ran a finger down the side of her face. 'Why don't you stay at mine tonight? Give your old man's temper time to calm down.'

'I'll have to nip back to grab an overnight bag.'

Max laughed inwardly. She was such a snob. Couldn't she do without a change of knickers and a toothbrush? Still, if it kept her sweet . . .

Rachel took out her phone. 'I'll ring Mummy to see if Dad's in or not. She's always on my side, no matter what I've done.'

He did laugh then. 'I'll wait for you and then you can crash with me. You'll have to slum it for the night, though.'

'I don't mind, as long as I'm with you.'

Max started the engine and pulled out of the parking space. Having Rachel on side for a while would be to his advantage.

After interviewing Rachel, Grace went back to her desk. It was getting on for five p.m. As she stifled a yawn behind her hand, her phone rang. It was a call from the duty sergeant saying a Mr Ramon wanted to speak to her. She tried to hide her surprise when it turned out to be Eddie. Keeping her head down and her voice low, she spoke to him. Afterwards, she sat back with a frown.

'What's up?' Perry asked, catching her eye.

'That was Eddie Steele. He says he has information for me. Wants us to meet this evening. What do you think I should do? He could be toying with me.'

'He isn't a suspect though, is he? If he was, that would be different. You'd have to declare it.'

'Like I did before? It still got me into trouble.'

'That was because Nick was being a dickhead. He shouldn't have pushed you to get information from them.'

'Maybe not but the damage had been caused. It took me a

250

long time to win some people's trust. I'm not sure I want to go through that again and I'd have to if I'm seen out with Eddie.'

'Then go in your own time.'

'Are you sure? There's a lot of stuff on that list that still needs checking.'

'You may be helping get info though.' He held out a hand, palm up. 'Go on, push off and have a night off . . . well, sort of.'

'Oh, I'll be back after I've seen him.' Grace passed him the list. 'Frankie's going to check in with the neighbours around the Townley house to see if any of them are home from work yet, and he can help you once he gets back. I have umpteen messages going backward and forward between Erin and Max on my sheet. I expect you have the same.'

'Yes and no. They were pretty consistent for a while, but then it became just the odd one or two.'

'I wonder what that means?'

'That they were an item and then they weren't?'

'But he denies ever being involved with her as a couple.'

'Maybe he broke it off. Any other numbers popping up regularly?'

'Yes, one.' She read out the number.

'I have lots of those too. We'll send that through to find out who it is.'

'Do you think it might be David West?'

'Anything's possible. There were a lot of men in those photos.'

Grace nodded and turned to leave.

'For what it's worth, I think Eddie is the only sane one in that family.' Perry smiled at her.

Grace was pleased at how he said that, showing he didn't include her as part of their clan. All of her life she had hidden from the Steele connection and now, again, it seemed it might provide a vital clue to their case.

'If he tells me anything I can't act upon, I'll come away. We can bring him and Leon in tomorrow if necessary. I won't jeopardise the case by speaking off the record.'

'Just find out what you can and report back. I'm interested to see what he has to say.'

Grace checked her watch. It was nearing five o'clock. She had time to freshen herself up and make a quick call to Simon before leaving.

The Red Lion was on the outskirts of the city. Another mile and the landscape changed into the Staffordshire Moorlands, the market town of Leek five miles further on.

Grace pulled into the car park, spotting Eddie's car already there. Her phone rang, Simon's name lighting up on the screen. He hadn't picked up when she'd rung earlier.

'Hey. Whatcha up to?'

Grace smiled at the warmth in his voice. He often answered his calls with the same words. It was code for: I've been thinking of you.

'Not a lot,' she replied as she always did. 'What about you?'

'Just tidying up some things for tomorrow's edition. Anything you can give me to add to it?'

'Yes, the senior crime reporter likes to dress in my clothes on his days off.'

'That's classified, I told you.'

They both laughed. It was good that they could tease each other. From the beginning of their relationship, neither had felt the need to ring several times a day to check up on the other, but often they wanted to say hello, see how one another were doing. There were no 'love yous' at the end of the conversation, just a 'see you later'. It made her feel comfortable with him and it often put her at ease when she was stressed just by hearing his voice. Like now.

'What time will you be in this evening? I assume it will be late?' he asked.

Grace looked at the pub door as an elderly couple came out. The man lovingly guided his wife across the car park as she seemed unsteady on her feet. It made Grace smile to see.

'It depends how much information I get out of my next call.'

'You have a lead? Care to share?'

'Never you mind, Cole. I'll text you later.'

They said their goodbyes and she got out of the car. Taking a deep breath and pushing her shoulders high, she went to face the man she loved to hate.

FIFTY-FOUR

Inside The Red Lion, the heat hit Grace as she left the miserably cold day behind. The lounge was half full, several people waiting at the bar to be served but not an edge of immediacy about it.

The pub looked as if it had been recently refurbished. A navy blue and claret colour scheme made it feel like a gentleman's club. There were rows of books along one wall with a nook fireplace. Grace could easily drop into the armchair next to the fire, put her feet up and go to sleep. She was already exhausted after working flat out since Erin's murder, but knew any intel she fished from Eddie would give her a boost of adrenaline.

It wasn't the role she played, but the emotion that tired her out at the moment. The constant thoughts flashing through her mind as memories came back at her. Those nights when her father had locked her in a room, and she'd slept alone and scared of what might happen. Those days when he had hit out at her if she so much as murmured a sound out of place.

At least she had been able to escape for a few hours during the week days – school holidays were the worst times – and she'd cherished the afternoons he'd be passed out when she got home and she could have a couple of welcome hours in her mum's company. It was much better than the times she had to cover her ears with her hands at the sound of fists on flesh, glass on walls, crockery on floors. She would never understand how she could conjure up these images in a flash: when she heard a song on the radio, or smelt cheap aftershave or the breath of a boozer.

Eddie waved to get her attention. She made her way over to him, knowing he turned other women's heads. He oozed sex appeal, the lines around his eyes making him distinguished rather than showing his age; clear skin that told of a non-drinker, and a non-smoker. Like her, he had probably seen too much and tried to ease off the addictive demons that controlled the mind.

Eddie also never failed to smell of something nice. She knew by now he wasn't flash like Leon – he didn't feel as if he had to make an effort to be liked or to fit in. Or be one up on his brother.

'I'm ordering a drink,' he said as he reached her. 'Would you like one?'

'This isn't a date,' she chided, pulling out a chair and sitting across from him.

His laugh made her shiver a little, reminding her of the times her father had done the same in her face before slapping her down for something trivial that she had or hadn't done to annoy him. She knew Eddie wasn't being nasty, but all the same. Some memories never faded, never died.

'Just a coffee for me, please,' she said. He went to the bar and she settled into her seat, glancing around. The room was full of diners; couples, a group of female friends. A family with twin teenage girls made her think about Erin and Molly. They had been as close as those sisters.

He was back in less than five minutes. Grace pounced on him as soon as he was seated again.

'So you have information for me?' she wanted to know. 'Unless you got me here under false pretences.'

'Would it be so bad if I had?'

'Yes, it would. I'm busy.'

'The murder case?'

'You know I can't talk about that.'

'Wouldn't ask it of you.' He took a sip of his drink. 'Have you worked anything out since I saw you this morning?'

'You mean what you and I discussed? I'm not at liberty to say.'

He laughed again, and this time Grace found herself smiling. She decided to be nice. Maybe that way he would tell her what he knew a little earlier.

She glanced at her watch purposely. 'I have to head off soon.'

'I'm worried about Leon after seeing those photos you showed me.'

Grace said nothing, knowing he had more.

'I'm not finding this easy, as you've noticed. I can't even begin to think about what he's been up to. I thought it had stopped, you see.'

'You have information about the parties?'

He nodded. 'You need to speak to a woman named Angela. Remember Clara, who worked for us at Posh Gloss?'

Grace nodded. She wasn't surprised that the name Angela would be linked to her.

'Angela was her replacement.'

Grace grimaced.

'Max Croydon gets the girls to the parties now and she sorts out the rest.'

Why does his name keep cropping up?

'Do you know where I can find her? Or Clara?' she asked.

'I haven't seen Clara since Jade's trial.' Eddie shook his head. 'And I honestly don't know anything about Angela.'

Grace wasn't sure she believed him but didn't let it show. 'Do you know where the house is that they're using?'

'There are several.'

Grace cursed under her breath. 'Your brother *has* been keeping himself busy.'

'He's always seen himself as some kind of superhero – or the king of the jungle.'

Grace snorted, restraining from an eye roll.

'I'd suggest getting yourself over to Sandon Crescent this evening. It's in Meir Heath. You might find something of interest going on.'

Grace sat forward a little. That was the address that Frankie had pointed out yesterday.

'What have you heard?'

'Let's just say there might be a party there tonight, at number twenty-five. I can't promise it's still on, but knowing Leon, he's not one to let a little thing like murder put him off.'

'Why are you tipping me off?'

'He might be my brother but I still find the whole thing repulsive.'

'I'll need you to make a statement.'

'I know you can't use any of this information in court. It's all inadmissible unless I was under caution.'

'Oh, so now we've gone back to being enemies?' she said.

'Not at all. I'm just telling it how it is. If you call me in for questioning, I'll deny all of this.'

'You can deny it but I'll ask you again, under caution.'

'I don't care about lying under oath. But there are certain lengths that *I* won't go to, even if it is to protect my family, do you catch my meaning?'

Grace nodded, unsure if she did or not. But she wasn't going to let him know. She needed time on her own, to think about the meaning of his words. Because he wasn't telling her everything and she knew there was more in his message.

Outside, she took her phone from her pocket, elated at what Eddie had told her about Leon. She was going to catch the bastards organising these parties, and she was going to nail Leon Steele in the process.

Although how she was going to explain where she'd found the information was another problem in itself.

FIFTY-FIVE

Grace was in Allie's office with Perry, the door shut.

'What the hell were you doing seeing Eddie Steele?' Allie fumed as she tore a strip out of her.

'It was my fault as much as Grace's,' Perry broke in before she had a chance to reply. 'I knew she was going there too.'

'Thanks, Perry,' Grace said. 'But this *is* my fault. I did go against orders.'

Allie looked at them both in turn and shook her head. 'I told you to come to me if anything like this happened, Grace. I'm extremely disappointed in you.'

'She's not the first officer to go against the grain,' Perry added.

Allie glared at him. 'If you are alluding to me, then I suggest you keep your mouth shut and your opinions to yourself.'

Perry was referring to a case in 2011 when Allie had got close to a prime suspect to gather information.

'You did what you did to get evidence. So did Grace.'

Allie glanced at her watch. 'We don't have time to discuss this. We need to get a team together for this party. Sam has gathered a list of properties in Leon Steele's name, so we'll start looking at them tomorrow, after we've done this raid.' She looked

259

at them both in turn. 'Let's keep this between us for now, but I'm warning you, Grace, don't step over the line again.'

Grace nodded, relief flooding through her. At least she was being allowed to stay on the case. There was no way she wanted to miss this raid.

'Did you have any luck with the neighbours in Park Avenue?' she asked Frankie as she got back to her desk.

'Not really. One side said they'd heard nothing.'

'Keeping themselves to themselves, just like Rachel said they would.' Grace rolled her eyes.

'The neighbour on the other side was a nice chap too.'

'A nice chap? You sound like you're in your seventies.'

Frankie smirked. 'He didn't want to get Rachel into trouble either. But he said he'd only heard the one party.'

'They *do* keep themselves to themselves, I'm impressed.'

An hour later, everything was set in place to raid the house in Sandon Crescent. Grace was travelling in a pool car with Perry, Allie and Frankie, Perry driving. There were no sirens on. They wanted to maintain the element of surprise. Two marked cars and a van full of uniformed officers followed behind them.

Grace expected no more than twenty people to be in the house but they were fully prepared for more. The enforcer had been brought along too, in case they couldn't get access straight away.

She only hoped the intel she'd received was good. She still wasn't sure if Eddie had been telling her the truth or setting her up to look a fool. She never would be able to trust him fully.

They parked up in the next street and Allie sent two officers dressed in plain clothes to walk the street. Behind her, Tactical Response were waiting for the signal to go ahead.

'We're past the house now,' a voice came over the radio.

'There are nine cars in the driveway and we can see people in the living room.'

Grace took a deep breath, adrenaline pumping through her almost as if she was in front of the house herself.

'On the count of three,' Allie told everyone. 'Go, go, go.'

Grace ran forward with the officers, along the road and into the drive of number twenty-five. A trained officer held the enforcer but they knocked on the door first to see if access would be granted. Allie was just about to give orders to use it when the door opened. Music could be heard in the background.

'Well, who do we have . . .' The man stopped talking, his mouth agog when he saw the police.

Allie held up her warrant card as officers flooded into the property.

'Does this house belong to you?' she asked the man. 'Are you Mr Trevor Merchant?'

'Yes, I—'

'We have reason to believe that this is an illegal party and need to look around. I'm sure you won't mind if we do that?'

Allie read him his rights as he floundered when words such as 'sexual exploitation' and 'grooming' were mentioned.

Grace had gone ahead and was already in the living room. People were shouting and screaming, some trying to flee, others busy arranging their clothing. Taking everyone by surprise meant that most people didn't have a chance to react. But she caught sight of one man running out of the back door.

'Police! Stop!'

She gave chase, Frankie behind her. They ran out into the rear garden, the lights illuminating a large lawn with a thick hedge border in front of a high fence. There were a number of places to hide but nowhere for anyone to escape. Frankie was looking behind the bins; Grace in each ornamental bush, pushing through it to see what she could spot. Just then she heard a kerfuffle behind her.

'Over here, Sarge,' Frankie shouted as he dragged a man from out of his hiding place.

Grace ran to Frankie's aid. The man lashed out at her as they tried to pin him to the ground. And then he turned his head towards hers, spittle flying from him along with a number of expletives.

She had the shock of her life when she recognised who it was.

'Well now, this is a surprise,' Grace said as she helped Frankie to secure him in cuffs. They pulled him to standing. 'Hello ex-detective Alex Challinor.'

SATURDAY

FIFTY-SIX

Grace was in the shower after a three-mile run on the treadmill. It was very rare in her job that she got to pound the streets of Stoke on a regular basis, so running indoors had to suffice. She was glad Simon wasn't into the sport too, though. It was always something she'd done alone to alleviate her stress as well as keep herself fit enough to chase down villains.

Her mind still hadn't switched off from the night before. At the most, she'd had a few hours' sleep before waking at five a.m. and finally getting up. Simon had been out for the count; she wasn't sure he knew she'd even got out of bed.

After her shower, she dressed and made two mugs of tea. Taking them upstairs, she opened the bedroom door with her bum to see him sitting up with the light on and his phone in his hand.

'Anything interesting come in?' she asked as she passed him the mug and lay on the bed next to him.

'Nothing I'm going to share with you,' he teased. 'These things have to work both ways.'

'They do, you cheeky git!' she admonished. 'I tell you lots of things.'

'I know.' He grinned. 'I'm glad that we work well as a team.'

'Trust is a good basis for everything,' she added, wrapping her fingers around her mug. 'What are you up to today?'

'First port of call is the monthly stats meeting. Unless anything came in overnight, which is why I'm checking my phone. You?'

'Pretty much the same things.' She sighed. 'I hope we get it sorted soon. It's messing with my head.'

'I know. You were talking in your sleep and tossing and turning.'

'Was I? Sorry. Did you make sense of anything?'

'No, you were muttering mostly. But you need to get some sleep. You look exhausted.'

'You're such a smooth talker.' She stifled a yawn, tempted to get back into bed with him. But there wasn't time. She needed to be at the office for seven, she was determined to make headway today.

FIFTY-SEVEN

'Okay everyone.' Allie beckoned for silence as they gathered for the morning team briefing. 'I want to start by saying thanks to everyone for a great effort at 25 Sandon Crescent. It's gone a long way to stopping these parties – if not for good, then at least for now. As you know, there was a lot happening last night so I'm going to run you through what we got from interviewing two of the people we brought in.

'The first person of interest is Trevor Merchant and, from David West's statement, we know that he is a big player in attending the parties, but not in setting them up. At first he wouldn't bend when we questioned him on who it was, and he denied knowing anyone named Angela Merchant. His wife is called Jeanette.'

'So basically he does the same thing as Rachel Townley,' Grace confirmed. 'His home is used for the parties and he is paid for that and also has the privilege of choosing any girl he likes.'

'Gross,' Sam shuddered. 'I mean, have you seen the state of him? He's an old pervert.'

'Who we are going to charge for sexually exploiting young girls.'

'What about Rachel Townley?'

'It will be difficult to prove she was involved with anything but providing a place for the parties.'

'Did she say how many she'd held?'

'She insists only the one. We can get the Financial Forensics Unit to look at her accounts if necessary. Although if she was paid in cash, it would be untraceable.'

Allie nodded. 'The second person interviewed was a blast from the past for some of us and an unwelcome return for us all. We picked up an ex-colleague, former DC Alex Challinor.'

A murmur went around the room and Allie held up her hand.

'I know, he's back like a bad penny. For anyone in the room who doesn't know, Alex used to work in Major Crimes here at this station until he was discharged for gross misconduct. He was seeing someone who was paying him for inside information and passing it on to known criminals. The woman turned out to be the killer on the case the Major Crimes Team were working on at the time.'

'Nearly came a cropper when she turned on him too,' Perry added. 'If it wasn't for Grace's quick thinking, he would have been a goner.'

'It was a team effort,' Grace told everyone. 'A complicated case, made even more so by the fact it was the Steele clan, my estranged family.' Grace swallowed down her emotion. 'It was a hard time for me, on a professional and a personal level, and I don't think I would have made it through as strong as I did without loyal officers around me.' She looked at Perry and then Sam. 'Alex skipped Stoke after he was fired but rumour has it he came back a year ago. It seems he's been working for the Steele family. He's now part of the team who looks after the bouncers at The Casino and Flynn's Nightclub.

'During the interviews, Alex blamed Trevor for everything

and vice versa. Alex caved first though, and finally admitted that he was one of the party organisers,' Allie went on. 'We had no real evidence to tie him to anything but he clearly knew from being on our side of the job what we would eventually find out. He obviously thought it best to tell us what he knew, perhaps to get a lesser sentence.'

'He'll serve time for this?'

'It's possible, even if he isn't the man behind it all.'

'Personally, I still think he's a dick,' Grace added, with a laugh to lighten up the mood. 'He played with fire too close to home and got his sticky fingers burnt . . . and any other cliché you can think of.'

Frankie chuckled.

'So . . .' Allie said. 'Now we have established that we're lucky he no longer works with us, we need to get on to some of the things he was telling us about and help to get the people at the top who are raking in the money from exploiting these girls. Perry, can you get everyone up to speed about how many people have been identified from the images on Erin Ellis's phone please?'

'So far we have David West, Max Croydon, Trevor Merchant, Rachel Townley, Molly Redfern and our victim, Erin Ellis.' Perry pointed them out to everyone.

'What came up on the phones, Grace? I assume we have both girls' fingerprints on Erin's leather phone case?'

'Yes – which tells us nothing more than they showed each other things. I'd say that was pretty normal with them being so close.'

'I agree. That will be the same with Molly's device. Do we have Molly's data too?'

'We do. There are reams and reams of text messages between her and Erin – trivial things like what are you wearing tonight, what time are we meeting, where are you, do you want anything from the shop before I knock for you.' Grace turned the sheets round so everyone could see. 'These are text messages too. All the blue markers are against Max Croydon.' She pointed to a group of dots. 'Can you see a huge cluster and then it suddenly goes down to once or twice a week? This could indicate two things. That they were an item and then they were not. Or that they were seeing each other in person more than texting as the relationship progressed.'

'It could also show that Max was friendlier when he was recruiting the girls and then lessened his contact.' Allie paused. 'Any other numbers popping up regularly?'

'Yes, one.' Grace read out the number.

'That came up regularly for me too,' Perry said. 'We'll ask the tech team for details of the owner.'

'Do you think it might be David West?' Frankie joined in. 'Perhaps he has a burner phone?'

'It might be. There were a lot of men in those photos.'

'There's someone called Chad, who we now suspect is Alex Challinor after checking his phone records,' Perry said. 'He wouldn't go by his own name in dealings like this. There are a few text messages out to his phone from Molly's about them meeting up. It seems he collected her in his car and then dropped her off at the end of the night, but there's no indication of where they went or if they were alone. Then there's several messages on Erin's phone from someone called Lion Man.'

'Wait a minute.' Grace sat forward quickly. 'Lion Man? Do you think it could be a code name for Leon? As in Leo the Lion?'

Perry began to flip through the list. 'The number only shows up a handful of times. But there's one message two days before Erin was murdered.'

'Maybe the break in communication with Max Croydon coincided with Erin getting pregnant?' Grace suggested.

'You mean Leon Steele was involved with Erin?' Allie said.

'It's more than a possibility. It would also give him a clear motive to murder Erin, or arrange to have her murdered, to cover up everything. She was the link to the parties, but through the baby a permanent link to him, if it was his?'

Everyone began to speak at once.

'It has to be Leon,' Grace said. Especially after Eddie had hinted about Leon thinking of himself as the king of the jungle last night. That was what he meant. Leon was Lion Man, she was certain.

'Grace, can you and Frankie fetch Molly in again? We don't have anything concrete but we need to see if she knows who Lion Man is. Go now to avoid people seeing you.'

'Yes, boss. On our way.'

FIFTY-EIGHT

Leon listened to the voice yelling down the line to him.

'I'm telling you, I'm out of here if they suspect the slightest thing. I knew I shouldn't have got involved.'

'Keep your hair on. I'll sort it.'

Leon disconnected the phone and gave out a loud groan. The call had been from Alex, telling him the party had been raided the night before. The party he had *specifically* told Max to call off.

Alex and that fat fuck Trevor had been arrested and given conditional bail. He could probably trust Alex not to grass him up but Trevor? He was all mouth and money, no balls about him.

At least the police didn't have enough evidence to remand them. There was likely a lot of work involved to get them to court, and he had no doubt the police would carry it out, but in the meantime, the police would be on to the parties now and that was the last thing he wanted with Erin dead as well.

Grace Allendale. That interfering bitch was at it again. Why did she always want to poke her nose into his business? She never came after what Eddie stood for. Although just lately, he'd been surprised to see his brother backing off the illegal stuff. Now he knew why. He didn't want to get into Grace's bad books.

Or maybe Eddie was leaving it all to him, to set him up, and keeping himself out of the equation for when something went wrong.

Eddie came into the office.

'What's up?' Eddie asked. 'You worried about something?'

'No,' he replied nonchalantly.

'Really? You're not at all concerned about the house being raided last night?' Eddie walked towards Leon.

Leon screwed up his face. 'How did you find out?'

'You think I don't know what you've been up to? I've known for ages. But I assumed you had it under control. What the hell has got into you?'

'I could say the same thing about you.' Leon ignored Eddie's question and prodded his brother's shoulder. 'Since Grace came on the scene, you've lost your edge. You used to be the man who everyone looked up to. Now you're after getting on her good side all the time, probably to the detriment of our family and the business.'

'You're the one who doesn't want anything to do with her,' Eddie replied. 'I'm fine with meeting her once in a while.'

Leon's eyes widened. 'You've met with her?'

'We had a drink last night.'

'Why?'

'I wanted to see if she would tell me anything.'

'About what?'

'What do you think?' Eddie glared at him. 'I told you to stop those parties ages ago but you never listen.'

'Did she say anything?' Leon looked around shiftily.

Eddie shook his head. 'Nah. So are you satisfied we weren't in cahoots behind your back?'

'Not really.' Leon almost growled. 'I know you. You're always trying to get one over on me. And let me tell you, it's not going to work. This business is run by both of us.'

'And our dear mother, Kathleen.'

'She has nothing to do with our side of things.'

'You'd be surprised,' Eddie muttered. 'She never misses a trick.'

'Then you'd better warn her off, too. I am sick of playing second fiddle to everyone else. I'm an equal in this firm and if you don't like that, then I'll buy you out.'

Eddie sniggered. 'You don't have the skill to do what I do.'

'That's where you're wrong. Especially if Grace is out of the picture.'

Eddie squared up to him. 'Keep away from her.'

'Or else you'll what?'

'Try me and find out. Trust me, you don't need me as your enemy.'

'You've *always* been my enemy.' Leon squared up to Eddie. 'From those very first days when that bastard used to make us beat each other up while he watched. You think I don't remember how hard you used to hit me?'

'It was the survival of the fittest,' Eddie protested. 'I had to do it, like you had to do it to me. He knew if I was holding back. I took many a beating on my own that you didn't know about just because he said I wasn't hitting you hard enough. I wouldn't do it. The only times I did was when I couldn't take another beating from him. But that doesn't give you the right to take everything out on Grace. She suffered at his hands too. You should give her a break.'

'I'll never welcome her into the fold.' Leon shoulder barged Eddie as he left the room.

'There's no need to make this personal, Leon.'

'It's too late.' Leon slammed the office door, stormed through the gym, and then pushed the outside door so hard it bounced back from the wall. The sound reverberated as he entered the car park.

He got in his vehicle and started the engine, wanting to put as much distance between him and Eddie as he could while he thought what to do next.

Eddie was his family, the only person he'd looked up to as a child, but even he didn't know the full truth. Leon had helped Eddie grow the Steele empire and yet he was never grateful. Leon always felt second best, like the poor relation. Eddie said something and he had to go with it. Well, not any more. He'd had enough of being second in command. He wanted things to be equal or it was over.

But first, he needed to hide as much as he could from the police. They weren't going to come between him and his livelihood.

Eddie sat at his desk but his mind wouldn't settle. How dare Leon bring their past to the table that way. The things they had endured as children at the hands of their father had made them close from their early years. It had been painful for them both, when George had pitted one brother against the other. Since then, age had mellowed Eddie, but Leon hadn't changed.

Alex Challinor had been a dark horse. Yet again, he had played the brothers off against each other. Eddie had no idea that Alex had been involved with the parties. He'd come back to Stoke with his tail between his legs. He'd begged for forgiveness and of course both he and Leon had welcomed him back, for their own separate purposes, it appeared. Eddie wanted him to keep his ear to the ground with the side he used to work on, the police.

It was time Leon learned to stand on his own two feet. He'd strip him of the Steele name if necessary, the power associated with it. Leon thought Eddie was the weaker of the two of them because he acted level-headed, fought with his mouth now far more than his fists. He also had other people willing to do the dirty work.

But Leon was the weak one, and had got himself into trouble again by not being able to leave young girls alone. It was a lucrative business, yet Eddie knew it was much more than that for his brother. Leon saw some of the girls to get his kicks. And it was enough to make Eddie sick.

It was time he spoke to Kathleen. That would give him leeway to set things in operation at his end. He had to stop Leon from ruining everything, no matter what it took.

FIFTY-NINE

Grace went downstairs to the interview suites with Frankie. Molly Redfern had been brought in by her mum again and was waiting for them. But deep in thought, the team briefing having thrown up so many things, she didn't know where to start. For one, if Leon Steele was Lion Man, why had Eddie warned her about him? That was out-and-out disloyalty, so her only assumption was that there must be cracks in the brothers' relationship.

'Do you think Molly knows more than she's letting on, boss?' Frankie asked as he swiped his security card to give them access to the floor.

'Yes, I do, but I don't blame her for not sharing with us either. She might have been warned to keep her mouth shut. Someone could even have said she would be next. We don't have a clue who attacked Erin Ellis in that walkway yet. The knife we found was the wrong one and we don't have any witnesses coming forward.' She counted on her fingers. 'It was half past nine in the evening. We've ruled out anyone who was seen in the vicinity and the man who went into the walkway from Leek Road isn't a suspect now, even if he does finally come forward. The attacker must have come from Sampson Street or the field next to it, but there were no muddy footprints anywhere. The weather was against us as everyone was in their homes. It's so frustrating.'

'And nothing from the post-mortem, only cause of death.'

'And the pregnancy.'

'But no fibres, hairs, etc.'

'Stabbings are fast and furious,' Grace explained. 'Sometimes the only thing left behind is the victim.'

'But we have a motive for Erin to be killed. She was pregnant, attending parties that no one wanted us to find out about. She could get the killer into a lot of trouble if he's in a relationship with someone else.'

Grace nodded her agreement. They went into the soft interview room where Molly was sitting on the settee, her mum next to her. Grace could tell she'd hardly been sleeping. Her eyes were puffy, cheeks red from crying: hair unwashed and hanging limp. She was wearing different clothes to when Grace had seen her yesterday, but she looked wretched. Lucy Redfern didn't look too great either.

For now, everyone was focused on finding out who had committed the crime. Once they had their killer, these two families, Erin and Molly's, would have catastrophic fallouts to deal with. When everything went back to normal, and everyone else went about their days with regularity, these people would be left devastated, a huge hole left in their lives.

But Grace couldn't let any of that affect her opinion of Molly until she had spoken to her again.

'Molly.' She sat down opposite her. Frankie sat next to Grace. 'We need to ask you some more questions. You do understand how important it is to help us find the person who killed Erin, don't you?'

Molly looked up through swollen lids and gave a slight nod. 'I don't know anything else I *can* tell you.'

'I want you to look at this photo again, the one we found

on Erin's phone. I know you said you didn't recognise anyone but I still think you might. I think you're too scared to say, and I get that. But we now know the names of some of these people. And we arrested several of them last night.'

Molly gasped. 'But they'll think I said something, and I never did.'

'We caught them through our own means. And right now, I think they have bigger things to worry about than that. I want to reassure you as much as I can.'

'You say you've arrested people?' Lucy spoke. 'Can you tell us who? Or how many?'

'I can't.' Grace shook her head. 'But Molly, I need you to look at this photo and tell me who that woman is there, the one with her back to the camera.'

Molly took the image from Frankie and looked at it again. 'Is Chad in trouble?'

'What he's been involved in is a very serious crime.' Grace didn't want to be too presumptuous by saying yes outright. There was also the name change, which she was keeping to herself for now. She wasn't going to tell Molly yet that Chad wasn't who he said he was, although she did want to get out of Molly the exact nature of their relationship.

'But he didn't do anything.' She looked at her mum and then down on the floor. 'Well, not with anyone else. He was always with me.'

'Even after you had been with . . . the other men?' Lucy almost spat the last three words out.

'Yes, he was nice.'

'The photo, Molly?' Grace encouraged her to look. 'The woman wearing the scarf.'

'That's Angela.'

'She was at every party?'

'Yes.'

'Do you know anyone who uses the nickname Lion Man?'

Molly's eyes widened but she shook her head fervently.

'Are you sure?'

She nodded and looked at her mum. 'I don't feel well.'

Grace took this as her cue to ramp things up, but not before giving Molly a long hard stare. 'Molly, I know that you're frightened, but you need to start opening up to us or else you're going to find yourself in trouble. Withholding information from a police investigation is a serious matter and you need to understand that if we don't catch Erin's killer and someone else gets injured, or killed, then it's going to be even more of an issue for you.'

'I don't know anything!'

'I think that you do.'

When Molly remained silent, Grace sat back in frustration and closed her notebook. Even though time was of the essence, there was no use pushing the girl when she was clearly too scared to talk.

'We'll leave this for now and you can go home,' she replied. 'But we will have to speak to you again.'

As they left the interview room, and Frankie showed the two women out, Grace felt like slamming the door in temper, but knew it was a childish thing to do. Nor was it in her nature.

But she knew Molly was lying. And now they had to figure out why.

SIXTY

Eddie parked up in front of Hardman House. He sat for a moment, bracing himself to go inside. Every time he came back to his childhood home, another part of him died. He wished his mother would sell the property and move to somewhere else. It held bad memories for them all. But Kathleen wouldn't.

He let himself in and she came out of the living room, into the hallway, to greet him. She wore the perfume that he remembered her wearing since he was a child, with a blue wool dress and black heels. Her hair was immaculate, her nails painted a vibrant purple.

'Eddie.' She kissed him on his cheek.

'Is he here?'

'I've had a message to say he's on his way. He'll be about ten minutes. Come through and I'll make tea.'

He laughed under his breath. Kathleen always acted like the doting parent when they had meetings like this. As if it was a Sunday afternoon and they were having something to eat together, laughing and joking, reminiscing and sharing anecdotes. It might be a coping mechanism for her, yet it did nothing but infuriate him. Things were never happy in the Steele family home.

'Has he told you about the party that was raided last night?' Kathleen turned sharply.

Eddie enlightened her on all he had found out from Alex after he'd called him. He watched his mother's face turn ashen.

'When he gets here, please don't start fighting,' she said. 'You know what his temper is like. He'll storm off rather than face us. I want him to answer some questions.'

'Don't worry,' Eddie replied. 'I intend to get to the bottom of this today. He's out of this family if he leaves without sorting things.'

Kathleen turned her back on him while she waited for the kettle to boil. Eddie stared out of the kitchen window. The old garage, the place where George Steele had held Eddie's sister when she was being abused by their father's friends, had gone. After Jade had tried to kill Alex Challinor there, and then left Leon for dead, Kathleen had pulled it down as soon as the police had released it.

Yet, even after what had happened with Jade, Leon hadn't wanted to stop the sex parties he'd started. Eddie knew it would be his downfall and he wasn't going to let his brother ruin what he had built. The Steele reputation was in danger of collapsing, but he would be there to patch it back together again. It was time to let his feelings be known.

A few minutes later, the front door opened and Leon came into the kitchen to join them. They were sitting across from each other at the table.

'What's going on?' Leon put his car keys on the worktop.

'Come and sit, Leon.' Kathleen pulled out a chair. 'We need to talk. I've made tea.'

'Your answer to everything.' Leon's tone was cruel but he did as she said, sitting down beside her.

Kathleen slid a mug towards him.

'We need these parties to stop,' Eddie said, wanting to get the scene over and done with. 'They're not part of what we do, nor what we stand for.'

'I told you before, you don't get to tell me what to do any more.'

'But Leon,' Kathleen exclaimed, 'things are getting out of hand and—'

'It's all under control.'

'Really?' Eddie said. 'Is that why you had a party here in summer?'

'I don't know what you're talking about.' Leon shrugged.

'Don't sit there and deny it.' Kathleen reached for his hand. 'We're trying to protect you.'

'Who gave them the tip-off about last night?' Leon jabbed a finger at Eddie. 'It was you, wasn't it? You said you'd seen Grace and—'

'You've seen Grace?' Kathleen questioned.

'I was trying to find out what she knew.' He raised his eyebrows as he looked at Leon. 'You really think I'd tell her anything?'

'I'm sure you would. You've been after an excuse to get rid of me for some time.'

'Don't be paranoid. I didn't say a word,' Eddie lied. 'For your information, it could have been anyone. Did you think about the fact Alex double crossed us last time he was working for us? He was getting money from everyone to pass things on.'

'It won't be him.' Leon held up his hand. 'He has more loyalty in his little finger than you have in your whole body.'

'Don't push your luck,' Eddie warned.

'I've had enough of this.' Leon scraped back his chair, picked up his mug and hurled it across the room. It exploded into tiny fragments, the noise deafening as hot liquid gushed everywhere.

'Leon!' Kathleen gasped.

Eddie stood up too, facing him across the table. 'We've had enough of *you*. Wasn't it sufficient that our father was into some weird shit without you going the same way?'

'It's all making sense now.' Leon nodded fervently. 'You told Grace so that you could get rid of me. You know that bastard Trevor Merchant is a wimp. He'll have told them everything. You led her straight to me!'

'You should have stopped this when Jade went mad.'

'Jade did not go mad,' Kathleen cried. 'She's your sister.'

'And you stood by and didn't help while our father abused her,' Eddie added.

'I couldn't do any different. You know that. It wasn't my fault.'

'You were weak,' Leon agreed. 'If you had helped us, then maybe none of this would have happened. It's your fault.'

'I didn't know,' Kathleen protested.

'Liar!' Leon's hands bunched into fists.

Eddie stretched across the table to stop him lashing out. 'Back off,' he warned. 'Lay a finger on her and you'll have me to answer to.'

'You? You're pathetic. When have you ever acted like a man?'

'More than you'll ever know.'

'What's that supposed to mean?'

Eddie ignored the remark. 'You need to clear up the mess around these parties and stop them for good, do you hear?'

'Oh, I hear, but it's not going to happen.'

'Then I suggest you get your stuff out of the office, and the gym.'

'What?'

'You heard me. If you don't want to play ball, then you're out.'

Leon shook his head. 'You're starting a war.'

Eddie said nothing. Instead, he nodded at Kathleen, who went to retrieve a sports bag from the far end of the kitchen.

SIXTY-ONE

'There's fifty grand,' Eddie said as Kathleen put the bag on the table. He unzipped it and showed Leon its contents. 'Take it.'

'You think I'll leave what I have here for so little?' Leon scoffed as he pushed the bag away. 'I can make more than that in a month. I've been earning twice as much as you for the past few years and—'

'I know.'

Leon glared at him.

'I know you've been lending money; that you've been getting the lads from the gym to deliver drugs for you. I've known about the cash and grabs from the cashpoints. I've known from the *minute* you've done everything.'

'So why have you never questioned me about it?'

'Because I thought one day you would see sense. But now, if you don't take this money and leave, I can guarantee that you'll get picked up by the police, for something regarding these parties or the fact that you've been involved with a dead girl!'

Leon lunged at Eddie, hitting him in the face.

Eddie ran around the table towards Leon and punched him in the jaw.

'Boys!' Kathleen cried, as they laid into each other.

They ignored her, punches raining down on each other. Eddie knew his brother was strong and had braced himself for it.

'Stop,' Kathleen screamed. 'Or I'm calling the police!'

It was over in less than a minute. Leon wiped his mouth, blood pouring from a split lip.

'Is this what you want?' He looked at Kathleen. 'To split the family altogether.'

'If you don't leave, you'll end up in prison,' she reasoned.

'You're not going to ruin this family,' Eddie seethed.

Leon laughed bitterly. 'Well you know, we're not *strictly* family.'

Kathleen paled. 'Leon, no.'

'It's time he knew the truth.'

'I said *no!*'

'If you don't tell him, I will.'

Kathleen held her head in her hands.

'What's going on?' Eddie looked at them both for an answer.

Leon sniggered, his lips curled into a snarl. 'George wasn't my father. Isn't that right, mother dear?'

Kathleen sat down with a thump. 'He's right, Eddie. George was your father but not Leon's.'

'And there's more.' Leon chuckled. 'My father is an ex-copper.'

Eddie's eyes widened in disbelief. 'Do I know him?'

'Please, Leon,' Kathleen pleaded. 'Not after all this time.'

Leon shook his head. 'Tell him, or else I will.'

'Who is it?' Eddie shouted.

'Tell him!' Leon roared.

'It's Nick Carter,' Kathleen said.

'The former DI on the murder team? What the fuck?' Eddie paced the room.

'I wanted to tell you, but I was made to keep it secret,' Kathleen said.

'By who?'

'Your father.'

'Well you could have told me when he was *dead*!'

'What use would it have been? There was nothing you could do about it.'

'And you see, not sharing the same father makes us totally different,' Leon chided. 'I'm not your family any more than Grace is. We're both your half-siblings.' Then he laughed. 'If you only knew what Nick had done for me over the years. He was as bent as George Steele.'

Eddie sat down as, all of a sudden, everything clicked into place. Nick Carter must have brought Grace back to the force to do his dirty work, get inside information for him. But Grace wouldn't toe the line, even though she couldn't have known that Leon was his son. Or at least he thought so.

No, he was sure. She was more loyal than his so-called family.

'Does anyone else know?' Eddie asked.

Kathleen shook her head.

'It's him that's been keeping you out of prison, isn't it?' Eddie said quietly.

Leon clapped slowly. 'Family *do* look after their own.'

'And you've both known all this time and never . . . does Grace know?'

Kathleen shook her head. 'And she mustn't find out.'

'So I suggest you keep your empty threats to yourself or I'll make sure I tell her,' Leon added.

'What good will that do you?' Eddie replied. 'They'll be

288

able to look over his cases, find you out for lots of things, no doubt.'

'He's left now, so that won't stick.'

'You don't think? No one likes a bent copper.'

'They don't have time to do their own jobs, let alone reopen old cases. And he's—'

Eddie pointed at the door. 'Get out, take the money with you and don't come back.'

Leon picked up the bag, staring at them both in turn. Then he spat on the floor at their feet, before leaving.

Once he'd gone, Kathleen wouldn't look at Eddie. But she began to speak all the same.

'It was when George was still married,' she said. 'You know that Leon is two months older than Grace. George and I weren't together as such. I . . . I was lonely and, well, you know the rest. Years later, when George told me Grace and her mum had left, he turned his anger on me. He forced me to marry him. I didn't have the guts to do what Grace's mum did. I wanted to leave but your father saw to it that I stayed with him. And he made us all pay for my one moment of weakness. That's why he was so cruel to Leon.'

'Why didn't you tell me?'

'I was sworn to secrecy!'

'But when George died—'

'When George died, Leon threatened me with all sorts. Where do you think he's been getting most of his money from?'

'He's been blackmailing you?'

She nodded.

'How did he find out?'

'George was drunk and goading him. They started to fight but as Leon was getting the better of him, he told him. He did it out of spite, to throw Leon off his game, and it ruined our family.'

'And no one thought to tell me?' Eddie prodded himself in the chest, unable to take it all in. 'I need a bit of space.'

He walked towards the door but Kathleen reached for his arm. 'But, I—'

'Leave me alone.'

SIXTY-TWO

Leon's car screeched off the drive in his haste to get away. How dare Eddie and Kathleen have a go at him about what he'd been doing. Did they think he was a child that had to be reprimanded? It was no concern of theirs what he got up to.

Stationary at a set of traffic lights, he tried to call Alex but there was no answer. He was probably screening his calls. Quickly, he tapped out a message to him. Then he tried to get his anger under control.

Had Alex told the police anything? He'd always struck Leon as the loyal type, but who would he stay faithful to this time? If his neck was on the line, would he lie or would he bargain with his ex-colleagues and tell them what they wanted to know?

Either way, Leon was in trouble and had to warn everyone else involved. He needed to get someone to check the other properties, see if they were clean, and get rid of evidence at each house involved. And he would have to get it done quickly, before they found the one place that would ruin him.

First, he drove to Max's flat. He wanted to know what had been going on, who had double crossed him and why. He parked a street away and walked round to the main road, wanting to maintain the element of surprise. The weather was cold, but with a warm sun for the time of year. He pulled the collar of his coat towards him and turned into Max's street.

He was a few doors away when he saw Max come out of the building. Leon dived into a shop entrance, out of sight, watching as Max ran to his car. As the car began to move, Leon stooped down so he wouldn't be seen. But as Max drove past him, he could see someone in the passenger seat. What the hell was Rachel Townley doing with a dick like Croydon?

He got out his phone and rang Max.

'Where the fuck are you?' Leon said when he answered the call.

'I'm in town. I'd arranged to meet with Alex. That twat double crossed me. I told him to cancel the party and he went ahead with it.'

Leon shook his head but reined his temper in. Max was lying about his whereabouts so he could be lying about Alex too. Out of the two men, he knew Alex was more likely to come good because he had more to lose. Max was young and stupid.

'It's okay – I can sort it.' Leon kept his voice calm, as if there was nothing wrong. 'Can you call in at the house later this morning? I have your money.'

Half an hour later, Leon arrived at home and removed his coat in the hallway. He'd hidden the money in the boot of his car while he decided what to do. Of course he wasn't going to leave Stoke, but he wasn't about to give the money back either.

As he hung up his coat, he heard Trudy's voice. Glancing through the open door, he could see her in the conservatory. She was talking to someone on the phone. She hadn't heard him so he stopped to listen before going in.

'I can meet you tomorrow when I'm out shopping. You can disappear for a while then.'

It went quiet while she listened to the caller.

'What time? Okay, and not a word to Leon about our arrangement, do you hear?'

Another pause.

'You knew what would happen once you killed her. I can't get you any more than that, but you'll have Leon's money too. You've doubled up doing one job, anyway.'

Leon sat on the bottom of the stairs, trying to work things out. What was happening to all the people he thought he could trust?

Was Trudy saying there had been a hit out on Erin? That's not what he'd ordered.

More than that, *was* his own wife double crossing him?

When he heard her saying goodbye, Leon rushed to the front door, opening and closing it as if he'd just arrived.

'Everything good?' he asked as he put his keys on the worktop.

Trudy turned to him, moving closer to peck his cheek. 'Yes, fine.'

Leon went to speak but thought better of it. Instead, he made coffee and took it into his office. Who had Trudy been talking to? And what was the conversation all about? What arrangement had been made?

He picked his phone up and made a call. But it went unanswered. He left a voice message.

Call at the house. Better there than at the gym.

Leon smirked. He could play games too.

SIXTY-THREE

Grace and Frankie had visited two of the properties that were owned by Leon Steele and had found tenants in them both. Without a warrant, they hadn't been invited into either, but as they were terraced houses it had been easy to have a quick look through the front window as they had gone past, to see that they were all furnished and seemed okay. However, Grace knew the tenants could be hiding things, so would go back to the office with the details and get warrants to search them all in one fell swoop.

Sam had also rung to say she'd found two properties registered under Trudy Steele. They were on their way to the first one.

'Leon could have joints all over the city that we don't know about, couldn't he?' Frankie asked.

'Not necessarily. The rules about buying houses have tightened due to the government trying to limit money laundering. I reckon he could only put them in his name or Trudy's without the VAT man interfering. Although he might have some properties from the George Steele days that haven't been transferred. I'll get Sam to check for that too.'

'Is that likely?'

'I'm not sure. You have to declare certain things once a death has occurred, but who's to say he did that? Leon's sneaky.'

'Doesn't all this bother you, Grace?' Frankie asked as they stopped behind a bus, waiting for passengers to disembark. 'The Steele name coming up all the time?'

'Of course it does but I'm happy that I can at least investigate it. They aren't my family, and I know I sail close to the wind, but I'm glad I'm allowed to. Well, kind of. I probably wouldn't be able to at any other station, but as Nick was okay with it, I got off with it.'

'I mean, doesn't it worry you that they might one day come after you?' Frankie shrugged. 'You know, get fed up of you being on the right side and—'

Grace's shoulder rose. 'I can handle myself.'

'That's what Leon thought before his sister got the better of him two years ago.'

'Adrenaline can be the cause of a lot of things,' she noted. 'But I think if they were going to do something to me, they would have done it by now.'

She kept her eyes on the road, not wanting Frankie to see her reaction. Of course she was worried about something happening to her. She didn't trust any of the Steeles to look out for her. To them she would *always* be on the wrong side. She worried constantly about Leon and what he was capable of. But she shut it out so that she could do her job.

She pulled up outside 11 Ranger Street. It was a dead-end of the city, the terraced houses run down and the area known for a lot of drug activity. But she noticed some of the houses were trying hard to look appealing in a dingy street mostly full of boarded-up windows. Several had brightly coloured doors; hanging baskets and boxes of flowers that seemed more out of place than welcoming. A wardrobe was outside number fourteen, piled high inside with black rubbish bags, a bicycle with its front wheel missing propped up against it.

She wondered if they'd got the right address. It didn't seem logical that Trudy Steele would want anything to do with a place like this. Was it something that she had no idea about?

Once out of the car, Grace knocked on the front door. No one answered so after a few seconds, she tried again.

She peered through the window. There was a settee, coffee table and a small TV in the front of the room, a table and four chairs in the back. A couple of nondescript pictures hung on the wall, a mirror above a cheap wooden fire surround.

'I can't make up my mind if it's occupied or not,' she told Frankie.

The door opened to the adjoining property and a woman appeared. Her clothes were cheap and ill-fitting, clinging to her body in an unflattering way, and she had long lank hair. She took a drag on a cigarette before speaking.

'There's no one in.' She looked Grace up and down. 'Are you the police?'

'Yes. Do you know who lives here?'

She shook her head, folding her arms underneath a heavy bosom. 'People visit every now and then but I never hear anything. Whoever it is, they're quiet.'

'Could you describe these visitors?'

'Sometimes a man, sometimes a woman. Sometimes the man brings a young girl with him. Sometimes the man and woman come together, with a girl.'

'The same girl?'

'Sometimes.'

'Anything else?' she pushed, wondering if the woman ever said anything but sometimes. 'Were they tall, small, fat, thin?'

'I don't stand on my doorstep staring at folk, you know,' she snapped.

'Okay, thanks,' Grace nodded, her mind already working overtime.

'If you need to get in, I'd suggest going around the back. Someone tried to break in there a couple of days ago and there's a smashed window in the door. I've phoned your lot twice but no one bothered to come out. Still, no one got inside after I'd had words with them. Some of us are decent people, looking out for each other, you know.'

'Did you get a description of the burglar?'

'No, I didn't see his face.'

'You've been most neighbourly.' Grace smiled, trying not to roll her eyes. The woman was aiming to be as unhelpful as possible yet wanting to tell them what she knew regardless. 'We'll take a quick look while we're here.'

The woman was gone before she'd finished her sentence. Grace smirked at Frankie.

They walked to the end of the street and around into the cobblestoned alley that split the properties from the terraced row behind. Negotiating a settee that had been dumped, they located the gate of the property they needed and pushed it open.

They were in a yard, weeds popping through between crazy-paving, and black bags and rubbish piled high against a wall. The back door, like the woman had said, had a broken window pane at the top.

'Let's go in,' Grace said. 'We can always say we thought there was a threat to life, to reduce the fact we don't have a warrant. What do you think?'

'Sounds a good idea to me,' Frankie concurred.

They slipped on latex gloves.

Grace took out her baton and broke the glass a little more to allow her hand inside safely. From here, she undid the lock and pushed the door open.

They entered through a small vestibule into a galley kitchen, treading carefully over the broken glass.

'Police! Anyone home?'

They stood still, listening, but there was no noise. Grace picked up a pile of post.

'Most of this is addressed to Trudy Steele,' she said.

They looked around and, finding the rooms empty, went upstairs. Frankie checked the small bedroom at the front, Grace the bathroom at the rear. There were a few toiletries on the side of the bath – deodorant, a bar of soap – but there was no toothbrush, nor toothpaste. No toilet rolls.

'Grace,' Frankie shouted through to her.

'What is it?' She moved quickly to join him. What she saw took her breath away as she stepped across the threshold. A camera was perched on a tripod, pointing at the wall where, through what appeared to be a two-way mirror, she could see a double bed.

'It's set up so that someone can film people without them being aware, isn't it, boss?' Frankie shook his head in disbelief.

'The sick bastards.' Grace's voice was so low it was barely audible.

The room next door had soundproofing on all four walls. Grace tried not to imagine what had gone on in there but still, images flooded her mind. Young girls with men. This had to be part of the sex parties – one-on-one invitations. Some watched; some participated. She wondered how much a front row seat would cost. And here again, the girls were used like pieces of meat.

On the far wall was a cheap bookcase, a row of DVDs all in plastic covers. Frankie was going through them as Grace joined him. She picked one of them up. Written on a white label sticker was the name Stacey. She picked up another; the name was Rebecca. Another: Fiona. Another: Hannah.

She flicked through them all, looking for two names in particular but hoping she wouldn't find them.

There was nothing.

Grace went back along the landing to the room she'd seen through the mirror. There was a lock in the handle, hidden from plain view. She turned the knob, finding it unlocked, and went in. It was dark, with no window, and furnished with red velvet bedding to give the feel of a seedy hotel room.

A fridge stood in the corner. Grace opened it to find a bottle of champagne. She looked around for glasses but could find none. She'd check downstairs later.

'Boss.'

Grace turned to see him standing in the doorway. Frankie held out a notebook. She knew what it would be before looking inside. Confirming her fears, she read of woman after woman being paired off with man after man. There was even a seating system and who preferred who. There were lists of phone numbers and email addresses too.

It was a larger version of the notebook they'd found on Leon Steele when Jade had left him for dead. Back then, there hadn't been enough evidence inside that to charge anyone. Finding this brought everything out into the open and would give the CPS ample evidence to prosecute.

'It *is* like history repeating itself,' she muttered. 'Leon was taking over from his father.'

Frankie opened one of the bedside cabinets. 'There's everything in here,' he said. 'Sex toys, lubricant. Christ, there's Rohypnol too.'

Grace had seen enough. She radioed through to the control room, updating them on the situation. Then she spoke to Allie on the phone.

'Allie is on her way to the Steeles' home,' she told Frankie afterwards. 'We're going to meet her there and take both Leon and his wife in for questioning.' She paused, trying not to let her mind wander as her eyes fell on the bed.

Frankie shook his head, unable to speak.

Grace shuddered as her darkest thoughts came to fruition.

'Leon and Trudy,' she said. 'They're in on this together, aren't they?'

SIXTY-FOUR

Max removed his seatbelt as he and Rachel pulled up outside Leon's house.

'Stay here,' he told her. 'I'll be ten minutes, tops.'

'You'd better be quick,' Rachel replied. 'If the police turn up, I'm off. I'm in enough trouble without—'

Max was about to get out of the door but leaned back. He grabbed her chin and squeezed hard.

'You'll do as you're told, or Daddy will find out everything you've been up to.'

'You're hurting me.' Rachel's voice was muffled.

'You're going to wait?'

She nodded fervently.

'There's a good girl.' Max let go, pushing her away at the same time. 'You'd better be here. I won't be long.'

He marched up the path to Leon's house. Every time he'd visited, he'd been envious of what Leon had. He wasn't short of money, that was for sure. The house was detached with four bedrooms, a large conservatory off the kitchen, and a huge back garden. Two cars were parked on the drive with new number plates.

When Leon answered, he pushed past him and into the house, closing the door behind him quickly.

'I need my money.' Max eyed him shiftily.

'And what makes you think I'm going to pay you after what you did?' Leon snapped.

'Hey, it was down to Alex, not me. How was I supposed to know the police would raid the party? Are you sure he isn't working for both sides?'

'He got arrested.'

'Could have been a cover-up.'

Leon was thrown for a second. 'Anyway, I wasn't talking about Alex,' he went on. 'I told you to beat Erin about enough to get rid of the baby. I didn't tell you to kill her. Now they might be able to identify whose child it would have been. Did you think of that?'

Max paused. 'Can they do that?'

'I don't know, but I expect so.' Leon prodded Max in his chest. 'You're a prick. You could have set either one of us up. It's your own damn fault.'

'What's going on?'

Max turned to see Leon's wife, Trudy, walking towards them.

'I need my money,' Max said. 'From both of you.'

Leon stared at him.

'If you want to know who told me to get rid of the girl, you'd better start looking closer to home.' Max sniggered. 'It's been under your nose all the time.'

'Come on through and let's talk this out,' Trudy beckoned him.

Max watched as she swivelled on her heels, the red soles visible as she marched away. She really was a piece of work. In her poncy designer shoes, she thought she was something special. He wasn't sure who was the worst of the two of them.

Leon wasn't going to be too pleased with her when he found out the truth.

Leon followed Max into the kitchen. He wanted to grab him and rip his head off but he held his clenched fists behind his back, out of sight. He'd worked out the logistics of what Max had said, but he didn't want to believe it.

He turned to Trudy. 'You told him to kill Erin?' His voice was filled with incredulity.

Trudy moved towards them. 'She was getting in the way, especially because she was pregnant.'

'You knew?'

'Of course I did. Word travels fast.'

'It wasn't mine.'

'You know that for certain, do you?' Trudy spat at him. 'I know you've been taking her to Ranger Street without me.'

'So what? It's only because you don't give me any satisfaction.'

'That's because I'm not sixteen.'

'Can we leave the family arguments until I've got my cash?' Max checked his watch. 'I have to get out of here.'

'Don't think you're getting anything from me,' Leon snapped. 'You went too far.'

'I'm not taking the blame for it. You're the one who has a thing for the young women. Everyone knows. The police will find that out, if they haven't already.'

Leon grabbed Max's coat and pulled him in close. 'Watch your mouth.'

'You don't scare me with your big man attitude. You've always hidden behind Eddie. Everyone knows he's the stronger of the two of you.'

Leon glared back at Max for a moment before pushing him away roughly.

303

'Trudy, give him what you owe him and get him out of my sight. And then you and I need to talk.'

'You don't get to tell me what to do.' Max pulled out a chair at the kitchen table and sat down. 'I want my money.'

'Like I said, you're not getting anything from me.'

Leon's breath quickened as the tension in the air intensified. He watched Max's eyes as they flitted around the room. Leon sensed he was searching for something to attack him with. Max was a fighter, but Leon could outmatch him. And he knew it.

But before they could square up to one another, Trudy grabbed a knife from a block. She turned to face them both.

They stood in a triangle in the middle of the kitchen floor.

'Put that down,' Leon said softly.

'Don't patronise me,' she spat. 'You think I don't have it in me to put the knife in you?' She glanced at Max next. 'Or you? Well, you're wrong.'

Leon looked at Trudy. For the first time in his life, he was unsure of her. She had matched him in the things she was capable of. Who was to say she wouldn't go through with this? She really was an ugly woman, inside and out.

It might be for the best if Trudy got rid of Max, anyway.

But Max had ideas of his own. He lunged at Trudy, his fisted hand smacking into hers. The knife flew across the floor and he went after it. He grasped the handle just as knuckles come down on his back. Then a kick to the ribs. He turned quickly, the hand with the knife up in the air.

'Don't come any closer,' he said.

Leon laughed at him. 'You're on the floor like a dog. How exactly do you expect to get the upper hand in this situation?'

Max stabbed the knife into the outside of Leon's thigh.

Leon roared in surprise. He reached for the handle, pulling it out and turning the blade on Max. He raised his hand in the air.

Trudy grabbed a saucepan and hit Leon on the side of his head.

Leon staggered across the floor, trying to steady himself on the table. As he dropped the knife, it gave Max time to get to his feet.

Leon's vision doubled as he tried to focus, the two of them standing in front of him. He never knew who came at him with the blade but it was the last thing he saw as he dropped to the floor.

SIXTY-FIVE

'What the hell is going on?' Grace asked as they drove towards the Steeles' residence, Frankie driving now. 'Are the family so screwed up that they're walking in their father's footsteps? I mean, I got away from it before I was damaged. But Eddie and Leon, they lived through it, day after day, year after year. I had no idea it had affected Leon as well as Jade.'

'And Eddie,' Frankie said, squeezing through cars that had pulled over when they'd heard their sirens. 'It must have done. He's the leader of the family firm. He might keep quiet but he must know what's going on.'

'You could say that about anyone though. We could all crack under circumstances like that. We know most killers don't set out to kill someone.'

'Maybe, but this is some weird shit.'

In Broad Street, Frankie parked a few metres away from the Steeles' household. Unsure what they'd be walking into, and knowing the hostile nature of Leon, Grace had insisted they put on stab vests before leaving Ranger Street. She felt for the handle of her baton, checked her cuffs were in the inside pocket of her jacket. Pepper spray was in the other one.

As they got out of the car, Grace heard more sirens and saw Allie turn into the street. A marked car followed behind her.

The door to the house opened and Max came running out. Seeing them there, he sped across the garden and hopped over the wall.

'Police. Stop!' Frankie charged after him.

Trudy Steele appeared in the doorway, her hands covered in blood. 'Help him, he's dying,' she sobbed. 'You have to help Leon!'

Behind Grace, Frankie came back just as Perry arrived. 'He got away in a car. Rachel Townley was in the passenger seat.'

Grace frowned but had no time to understand the logic.

'Come with me.' Perry reached for his radio as he raced back to his car.

Grace was torn. She wanted to go with Perry to chase down Max but equally she wanted to assist Leon. Already she could see other officers running towards the house, so she wasn't really needed on the scene – but, if . . .

She couldn't abandon Leon.

'Go with Perry,' she told Frankie. Then she drew out her baton and followed Trudy into the house.

In the kitchen there was blood all over the floor. Trudy dropped down next to where Leon was gasping for breath.

'Step away,' Grace said to her as she slipped on latex gloves. She kneeled down next to Leon.

'Who did this to you?' She could see his eyes glazing over.

He tried to speak but she couldn't make out what he was saying. Blood poured out of his stomach. She put a hand over it and pressed down, hoping to stem the flow.

Leon grabbed her arm. Behind her Allie and another officer were restraining Trudy in handcuffs.

'It wasn't me who did this. It was Max!' Trudy cried. 'Let me go to my husband.'

'Eddie . . .' Leon gasped.

Grace leaned in closer to hear him.

'Tell . . .' he whispered. 'Tell . . . my brother . . . I love him.'

Leon took a few deep breaths as he fought for his life.

'Breathe with me, Leon,' Grace asserted. 'You need to stay awake. Open your eyes, and breathe with me. Come on: one, two. One, two.'

His chest was rising and falling as she counted but the effort was exhausting him and still the blood poured out.

An officer passed her a tea towel and she pressed it onto the wound. Leon groaned, and Grace almost cried with relief that he was still with them.

But as she heard ambulance sirens in the distance, Leon's hand flopped from his chest onto the floor.

'Leon?' She slapped at his face. 'Leon, wake up!'

His eyes fluttered open and then closed again.

'Leon! Stay with me!'

With blood oozing out of him, Grace sat back on her haunches, still putting pressure on the wound but feeling help-less, distraught, inept. Two paramedics came rushing in as Trudy began to scream.

As the paramedics took over, Grace pinched the bridge of her nose, squeezing her eyes shut. That wasn't supposed to happen. Now she wouldn't get justice. The bastard should have rotted in jail.

So why was she trying to hold in tears?

Max glanced at the rear-view mirror to see the police were too far away to catch him. He accelerated the car regardless, crashing over a hump as they gained speed.

'What's happened?' Rachel held on to the car door as she bumped up and down in her seat. 'Slow down, will you?'

'The cops are chasing me. Leon's wife's just stabbed him.'

'What? No way!' She turned to look behind her when she heard sirens. 'Why are the police chasing *you*?'

'Because I have a record and they're bound to blame me.'

He took a corner too fast, ending up on the wrong side of the road, narrowly missing a parked car.

'Slow down!' Rachel yelled. 'You're going to kill us!'

'Don't tell me what to do! This is all your fault.'

It was time to play his cards. A few months ago, Rachel had let it slip that her parents would be away all summer. Max said it would be the perfect place for the next party.

Unbeknown to her, Max had damning evidence that he knew she wouldn't want her parents to see: during the party at her house, he'd asked her to go with two of his friends. After plying her with alcohol, she'd still been hesitant but was okay with it. While all three were in her parents' bedroom, he'd secretly filmed and taken photos of her. From what he knew of her parents, they would disown her if the footage was ever leaked.

He quickly filled her in as he negotiated more roads, the police never far behind him. He'd be out on a main road in less than a minute. He could abandon the car and make a run from there.

'I trusted you!' Rachel reached for the door handle. 'Let me out of this car right now.'

'No!' Max leaned over to stop her, losing control. He went up the kerb and crashed into a lamppost at the side of the road. The airbags deployed with a loud hiss.

He scrambled for the door handle but before he had time to get out, Frankie and Perry were pulling them both from the vehicle.

Rachel was screaming and he was pushed to the floor and handcuffed.

'Nice try, Croydon,' Perry said as they both got to their feet after he'd read him his rights. 'I think you have some explaining to do.'

Frankie had cuffed Rachel but she wasn't going quietly. 'He was threatening me,' she shouted. 'I've had no choice but to do as I was told. I had nothing to do with anything.'

At the station, Max Croydon, Rachel Townley and Trudy Steele were downstairs in different cells waiting to be interviewed.

Grace sat at her desk, staring into space, the events of the morning catching up with her. Despite the paramedics working on him, Leon had died at the scene from his injuries. He had lost too much blood. Someone needed to tell the family what was going on. Eddie was going to be devastated, and her name was yet again going to be mud once details of his death came out, but it wasn't anything to do with her.

Now came the hard work, especially as it wasn't clear what had happened. It could have been Max or Trudy who had taken a knife to Leon, and it was going to be hard to prove either way. Unless the evidence overwhelmingly pointed to one of them, the onus would be on the officers to break them during their interviews. Grace couldn't join in with their questioning but for once she was glad to step back. This was definitely too close to home.

And now there were two murders to solve.

'Nice job,' she greeted Perry as he came back into the office.

'Same to you.' He sat down next to her. 'Sorry to hear about Leon. Are you okay?'

'Yes and no, but I'll be fine. Thanks.' She gave a faint smile.

Allie joined them to talk tactics.

'Interview time, although I reckon it's going to be one word against the other.' She looked at Perry. 'Do you want to speak to Trudy and I'll try and crack Max?'

Perry nodded.

'I'm sorry you can't join us, Grace,' Allie added. 'But rest assured, we all know how hard you've worked to get to this stage, and how emotionally invested you've been. It can't have been easy, especially after what's happened with Leon. I've sent a DS from the fraud team to break the news to the family. I think it's better all around that it's someone they're not familiar with.'

Grace nodded her thanks.

'Dave Barnett is processing the crime scene now but I thought we'd start our questioning before any of it comes back. See what they have to say for themselves. It won't be cut and dried, but if the evidence is there afterwards, and they've been untruthful, then the CPS may be on our side for longer sentencing.'

'Just make sure you charge them both,' she said.

Grace busied herself making coffee for everyone. She checked through her emails before going into the room downstairs in the custody suite that they used to transmit footage to a monitor. The interview was streaming, and she watched as Allie ran through the necessary formalities with Max Croydon and his solicitor before getting right down to business.

SIXTY-SIX

'Why were you visiting the Steeles this morning?' Allie asked Max Croydon.

'I often call. They're friends of mine.'

'It can't have been very social. You left your girlfriend outside.'

'She's just a friend.'

'Right.' Her tone was one of disbelief.

'We were going to have coffee but I realised as soon as Leon let me in and we'd gone through to the kitchen that I'd arrived in the middle of an argument between the two of them.' Max sat forward. 'The atmosphere was . . . icy . . . to say the least.'

'Did they mention why they had been arguing?'

'Of course not. I assumed it was just a domestic. Leon and Trudy are both as fiery as each other. They can start a fight at the drop of a hat.'

'Did you try to stop them?'

'I know better than to interfere. You should have seen Trudy, she was like a woman demented. There was no love lost between them, which is surprising considering what they do together.'

Allie played it as if they didn't know about the house in Ranger Street. 'What do you mean by that?'

Max sat back and folded his arms.

Watching from the monitor, Grace realised Max thought he had the upper hand. Which then gave Allie the element of surprise.

'They own a house,' he went on. 'At first it was for their pleasure. They used to film themselves getting it on.'

'Like a sex pad?'

Max nodded. 'They were into some weird stuff. They bought the house a couple of years ago. It was supposed to be just for them, but I guess they got bored with each other.' He sniggered. 'Too much of the same thing can turn anyone off.'

Allie waited for him to speak again.

'They started to bring girls back and Trudy would watch and film him having sex with them. But then she found out he was bringing Erin there more regularly, just the two of them. And when I told Trudy that Erin was pregnant . . .' Max drew his index finger across his neck. 'Well, it was only a matter of time before she was a goner.'

'Do you think the baby could have been his?'

'I told you before. Erin was a sleep around. It could have been anyone's. But Leon had taken a shine to her. He'd started seeing her a few times. I don't know what happened, whether he felt sorry for her or something, but he started to care too much. The next thing I knew there was a hit on her name.'

'A hit? To kill her?'

'Yes.'

'Who gave the orders?'

'Trudy did.'

Allie wondered why he gave up Trudy's name so readily. There was no reason why he shouldn't if it meant covering his own skin, but even so.

'She wanted rid of all the evidence linking Leon to Erin,' Max continued. 'Imagine if it came out that the baby was his, she'd said.'

'She said that to you?'

Max coughed. 'It's what I heard.'

Allie could see he thought he'd let a little too much information out.

'So you must know who killed Erin Ellis then?'

'No. I don't have a clue.'

'You had nothing to do with her murder?'

'That's right.'

'And you're also saying it was Trudy who killed Leon Steele?'

'Yes.'

'You have a memory that's convenient for some things and yet you can't recall others. It seems a bit too selective, to me.'

Max shrugged. 'Trudy was jealous of Erin and wanted her out of the picture. The fact she was pregnant was the last straw. She's a very jealous woman.'

Allie stayed quiet for a moment before launching in, pushing him more. 'Let's quit the lies, shall we? I believe it was you who took a knife to Erin Ellis, maybe on Trudy Steele's say so. When you came to the house for your money, Leon saw Trudy giving it to you and wanted to know what it was for. That's when a fight blew up between the three of you – not for the reasons you said, but because you'd been found out.'

'I didn't carry out the hit. I was as surprised as you were to hear that she'd been murdered.'

'So why did you run when we arrived at the scene earlier?'

'Because you were bound to blame me for Leon's murder. My prints are all over the knife.'

'We don't know that yet.'

'I didn't kill him. I didn't kill either of them!' Max was getting agitated now. 'Look, Leon told me to rough the girl up a bit. Trudy asked me to kill her. But I did neither. I was collecting money as if I had.'

'You expect us to believe that?'

314

'I'm telling you. I didn't kill her. I didn't kill either of them. I was just after the money for the girl. It could have been anyone who took a knife to her, but it wasn't me.'

'And what happened at the Steele property?'

'When Leon found out that Trudy had put the call out to get rid of Erin, he was furious. He and Trudy started to argue. I sat down at the table to wait for my money.'

'Even though you had nothing to do with the murder of Erin Ellis?'

'Yes. I know how stupid it was now, but I thought if I got the cash from both of them by telling them they were playing each other, I could skip town.'

Allie shook her head in disgust.

'When Leon got too much, Trudy picked up a knife. I stood up and tried to calm the situation, standing in between the two of them. Leon was shouting obscenities over my shoulder at Trudy. She was trying to get at him and pushed me to one side. I grabbed the knife from her and threw it across the floor.'

Max was acting out the scene with his hands.

'She yelled out in such a rage. I could see her looking for something else to use and then she grabbed for a saucepan. She cracked Leon across the head with that.'

'What did Leon do?'

'He was knocked to the floor. I helped him up but Trudy ran across to the knife and picked it up again. That's when she ran at Leon and stabbed him in the leg. I thought that was bad enough but as he swore at her, she stabbed him in the stomach.'

Through the monitor, Grace watched Max sit forward, glancing at Allie before bowing his head. She could almost see his brain working as he wondered what more he could say that would incriminate him less and implicate Trudy enough to take the full blame.

315

By the side of her, the door opened and Grace's concentration was interrupted.

'I thought you might like to know.' Frankie stood in the doorway. 'We found a DVD of Erin Ellis and Leon Steele in Rachel Townley's car. It was in a holdall we reckon belongs to Max. It was filmed in Ranger Street. Looks like Max took it for his own purposes. Whether to blackmail Leon to keep away from him, or to sell on, who knows.'

'Thanks, Frankie.' Grace nodded.

Frankie stood for a moment. 'Are you sure you'll be okay? I can stay with you if you'd like some company. It's been a shocking day for you.'

Grace smiled. It was thoughtful of him to ask.

'I'll be fine, but thanks anyway.'

She waited for the door to close again before letting a few tears fall. She wasn't sure she could hold it all in until she got home. But she wouldn't miss Perry interrogating Trudy Steele.

Not for anything.

SIXTY-SEVEN

In interview room six, Perry was in full swing, but he was finding it difficult to be heard. Trudy Steele hadn't stopped ranting yet, despite her solicitor trying to intervene and get her to calm down.

'I can't believe Leon is dead,' she cried.

'We're all sorry for your loss, Mrs Steele.'

'No you're not.' Trudy wiped at her nose with a tissue before continuing. 'Leon had it so tough. You have no idea what he went through as a child. He was bullied by his father, his mother did nothing to stop it and his brother joined in. He was always being beaten for something he hadn't done. That's why he turned out like he did. He could be like an animal with me at times. He was cruel, vindictive, coercive. He did things to me that I'm too ashamed to admit.'

'Things you didn't consent to?'

'Look at me.' She prodded her chest. 'I'm less than nine stone and five foot three. Leon was a tower of strength. He overpowered me all the time.'

Perry frowned. 'Are you saying you did what you did because you were scared of him?'

'No, I'm telling you that I'd be *too* scared to harm him. Leon controlled me.'

'I understand that. Was it too dangerous to leave?'

'Yes. I was helpless. He gave me no money, he would lock me in the house and I couldn't get out. He would leave me inside for days on end while he went about his business.'

Perry scowled, knowing instantly that she was lying. Even with his little knowledge of the beauty industry, he could see she used Botox, was dressed in the latest designer clothes and her hair was styled and cut expertly. Her nails were also long and manicured. She couldn't do all that without leaving the house.

'What about your children?' he asked. 'Surely they would have seen this happening?'

Trudy shrunk back in her seat a little.

'It was never in front of them. They're not in much now they're older anyway.'

Watching on the monitor, Grace could see Perry was having his doubts.

'And you never told anyone?' he went on.

Trudy shook her head. 'I was ashamed.'

'I can understand that too. But, to me, it seems you had more reason to attack Leon in that moment than Max Croydon.'

'No! I wouldn't dare to stab Leon. What if I had attacked him and he'd survived? He would have retaliated. He could be crueller than you will ever know. Jade wasn't the only one in the Steele family damaged because of George.'

'Tell me what happened today then, Trudy.'

'Max came to the door. Leon let him in and as soon as they were in the kitchen, they started to fight.'

'Do you know what about?'

'I didn't have time to hear. I was trying to stop them. Leon was getting the better of Max and that's when Max grabbed a knife from the block on the worktop. He stuck it in Leon's leg so I hit Max with a saucepan. I thought it might knock him out but he came back at Leon with the knife again.' She looked at Perry, tears pouring down her face. 'That's when Max stabbed Leon in the stomach. I tried to stop him, but he was too strong.'

'Are you sure about that, Trudy?' Perry questioned. 'Max doesn't have a head wound, and yet Leon does . . .'

'I-I, yes I hit Max.'

'So why did Leon have a head wound?'

'I can't recall everything! It all happened so quickly.'

'Perhaps you could have hit Leon with the saucepan and then not remembered?'

'You're putting words in my mouth.' Trudy glanced at her solicitor in exasperation. 'Do I have to answer all these questions? My husband is dead. I'm in shock.'

'It's okay, Trudy,' Perry said, holding up a hand to the solicitor. 'I don't want to cause you any unnecessary stress. I've found in my line of work the evidence never lies. We'll go back and question Max again. And then we'll look into your family and background. Then we'll question you further as to how Leon got that head wound. Because Max said it was you who hit Leon.'

'He's lying. They were fighting and he stabbed Leon.'

'When our officers got to your home, Leon was on the floor, bleeding from his wounds. Why hadn't you called for an ambulance?'

'I was about to, when I heard sirens. I ran outside for help, and to get away from Max.'

'Did Max try to stop you?'

Trudy paused for a moment as if she was recollecting, before nodding.

'He grabbed my arm as I went past but I punched out at his hand until he let me go. I couldn't stay in there with him and I had to get help for Leon. So I ran to the front door. That's when we saw the police and Max made a run for it. I'm telling the truth.' As if remembering about Leon, Trudy's face crumbled. 'I can't believe he's gone. I did love him.'

'Tell me about the girl, Erin.'

'I don't know anything about her.'

'I think you do.' Perry pushed a box of tissues towards Trudy but continued with his questioning. 'I think you and Max are in this together. I think Erin's murder was planned to get her out of the picture and I think Leon's death was spur of the moment, but a good call for one of you. And my money is on you. I think it was you that killed Erin *and* Leon.'

'No!' Trudy sat forward. 'I would never – I could never. You have to believe me. It was Max. Max killed Erin.'

'Max said that Leon just wanted him to beat her up, enough so that she would lose the baby.'

'He's lying.' Trudy shook her head fervently.

'So it was Max's idea to kill Erin?'

'Yes. He wanted her dead.'

'Whereas you . . .'

'I was worried, yes, but I wouldn't want to harm her.'

'Why not? Surely your husband being the father of Erin's baby would have been detrimental for you and your future with Leon?'

'She wasn't pregnant with his baby.' Trudy laughed hysterically. 'He didn't see her that much.'

'Not even when she was at the party at 7 Park Avenue? Or 25 Sandon Crescent? Or how about 11 Ranger Street?'

Trudy stared at them, tears beginning to fall down her cheeks. She wiped at them furiously.

'We've had evidence come to light. A DVD showing Leon and Erin together at your house in Ranger Street. It was recorded two months ago.'

'I don't know about that. I didn't have anything to do with that house.'

'So your prints won't be anywhere at the property?'

She shook her head but there was uncertainty in her eyes.

'Maybe you had the house cleaned so that we wouldn't find traces of you as Trudy. Fine, but will there be a trail left behind of you as Angela Merchant? Because that is you, isn't it?'

Trudy's shoulders sagged.

'You were in charge of the parties, getting the girls and the men there, weren't you? You, Alex, Max and Rachel.'

'Rachel?' Trudy scoffed. 'She was just a toy. Max had a thing for good-looking women and she obviously got drawn in by his bad boy image. But she was stupid. Any fool could see he was using her. She should have been more savvy.'

'So it was just you who saw to the financial side of things? That's before we start looking through the recordings that you did at Ranger Street.'

'You have no proof.'

Perry leaned to his side and picked up an evidence bag. He watched Trudy's face drop when she saw what was inside it.

'We found this notebook at Ranger Street. Is this your handwriting?'

Trudy squirmed in her seat but said nothing.

'All the numbers relate to discs we've found with the girls' names on them. There's so much more detail here than in the one we found on Leon two years ago. Thankfully, you're very thorough.'

'It wasn't me,' Trudy said. 'I didn't kill the girl.'

'But you killed Leon, didn't you? Perhaps in a fit of rage,

321

when he found out you were involved. He didn't want Erin Ellis dead, and you had ruined everything. You were jealous that he wanted to be with her rather than you. And the fact people would find out it could have been Leon's baby would make you look a fool. That wasn't acceptable, was it Trudy?'

'It wasn't like that.'

'Did he not love you any more?' Perry continued. 'Was that what this was all about? Was that why he was mad that you'd set out to murder her?'

'He didn't love her. He loved me!'

'So you killed the one thing that was coming between you both . . . and then you killed him.'

'He was my husband! I wasn't going to let some slip of a girl pretend that she had been sleeping with him.'

'That's why you wanted her dead. If the baby was Leon's, you couldn't deny their involvement any more.'

'Yes, I wanted her dead, but I didn't kill her.'

'But you did kill Leon.'

'No, I—' Trudy banged her palm on the table.

'He had let you down again; made a fool out of you, I get it. Only this time, if the baby was his, there would be no hiding it from everyone. You hit him with the saucepan intending on killing him.'

'He was stronger than me!'

'So you took a knife to him while he was down. It was a way out for you, wasn't it? After all the years he had treated you bad, this was how it could be over.'

'Yes, it was me. I killed him!' She stood up and leaned across the desk. 'He deserved to die after what he'd done to me.'

Grace was standing up as she watched the monitor. She'd been on pins waiting for the interview to finish, not wanting to leave until it did. But the jealous rage that had finished off

322

Trudy Steele had made her realise what had happened with Erin Ellis.

Needing to speak to Allie, she rushed upstairs. They had to get to Sampson Street.

SIXTY-EIGHT

Grace sighed as Allie pulled up in Sampson Street. 'We're going to wreck a whole family,' she said.

'Yes, but at least another will find some closure,' Allie replied.

They walked in silence to the Redferns' front door.

Lucy greeted them and showed them through to the living room, where Molly was curled on the settee and Phil was in the chair by the window. Molly sat up when she saw them, more nervous than earlier that day.

Grace sat down on an armchair. Allie chose to stand.

'Molly, we've had some major developments in the case regarding Erin,' Allie said. 'It's time you came clean once and for all. We know what happened but we'd like to give you the chance to tell us first.'

'Mum.' Molly began to cry.

Lucy went to sit next to Molly and wrapped an arm around her. 'Can't you see how stressful this is to keep going over and over for her? She's lost her best friend.'

'I understand that, Mrs Redfern, but we must ask these questions.' Allie nodded at Grace to continue.

'We think that you and Erin got into a fight about her having the baby.'

'No.' Molly shook her head.

'You were arguing before you went into the walkway and then when you entered it, things got nasty and it ended up in a fight. It was you who stabbed her, wasn't it?'

'She was my friend,' Molly replied, as the colour drained from her face.

Lucy went to protest but Grace held her hand up to stop her.

'Friends don't keep secrets, do they, Molly?' she continued. 'We know from Erin's diary that she was seeing someone else besides Max. Were you consumed with jealousy, and the rage come out of you when she said whose baby it was? Because she thought it was Lion Man's, didn't she?'

'She wanted to sleep with everyone and she wouldn't listen,' Molly said. 'She didn't care. She just wanted attention.'

'So you argued when you were in the walkway and then you took out a knife and you stabbed her.'

'No!' Lucy cried.

'I—' Molly faltered.

'I know you didn't intend to kill her, but she made you so angry. Afterwards, you deleted the photos of anything to do with the men and the parties from both yours and Erin's phone, and then you hid the knife down the drains. That's why you didn't call an ambulance straight away, isn't it? You did have your phone on you, but you were busy hiding evidence of what you'd done.'

Molly was sobbing openly now. So too was Lucy. Phil hung his head down as if he didn't want to hear any more.

'Because it was hurting you, wasn't it?' Grace continued. 'All the attention she was getting.'

'She was supposed to be my friend.'

325

'You were annoyed that Erin was going to Ranger Street with Lion Man, weren't you?'

'She kept going on about it, as if it was some kind of special treat that only she was allowed. I asked Chad to take me but he told me I couldn't go and that I wasn't to mention it to anyone. He got really angry with me. But Lion Man said he'd take me instead.'

Grace leaned across and took her hand. 'Molly, I need to hear in your own words what happened in that walkway.'

SIXTY-NINE

Last Wednesday evening

Molly pulled away when Erin tried to link an arm through hers. 'What were you and Leon talking about earlier?' she snapped. 'You looked very happy, given the circumstances. You should have told him by now. Besides, everyone will know soon – you're so skinny that you're beginning to show already.'

'You're not to tell anyone,' Erin emphasised. 'You said you wouldn't.'

'But he should know. It's only fair that he does.'

'I will tell him, just not yet.'

'Why, because you think he'll want you to get rid of it?'

Erin stepped away from her. 'You can be really cruel at times.'

'You're the one who's pregnant and won't tell anyone until it's too late for you to have an abortion.' Molly marched ahead for a few steps.

'That's not the reason why.'

Molly stopped and turned back. 'Yes, it is. You've been after Leon since Max got fed up of you and went off with Rachel. And now you've trapped him.'

Molly continued to walk, Erin keeping up at her side. They turned into the walkway that would lead them home.

'You're only annoyed because you like him,' Erin countered.

'Well, he must like me too, because we went to Ranger Street last week.'

'What?' Erin stopped. 'You're lying.'

'I am not,' she fibbed. 'He took me upstairs to the red room. We had a glass of champagne and then we had sex in the middle of that huge bed. He was making me laugh because he said no one could hear us. The walls were soundproofed, he said.'

'You're lying!' Erin's voice rang out along the narrow pathway. 'Someone's told you what the room looks like. I bet it was Rachel. You seem very friendly with her now you know that she split me and Max up.'

'Rachel is far more mature than you'll ever be.'

'You're only jealous because I'm having this baby.'

'It might not be his.'

'It is. I know it is.'

Molly turned to see Erin with her phone in her hand. 'What are you doing?'

'I'm ringing him to find out if you're telling the truth. I think you're trying to split us up because you're jealous.'

'Envious of a tramp like you who gets pregnant at the first sniff of a man? I don't think so.' Molly pointed at Erin. 'You're infatuated by him and he's conning you.'

'I'm going to ring him.' Erin started to scroll through her contacts.

Molly couldn't believe her eyes. 'You can't do that.' She snatched the phone from Erin.

'Give it back.' Erin held out her hand, tears welling in her eyes. 'You're supposed to be my friend and you've been going behind my back and sleeping with him as well.'

'He likes me too.'

'Give me my phone.'

'No.' Molly clicked on the photos icon and began to delete some of the images as she kept it out of Erin's grasp. 'You're going to get him in trouble if you call him. He does have a wife and kids, you know.'

'But once he finds out I'm having his baby, that will change everything.'

Molly wondered who was the smartest between them. Was it her for trying to be Leon's special girl? Or was it Erin for trapping him, having something that would tie her to him for the rest of their lives? No one could hide a baby. Envy bubbled up inside her.

'You don't know it's his,' she argued. 'You shouldn't have got pregnant when you were sleeping with so many men.'

'And you shouldn't have been seeing him at all because you knew I was.'

'He's clearly going off you and getting in to me.'

'Like he would do that.'

'What's that supposed to mean?'

'Just give me my phone!'

'If you want it, go and find it.' Molly drew back her hand and threw the phone into the hedges.

'You utter cow!' Erin pushed Molly out of the way. 'I'm going home to tell my mum. She'll have to come and help me look for it.'

'I bet Mummy dear would love to know her precious child is up the duff,' she shouted.

'Leave me alone.'

'I think I might tell her.'

Erin spun round then. 'You wouldn't dare.'

'Watch me. I've already told Max and Chad, and Jeff. I'm going to tell everyone else. You're a slut, Erin Ellis.'

Erin slapped Molly hard across the face.

Molly gasped as she held on to her cheek. They had argued many times but neither of them had ever struck the other.

'You bitch,' she said quietly. Then she launched herself at Erin.

Erin balled her hand into a fist and punched Molly in the eye.

Molly tried to defend herself but Erin was too strong. She bent her head as fists came down on her back. She had never seen Erin so angry.

Her hand reached inside the pocket of her jeans, her fingers clasping the knife she carried for protection. In a moment of madness, she reached for it, flicked out the blade and plunged it into Erin's chest.

Erin gasped at the force. Her eyes widened with fear and she groaned before staggering backward a few steps.

'Erin!' Molly said. 'Oh, Erin, I'm sorry.' She pulled the knife out, dropping it on the grass.

Erin fell to her knees before falling to the side.

Molly bunched her hair in her hands and pulled at it as she stared at her friend in disbelief.

As Erin's breathing became laboured, blood pouring from the wound, Molly glanced around to see if anyone had seen them. But the alleyway was quiet.

'Please don't die.' Molly kneeled and cradled her friend in her arms. She looked down at her, seeing the pain etched on her face and then screamed into the night.

In Sampson Street, were lights, people. But all she could hear were the sickening sounds made by Erin as she gasped for breath. Molly watched the blood seeping through Erin's fingers as she held her hands against the wound in her chest.

Erin coughed and tried to take a deep breath. It rattled inside her chest as if she was drowning.

Molly sobbed. Why had they even started to argue? She

always had to take things too far. Now everything was going to come out, whether she liked it or not. Nothing was going to be secret soon.

Gently she laid her friend's head down on the tarmac. As if she sensed what Molly was about to do, Erin tried to talk.

'Don't go,' she whispered, coughing from the sheer effort.

Tears poured down Molly's face. 'I won't be long, I promise.' She was too scared to call an ambulance because she'd be in so much trouble. And Sara would know best what to do. 'I'm going to fetch your mum.'

'No.' Erin held up her hand.

Molly gave it a quick squeeze but stood up anyway. She turned and, with one last glance back, ran. It was the hardest thing she had ever done, leaving Erin there, knowing that she might not be alive when she got back. But she knew what she had to do first. She picked up the knife, wiping it as clean as she could with the sleeve of her denim jacket. Then she ran towards Sampson Street, all the time making up a story and a mental picture of a man attacking Erin. She would pretend he looked like Thomas Haddington. He'd been really nasty to her the last time she'd seen him.

She stopped and looked back. Why had she thrown the phone into the hedges? She could have got rid of it but now she wouldn't be able to find it in time. But she had the knife. She would hide that, and then get rid of it later.

SEVENTY

Grace looked at Molly as she sat on the settee next to her mum. Tears poured down Lucy's cheeks, the disbelief etched across her face as she'd removed her arm from around her daughter's shoulders a few minutes ago.

Molly had ripped at a tissue as she'd confessed. A small pile of white shreds lay in between her feet on the carpet. Phil had sunk in a chair across from them, his head in his hands.

'It's the reason why we could find no evidence, isn't it, Molly?' Grace said. 'There was no one seen coming in or out of the pathway. Your trainers and clothes had blood on them because you'd comforted Erin, but *after* you'd stabbed her. There wasn't a trace of anything from anyone else because it was you who killed her. It was your knife, wasn't it?'

Lucy gave out a sob. 'Please tell me this isn't true, Molly,' she cried. 'We can—'

'I'm sorry, Mum!' Molly spoke through her tears.

Lucy clearly didn't know what to do. Grace assumed her disbelief was turning to acceptance. Her daughter had murdered her best friend. It didn't seem feasible. But it was true.

'Molly Redfern, I'm arresting you for the murder of Erin

Ellis.' As she recited the remainder of the arrest statement, her words were drowned out by Molly's cries.

'I didn't mean it, Mum,' she said. 'Mum! Dad!'

Grace watched as she pleaded with her parents to help her, to say it was all a misunderstanding. Everything would be all right. Because that's what parents do.

But not this time. Lucy seemed shell-shocked, unable to look at Molly. Phil stood up and she followed suit. He opened his arms and his wife broke down inside them.

'Where is the knife, Molly?' Allie asked.

'It's buried at the bottom of our garden.'

Lucy's sobs pierced the air.

'Can you show me?'

Back at the station, Grace was sitting at her desk again. Molly Redfern had been booked in to the custody suite and was awaiting the arrival of her legal representation.

'What made you think it was Molly?' Allie asked.

'I thought all along it was someone from those parties,' Grace admitted. 'It made sense that one of the men would want to get Erin out of the way as she was pregnant. But nothing seemed to fit into place until Trudy Steele was interviewed. The way she spoke out about her jealousy over Leon taking Erin to Ranger Street without her, I realised that it might have been the same for Molly. But also, I'm not sure I believed Trudy's story about Leon being cruel to her. I thought she was making some of it up, perhaps to make us feel sorry for her. So I thought I'd try and gently break Molly down too. It would only have been a matter of time before it got too much for her to keep to herself.'

Allie smiled but it morphed into a sigh. 'I bet Molly was probably relieved to let it all out.'

'Her dad told me before I left that she'd tried to take her own life yesterday. She was desperate for a way out.'

'Well, at least now she might get some support. I can't help feeling sorry for her, under the influence of those men and pitted against her best friend all the time. They knew how to play to their insecurities. It's such a sad case.'

Grace nodded. Although one young girl's life had been lost, they had stopped other innocent girls being dragged into a seedy world of sex, drugs and alcohol. For now.

SEVENTY-ONE

Two weeks later

Lucy waited until it was dark before she went out of the house. She pulled her coat closer around her as she ran across the road to dodge the rain. It had been a miserable, grey day, pouring down for most of the afternoon. Christmas would be upon them soon and this year would be the first time she wouldn't be looking forward to it.

She and Phil were coping okay, all things considered. For something so tragic, they had drawn together closer, comforting and reassuring each other in equal measures. Their families had rallied round them too. Not a one had said a bad word, even if they thought it in private.

Some of the neighbours had shunned them, but most had been understanding, and in shock as much as they were. Even so, neither of them felt that they belonged in Sampson Street the way they used to.

At Sara's house, Lucy took a deep breath and rang the bell. It was two weeks since she had last spoken to her best friend.

She wasn't certain if she would even listen to her, but she had to try.

The hall light came on and she saw a shadow through the glass pane. When Sara opened the door, all the words Lucy had rehearsed disappeared. Her mouth hung open as she saw how pale her friend was; how much weight she had dropped since Erin had died.

Lucy took a deep breath. 'For the past fortnight, I've wanted to come across and say how sorry I am and how much I miss Erin. I've wanted to say I wished it had never happened, and that I was there for you if you needed me.' Tears dripped down her cheeks. 'I've wanted to say I couldn't believe what Molly had done. But as I stand here now, all I can think is: what kind of mother doesn't see the signs that their daughter is a killer?'

'I could say similar, too.' Sara folded her arms, but then her expression softened in pain. 'I didn't notice that Erin was pregnant.'

'They kept so much from us, didn't they?'

Sara nodded. 'They were scared.'

'But I should have noticed what Molly had done. I didn't even suspect her – how terrible is that?'

'She loved Erin as much as we did. She would have been desperately upset at what happened.'

'I know, but—'

'This isn't your fault, Lucy. The girls had been coerced into something beyond their control. The only reason Molly was carrying a knife was for protection against those awful men.'

'It doesn't make it any better.' She was crying openly now.

Sara held out her arms. In seconds, they were both sobbing.

It felt good to embrace her friend, knowing that whatever happened from now, she had at least been able to do this.

'I know it's not the same because I can see Molly every month, but I'm going to miss them both so much,' Lucy said as she stepped back, wiping at her eyes. 'I wanted you to know that Phil and I are putting the house up for sale.'

'You don't have to do that.'

'It's too painful to live here now, so close to where it happened. Some of the neighbours look at us as if we're going to murder someone too. But worse . . . I can't stop thinking about how it was Molly. And yet she loved Erin as much as we did.'

Sara nodded. 'I was thinking the same thing, actually. A fresh start might do me and Nat good. Yet I can't move from here because it *is* so close. I know it sounds silly but I can go through the walkway and feel her there. It's a comfort.'

Lucy understood what it was like to have the heart ripped out of your family – she really did.

'How is Nat?' she asked.

'He's coping. It's hard for us but Rob is coming back soon for the funeral.' She paused. 'You're both welcome to come, you know.'

'I'd like that.'

They smiled at each other. There was no need for any more words. It was enough.

Eddie lay awake the next morning. It had been a trying fort-night, to say the least. Finding out that Leon had been killed by Trudy, and that they were both in a way responsible for the death of Erin Ellis, had been a bitter blow to take. He'd blamed himself at first. If he hadn't interfered by giving Grace infor-mation, his brother would still be alive.

He missed Leon deeply. It hadn't all been war and game playing. He remembered the time when he had held his nephew for the first time, and the look that had passed between him and Leon. The proud brother moment. They had been close, at points.

It was sad to see how one man could have such an influence

over so many people, even after his death. George Steele was Eddie's father by nature but had never been a dad to him. Even now, the smell of his father's cheap aftershave could trigger a reaction that could make him retch. He was a bully. No one would truly know how much pain they had all suffered at his hands.

The news about Nick Carter had also been a terrible blow. How Eddie had found out from Leon still haunted him, but it was the way he'd been played for years that really tortured him. Leon and Kathleen had kept it from him. He felt like collateral damage. If anything had happened to him in his earlier days, when crime was all he lived for, he would have gone to prison. There would have been no one there to help him out.

And yet, he still felt protective towards Kathleen. George had made her into the woman she was today – and Jade, to a point. She'd been damaged by him too.

He couldn't believe how much he had mellowed since Grace had come into his life. Even his wife had commented on it, and they were getting on better as a result. Losing Leon and Trudy had hit her just as much. It was time to start looking after his family, putting them first and keeping on the right side of the law. He didn't want to end up in prison too.

Eddie reached for his phone and sent a message.

SEVENTY-TWO

Grace hadn't been surprised when she received a message from Eddie asking her to call in and see him. Even though she knew she shouldn't, she was going to go. It would be the last time, so she didn't let herself feel guilty about it. There was unfinished business to discuss.

When she stepped inside Steele's Gym, her stomach lurched in a familiar way as she tried to forget what it all stood for. She marched across the floor. The door to the office was open so she knocked on the frame and went in.

'Grace.' Eddie's smile was warm. 'Come and take a seat. Would you like a coffee?'

'No, thanks. I won't be stopping long.' She'd give him twenty minutes at the most. 'You wanted to see me?'

'Yes, now things have gone quieter, there's something I need to tell you.'

Then there was silence.

'How are you doing?' she asked him eventually.

'Now that my brother is dead, my mother is a hypocrite and my sister-in-law and sister are in prison?' His tone was bitter. 'Not too good, to be honest. But Leon had to be stopped. He

339

was bad blood, and I'm not like that. I need you to know I wasn't into it, and I never helped him. I constantly warned him about it but he wouldn't listen.'

Grace moved around on her chair. 'You wanted rid of Leon, didn't you?'

'I did, but not this way. I hated what he was doing. He was the cruel one of the two of us.'

'Yet you knew what he was up to, and did nothing?'

'Kathleen went away last summer. I found out afterwards that Leon used the family house to hold a party. I could never forgive him, bringing that sort of stuff to our doorstep after what happened to Jade.'

Grace shuddered inwardly at the mention of her name. She still found it tough to talk about her.

'I knew if we argued about it, one of us would end up going too far,' Eddie continued. 'Especially when things were coming to light after Erin Ellis was murdered.'

'Did you ever think he had killed her?'

'Once or twice. He was capable of it.'

'I must admit I was surprised to learn that Trudy was so involved.'

Eddie nodded. 'The only way I could think of putting a stop to it all was by leading you to Sandon Crescent. I heard Leon on the phone to Max telling him to cancel the party. But I persuaded Alex to go ahead with it.'

'You wanted us to send Leon down. Get him out of your hair.'

He nodded. 'I didn't want him dead though.'

Grace wondered what effect Leon's death had had on him. The brothers might not have got on at times but they had been close when they were younger. She imagined going through that kind of trauma together played a huge part in it.

'There's something else you should know,' Eddie said. 'It's about Nick Carter.'

Grace tried not to let her jaw drop as he told her what he knew. How had Nick had the audacity to have a go at her about her family when he was Leon's father? She couldn't help but wonder if he'd assisted Leon in any way. He could have covered up for him over the years.

Back then, when everyone was thinking that she was the bent copper among them, not only was Alex Challinor corrupt, but Nick was too.

Now she realised why she'd got the job. It must have made his day when she put in for it. And all that talk about him sticking up for her with the DCI. That was for his own benefit.

'The sneaky bastard,' she muttered.

'It was a shock to me too,' Eddie admitted. 'And how Leon told me, to get one over on me? Well, let's just say there was no family loyalty, no love lost after that.'

The silence was back again. Grace could hear music in the background now, the odd thump of a glove on a punch bag.

'Do you think there is any way we could call a truce?' Eddie asked.

Grace was shocked at what he'd said, but also at the feel of her stomach lurching. He was her half-brother – Leon hadn't been related to her at all – but still, Eddie was on the wrong side of the law.

'I don't know.' She sighed to show her frustration. 'It's very complicated. And how do I know you're not setting me up again? Making out that you've gone legit to keep me from your trail?'

'Do you think that?'

'You've done it before.'

'Only when it served a purpose.'

'When the outcome was going to be good for *you*, you mean.'

'I was on your side most of the time.'

Grace shook her head. 'No, you were on Eddie's side.'

He smiled and she couldn't help but return it.

Now that Leon was out of the picture, Eddie was promising to stay out of her way. Did he mean that he would go clean? Had it always been Leon behind everything? She bit at her bottom lip as she wondered what to say next.

Grace would never stop watching him and he would never trust her not to. It was a mutual thing. She decided she *couldn't* trust him. But she wasn't going to let him know that.

She nodded. 'Okay, a truce it is. You stay away from my job and I'll stay away from you.'

He held out his hand. 'It's a deal.'

She wasn't prepared for the rush of emotion that crashed through her when her fingers slipped around his. There was some connection there but, sadly, it could never be more than that. No visiting the family. No spending time getting to know his wife, or his two boys. It wasn't fair, but it was the way it had to be.

'I have something to tell you, too,' she said. 'I was waiting until after Leon's funeral but now seems a good time. I was with him when he died. I sat by his side, holding his hand as the paramedics worked on him. But before that he'd spoken to me. His last words to me were: "Tell my brother I love him".'

Tears glistened in Eddie's eyes as he struggled to hold in his emotion. She squeezed his hand quickly before turning to leave.

'Thanks, Grace.'

She held in her own tears as she left, for good this time. Outside, she got into her car and sat behind the wheel, knowing she could at least relax for now. From where it all began, with Operation Wedgwood two years ago, they had finally pulled the plug on the sex parties. Leon had been untouchable then, but this time they had found the evidence, and he had been killed because of it.

Leon's death still haunted Grace's dreams. She'd woken up several times, crying at how she'd been trying to save his life over and over, but couldn't. But she knew the memories would fade eventually. And at least she could put to bed a few ghosts of her own. There was no one in that group now who could exploit a woman so that she would end up like Jade Steele, damaged enough to want revenge on every man who had hurt her.

She closed her eyes as images of her own capture pressed to the front of her mind. Back in the room that she had been imprisoned in as a child. Yet again, she said a silent prayer to her mum, the woman who had been brave enough to risk everything to lead them to safety, away from the violence of George Steele.

Grace would have to forgo seeing her half-niece Megan, which was a shame, but at least she still had Simon's daughter Teagan. And a special place in her heart had been created for Simon, next to her memories of Matt, who would always be there too. Her mum took up the final space.

She was glad to have nothing to do with Kathleen Steele. Kathleen had thought that the police were stupid. Grace realised she must have known what was going on and again, turned a blind eye. How could she keep lying to protect herself after all she'd suffered as a wife in an abusive relationship? It was beyond comprehension. Usually victims like that were much better at stopping things, not letting them go on. Kathleen Steele would have to move on with her life instead of hanging on to the past. What was done was done.

Grace wondered how Eddie really felt without Leon. Did he miss having his brother around or had he really become too much of a liability? After all, Eddie had led her to Leon.

She would never know, as she wasn't going to see him again. But she was going to tell Allie what he'd told her about Nick. Her boss would know what had to be done.

As she started the car and drove towards the exit, Grace looked across at the building one more time. She hoped Eddie would keep his word. She didn't want to put all the Steele family behind bars. But she would if it was necessary.

SEVENTY-THREE

Six months later

It had been a busy time since the charges had been brought in connection with Operation Doulton. Over the past few months, several young women had come forward after the death of Leon and arrest of Trudy Steele. Grace had helped the Major Crimes Team to collate and put together the evidence needed to get the perpetrators put away. As word got out, more girls came forward, more names were gathered and the case took on a life of its own. The evidence against the accused was damning. There were a lot of young girls and women in the city, many she doubted they knew about, who were living their lives as they were supposed to now. Getting back their teen years, rather than becoming vulnerable sex slaves.

Grace hadn't seen Eddie since that day they'd met up two weeks after Leon had been killed, and Trudy had subsequently been charged and remanded in prison. The murder of Leon and the sentencing of Trudy had left two boys without parents, so now Kathleen was looking after three of her grandchildren – the boys and Megan. Grace couldn't imagine it was ideal yet, regrettably, it was the position they were in, and they were all teenagers, soon to be grown-ups in their own right.

Grace had been present at Molly's trial last month. It had been heartbreaking to see Molly as she was given a five-year sentence. She had been mixed up in this because of those men. They had lured her and Erin, given them money, drugs and alcohol, and a lot of false stories and promises. Preying on a girl like Erin, whose parents had recently split up, was par for the course. She was glad none of them would be able to do it all again.

The one thing Grace had been totally blindsided by was Trudy being involved. To her, Trudy had seemed like the innocent wife, whose husband was off having affairs everywhere. But when it had come to light that she knew what was happening all along, it made her in some ways more callous than the men.

Grace had settled into her new role with Frankie. Her position in the Community Intelligence Team had become a permanent one. For now, the role was working well. She and Frankie were making waves in a good way with the communities they served. People were trusting them more after the media spoke about the Doulton case. There were a lot of single parents on the estates and the fact they had helped to stop this gang was good in their eyes.

She heard the front door open and close, car keys thrown on the hall table.

'Please tell me you have it,' she shouted to Simon.

'Yes, here it is.' He handed her a copy of that day's *Stoke News*.

'You know that's not what I want first.' Behind his back was a brown paper bag. She sniffed. She could smell bacon.

'I'll dish brunch out while you read it.'

'How did I manage to find you?' Grace grinned. 'You're perfect for me.'

He leaned down to kiss her and then went through to the kitchen. Grace scanned the front page and then went on to page five to read the rest:

GROOMING GANG JAILED – Simon Cole, Senior Crime Editor, Stoke News.

One woman and three men were given a combined total of twenty-eight years imprisonment at Hanley Crown Court yesterday.

Trudy Steele, 37, was jailed for fifteen years for her part in the sex ring. She also received a further life sentence for the murder of her husband, Leon Steele, 39. Former detective constable Alex Challinor, 42, was jailed for three years; Jeffrey Harvey, 46, for two years; and Max Croydon, 25, eight years, for their parts in the grooming ring. Trevor Merchant, 52, took his own life two months before the trial started. He was facing charges of procuring prostitutes, running a brothel and sexual exploitation.

The court heard how the gang had groomed girls as young as fourteen, luring them with gifts and money and handing them free food and a place to hang out with friends at Potteries Takeaway. Following the death of Erin Ellis last year, the police were able to gather more evidence to shut the grooming ring down.

'We've been watching this group of people for quite some time now, building up evidence, and finally we were able to arrest the ringleaders. Now, today, we have put them where they belong,' DI Allie Shenton said. 'I'm pleased with the sentences. The streets of Stoke-on-Trent are much safer now.'

'It's been an emotional case, which also resulted in the death of sixteen-year-old Erin Ellis, killed by her friend Molly Redfern, who was also sixteen,' DS Grace Allendale said. 'It wasn't easy dealing with the victims and the things they had

gone through. But equally, it wasn't us who had to deal with the gang's exploitations. These people preyed on young and vulnerable girls, sucking them into a life of prostitution, drugs and alcohol abuse.'

'It was a huge team effort,' DS Perry Wright concurred. 'We had multiple divisions involved and it was this extensive collaboration that enabled us to pull it all together.' DCI Jenny Brindley added, 'I couldn't be more proud of every officer who worked on this case.'

During the sentencing, Judge Patrick Hughes added his thanks to Staffordshire Police, who had worked relentlessly behind the scenes to bring the accused to justice and to help change the lives of many young teenagers who had been embroiled in something they should never have to face in their entire lives, let alone before they had grown up. He finished by saying that he hoped the long sentences were a warning to anyone who thought it was a good idea to exploit women and girls this way, and that the police would continue to hunt down these gangs and put a stop to them.

Grace went to join Simon in the kitchen and sat at the table where there were mugs of tea waiting. She watched as he unwrapped the silver foil around each parcel of bacon, cheese and oatcakes.

'Your article is excellent,' she said, eagerly awaiting her first mouthful.

'Thanks, I was pleased with it too. Imogen helped me out with it.'

Simon had taken on a junior reporter now. He was determined to give her a good start, and not think she was working for a dinosaur despite their twenty-year age gap. Imogen was a lovely girl and Grace got on really well with her and her boyfriend Jake.

'Well, it's not bad for the senior crime reporter and his side-kick,' Grace teased. 'You make a great team.'

'You reckon?' Simon hugged her. 'I think *we* make a great team, too.'

'We do,' she admitted. 'We're the best.'

He tilted up her chin so she could look him in the eye. 'So let's make it permanent.'

'Are you proposing to me, Cole?' she teased. 'Because if you are, then you'd best do it properly and get down on one knee.'

'Only if you'll say yes. My ego couldn't stand being rejected.'

Grace smiled. There were no ghosts hanging over them now. She would never forget Matt; he would always have a corner of her heart, but Simon had become a huge part of her world and Teagan was like a daughter to her now.

Simon cut one of his oatcakes in two. He handed a half to Grace, picked up the other one and entwined an arm with hers so that they were facing each other and the food.

'I don't have a ring but this is my most treasured possession at the moment. So this will have to do. Grace, will you marry me?'

Her eyes lit up as she grinned widely at him, ready to take a bite. 'Okay, let's do it.'

AUTHOR NOTE

To all my fellow Stokies, my apologies if you don't gel with any of the Stoke references that I've changed throughout the book. Obviously, writing about local things such as *The Sentinel* and Hanley Police Station would make it a little too close to home, and I wasn't comfortable leaving everything authentic. So, I took a leaf out of Arnold Bennett's 'book' and changed some things slightly. However, there were no oatcakes harmed in the process.

ACKNOWLEDGEMENTS

I can hardly believe that *Good Girl* is my fifteenth crime novel – it feels like it was only yesterday when I was tentatively publishing my first in 2011 and hoping that one or two people might like it.

Thanks must go first to my agent, Madeleine Milburn. Thank you for coffee, cake, lunches finished off with Tiramisu, Pimm's, pick-me-ups and everything else that looking after me as an author entailed. Thanks to Team Avon, especially my editor, Katie Loughnane, who made this book a dream to work on.

Particular thanks must also go to the close trio of friends I am very lucky to have – Alison Niebiezczanski, Caroline Mitchell and Talli Roland. I'd also like to thank, as ever, Martin Tideswell for his cheerleading, friendship and support.

I want to say a huge thank you to anyone who has read my books, sent me emails, messages, engaged with me on social media or come to see me at various events over the country. Without you behind me, this wouldn't be half as much fun. I love what I do and hope you continue to enjoy my books. Likewise, my thanks go out to all the wonderful book bloggers and enthusiasts who have read my stories and taken the time out of their busy lives to write such amazing reviews. I'd love to give you all a personal mention, but I fear I might miss someone. But please know I am grateful to all of you.

And then, my Chris. Without your support, and endless cups of tea, I know I wouldn't have got this far. Love you to bits, fella.

A LETTER FROM MEL

First of all, I want to say a huge thank you for choosing to read *Good Girl*. I have thoroughly enjoyed writing about Grace and her team and I hope you enjoyed spending time with them as much as I did.

If you did enjoy *Good Girl*, I would be forever grateful if you would leave a review on Amazon. I'd love to hear what you think, and it can also help other readers discover one of my books for the first time.

Many thanks to anyone who has emailed me, messaged me, chatted to me on Facebook or Twitter and told me how much they have enjoyed reading my books. I've been genuinely blown away with all kinds of niceness and support from you all.

You can sign up to my newsletter and join my readers group on my website www.MelSherratt.co.uk or you can keep in touch on Twitter @writermels and Facebook at MelSherrattauthor.

Thanks, Mel

Loved *Good Girl*? Then why not get back to where it all started with book one of the DS Grace Allendale series . . .

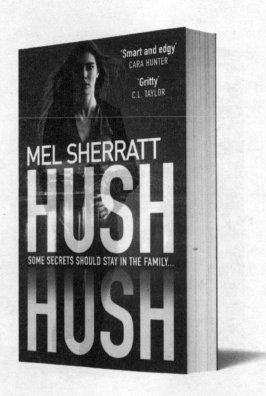

Available now in paperback, ebook and audio.

**Can they catch the killer before another
young woman dies?
Time is running out . . .**

The second instalment in the DS Grace Allendale
is available now in paperback, ebook and audio.

**The truth could be as shocking
as the lies . . .**

The third instalment in the DS Grace Allendale is available
now in paperback, ebook and audio.